Murdermoon

A McCall / Malone Mystery

Glenn Harris

Copyright © 2020 by Glenn Harris

First Edition 2020

Paperback Edition ISBN-13: 978-0-9969155-7-1

www.glennharris.us

Cover design: Cathleen Rehfeld

Murdermoon

CHAPTER ONE

"Clint, is that who I think it is?" asked Devon Malone.

I looked past her out the passenger side of the Subaru Outback and saw a short, middle-aged woman with straw-colored hair and a very determined expression striding down the no-tell motel walkway toward the room we'd been surveilling. She was dressed all in black: boots, pants, t-shirt with vest, ball cap. If the PTA had a Special Ops unit, she could be a member.

"That's our client," I said.

My partner, and brand-new wife, shifted in her seat and squinted. "Is she carrying what I think she is?"

I looked more closely. "That's a gun," I said. Maybe the PTA did have such a unit.

It was the first Tuesday in August, a sticky-hot afternoon in Portland, Oregon, and I still wanted to go on a honeymoon one of these days.

But it would not be today, just as it had not been any day since our Ferret-officiated wedding ceremony. It was like the entire Portland metro area was determined to keep the McCall-Malone Detective Agency too busy to take time off. The phone had started ringing as soon as the last wedding guests left, a big disadvantage of getting married in the office, and hadn't let up since.

At least we were making a lot of money, currently by documenting the extravagant infidelity of one Bernard Mondragon, local real estate agent and husband of Martha Mondragon—who had apparently decided that she needed no further reports from us.

Malone and I bailed out of the Subaru and hurried to intercept her. "Let me take the lead," Devon muttered as we approached. "If she shoots me, shoot her back."

"And then call 9-1-1 for everybody. You got it."

Mrs. Mondragon saw us coming and I could tell from the firming of her lips that she didn't intend to let us stand in her way. At least she hadn't pointed her Sig Sauer—a popular choice for women—at us. Yet.

Malone, as the designated negotiator, was a little ahead of me and held up her hands as she stepped in front of our client. "Wait up, Martha," she said. "We should talk about this."

Mrs. Mondragon did stop, but only to glare up at my partner who topped her by a good six inches. They were dressed much alike, all in black, but my partner's long, lean body contrasted sharply with the smaller, round one that confronted her.

"There's nothing to talk about. I appreciate what you two have done and I put your final check in the mail before leaving home, so your work is finished and you can go back to your office now."

"Leaving you to do what?" Malone was edging forward as she spoke. "Shoot your husband and the prostitute that he's with? A double murder right here in downtown Portland? With plenty of potential witnesses?" She gestured at the traffic that was passing by and eased forward a little more. "Not to mention," she went on, "that the two private investigators you employed saw you here with a gun right before the shooting."

Mondragon took a step back. "You'd rat me out?"

My partner snorted. "Rat you out? Do you think you're in an old gangster movie? That's a real gun you've got there, I assume with bullets in it, and Oregon has the death penalty for first degree homicide. There's a moratorium on executions right now, but still...."

Our client was beginning to tear up. "You don't know what it's like to be betrayed this way by your husband."

"True," Malone agreed, "and if I ever found out he'd betrayed me I probably would shoot him myself—but I'd know how to get away with it. You don't."

She had not even flicked a glance in my direction, but I duly filed the information for future reference.

Meanwhile, Martha Mondragon was getting more animated, as was the gun she was holding. It was still pointed toward the ground but working its way up toward my partner. My own hand came to rest on my Smith & Wesson as I thought of a possible distraction.

"I have an idea," I announced. Both women looked at me and the gun settled downward again. I focused on Malone. "You can take photos with your phone, right, and send them to other phones?"

"Yeah."

I looked at Mrs. Mondragon. "And your husband probably has a phone like that with him in the room, right?"

"Yes, he has a smartphone. Doesn't everybody?"

Not everybody; I don't, for instance, but I let that go. "How about Devon takes a photo of you standing in front of the motel room door, with your weapon and the room number plainly visible, and e-mails it to your husband inside? Then we all go sit in my car to watch and see how he reacts."

Malone laughed. "You want to scare him straight?"

"If he gets a photo of her right outside the door with a gun, it's got to have some impact." At the very least, we'd have our pistol-packing client out of sight.

"Well, hell. It might work. What do you think, Martha?"

The woman looked down at her gun. "I guess we could try that. But what happens then?"

Malone shrugged. "Either he changes his behavior or you change your marital status. Either way, he's still alive and you're not in prison."

It took less than a minute for Martha Mondragon to pose in front of the door, her Sig Sauer pointing at the room number and her expression appropriately grim, as Malone took the picture.

Then the three of us piled into the Subaru, Mondragon in back. "Can I see it before you send it?" she asked Malone.

"Sure." She held up her phone for easy viewing from the back.

"Oh, I like that. Can you send it to me, too?"

I grinned to myself. She'd have something to show her fellow PTA members.

"Tell you what," said my partner, "I'll trade you for the number of your husband's phone—and your gun." Oh, good idea.

"What do you mean? I just paid six hundred dollars for this thing. You can't have it."

"I'm not going to keep it. We'll send it and the photo to you along with the final report. It's just better that you don't have it right now, while we're sitting here in the middle of Portland."

"I guess that's okay." Mrs. Mondragon handed the gun over to Malone, who placed it carefully in the glove compartment, and then turned her attention back to her phone. She entered hubby's number as our back-seat guest recited it and pushed send.

"We may have to wait a while," I cautioned. It depended on how busy Mr. Mondragon happened to be at the moment, but I didn't say that out loud.

We sat there, the three of us staring expectantly at the motel room door—which opened very slightly in under sixty seconds. Apparently he hadn't been that busy. After another moment, it opened a little more and we could see a bit of a balding head, followed by a portion of a shirtless and very scrawny torso.

Finally Barnard Mondragon stepped fully into the doorway. Thank goodness he was wearing pants. He looked around, his expression just this side of terrified, and down at the phone in his hand. He turned to look at the door itself, confirming that that's where the photo was taken. One more look around and he disappeared back inside.

"Well," his wife said from our back seat. "That's that. Can

you drive me back to my car? I don't want to wait and see what his whore looks like."

"You got it," I said and started the Subaru.

"But I am looking forward to waiting at home to hear what Bernie has to say about the property he was showing today. I guess it's good that you keep my gun for now. But don't forget to return it. Maybe I can get my money back."

"Or you can sell it," I said. "Unfortunately, there's always a market for handguns."

"I suppose so."

Malone twisted around a little to look back and offer Mrs. Mondragon her hand. "Good luck, Martha."

They shook. "Thank you, both, for doing your job—and for saving me from myself, which wasn't your job."

"You're welcome," we echoed each other.

She sat back and I could see in the rearview mirror that she was smiling a grim smile. "But I'm not the one who's going to need the luck," she muttered.

CHAPTER TWO

"Another case satisfactorily concluded," I said as I hit SAVE on the final Mondragon report and sent it to the printer. "Maybe we'll get to our honeymoon one of these days soon."

Malone and I sat on opposite sides of the partners desk in the large one-room office of our detective agency. We were located above Previously Owned Books on the corner of 3rd and Stark—a good location near the periphery of downtown Portland. It was eight-thirty on a Wednesday, the morning after our downtown motel photo session.

"You and your obsession with honeymooning," scoffed my wife—whom I still mostly thought of as partner and backup rather than wife, at least when we were in the office. Dressed as usual in black jeans, boots, and t-shirt, her brunette hair hanging shoulder-length, she certainly looked more martial than marital. "Didn't you have one of those when you got married the first time?"

"Well, yeah," I agreed, "but it's kind of expected even the second time around."

"By who? You know you're being the girl in this, right?"

"Reverse sexism!"

"I'm not sure that's possible," she responded to my accusation. "Look, why not do something different this time? Personally, I think talking down armed and angry clients is much more fun than sipping drinks with little umbrellas on a beach somewhere. Besides, we've got more cases to satisfactorily conclude."

I had to laugh. "This is us, isn't it?"

My wife and partner grinned at me. "Yep. This is us."

And, right then, speaking of more cases, there came a knock on the pebbled glass in the upper panel of our office door. The knob turned and the door began to open before I had a chance to call out an invitation to enter.

First I saw a cane, then a fragile-looking arm, and then a classic little old lady was standing in our doorway, a big smile on her face. She was wearing a colorful patterned dress that fell well below her knees with a matching ribbon holding her white hair in a long ponytail. The bright green purse slung over her right shoulder was just slightly smaller than the typical airplane carry-on.

My first thought was that she probably had the wrong office. We don't usually get clients who are so very old or so cheerfully flamboyant.

She looked from Malone to me and back to Malone. "You the detectives? Who's McCall and who's Malone?"

Well, okay, so she had the right office. I stood as my partner assured her that we were indeed the detectives and we introduced ourselves. I thought our elderly visitor might need some help getting from the door to the desk, but she handled the cane with assurance as she crossed the room and took the chair nearest Malone. She carefully settled herself, leaning her cane against the desk and lowering the massive purse from her shoulder to the floor.

She beamed at my partner. "I like your outfit. You look tough." She then settled her gaze on me, taking in my khaki pants, tan polo shirt, and brown loafers without further comment.

"What can we do for you, Mrs....?" I prompted. Maybe find your missing cat?

"It's Ms., thank you very much." She leaned forward on the cane and stuck out her right hand. "Agatha Pepper." Her grip was unexpectedly strong when we shook. Her eyes darted around the office, making me think of a little bird with a white crest. "This is just what I imagined."

Given her age, that didn't surprise me. I had gone for the Maltese Falcon look when I first set the office up and it hadn't changed much when Malone joined the agency. Besides a few modern touches like our PCs and the phone system, there was the old and somewhat battered partners desk, two upholstered visitor chairs, an old couch against one wall, a couple of metal four-drawer file cabinets for hard-copy reports and notes, a small utility table with coffee maker and office fridge, and an antique hall tree in the corner, currently holding my sport coat and Malone's leather jacket. The big double window on the far side of our desk from the visitor chairs looked over Stark Street's vehicular and pedestrian traffic.

I tried again. "How can we help you, Ms. Pepper?"

She sat back and her eyes widened, as did her smile. "Why, you can find out who's trying to kill me," she announced as if we should have inferred that already.

So much for the missing cat.

Malone responded while I was still at a loss for words. "You seem awfully cheery for someone who's the target of a killer."

Which was about what I would have said if I'd been faster. I wasn't at all certain that we had a viable client here.

Agatha Pepper raised both hands as if to take in the total ambience of the McCall-Malone Detective Agency. "I just love this," she chortled. "Me, Agatha Pepper, sitting here with real private detectives."

I glanced over at my partner and then focused again on our elderly visitor. "Why do you think someone is trying to kill you?"

"I don't think so. I know so. In the last two weeks, I've had a near-fatal case of food poisoning, been the victim of a hit-and-run"—she hefted the cane—"and my house caught on fire in the middle of the night. That would have killed me right there if Morty hadn't woken me up."

"Morty's your husband?" I asked.

"Morty's my beagle."

"Ah."

"You've talked to the police?" Malone asked.

Ms. Pepper made a *pfft* sound. "They don't take me seriously. The food poisoning was at a restaurant and appeared to be nothing more. I couldn't identify the car that hit me and my injured leg will recover." She flipped an age-spotted hand toward the cane. "The fire was ruled accidental, although it *could* have been arson. All coincidence, as far as the police are concerned. I thought they weren't supposed to believe in coincidences. They never do on TV."

My partner offered one of her classic snorts in reply to that. "I used to be a police officer, Ms. Pepper, and it's not like it is on TV. Coincidences do happen, as do streaks of bad luck." She held up a hand as our visitor's face began to transition from smile to frown. "But I can assure you that we'll take you seriously. Attempted murder also happens."

The big smile was firmly back in place as Agatha Pepper leaned forward to pat Malone on the knee while looking my way. "You're lucky to have such an attractive and smart wife."

Whoa. We hadn't said anything about being married. We'd had to work out how we were going to refer to one another, given the new marital situation: when the occasion was business, we were partners, and when it was social, we were husband and wife. Did the old lady do a background check on us? "How did you know we're married, Ms. Pepper?"

Now she looked smug in addition to cheerful. "Matching wedding rings. That would *really* be a coincidence if you aren't married."

Which told me that she's a very sharp and observant old lady. Who therefore should perhaps be taken seriously.

"Okay," I said. "Very good. Do you have any idea why someone would want to kill you?"

She sat back and shook her head. "No idea at all. I'm a research librarian. Retired. No enemies. I used to have one. Matilda Baggins hated me because she wanted George and I got him. But she's been dead for years now."

"George?" Malone prompted.

"My late husband."

"Any other family?"

"Not living, no. Except Morty, of course. I've given no one reason to kill me, I assure you."

"And yet," I said, "you believe someone is trying to kill you."

She looked at me as if I'd asked a really dumb reference question. "If you could have been killed three times in two weeks from apparently unrelated external causes, wouldn't you be a bit worried?"

"Point taken." Another thought occurred to me. "Are you hiring us for protection as well as investigation?" That would be much more expensive, especially with my two old mentors now fully retired. We'd have to contract manpower from another agency, probably.

Ms. Pepper raised an eyebrow at me. "You mean bodyguards? That would be fun but, no, I've temporarily moved into a hotel downtown. No one but you two will know that I'm there and they have good security. Plus room service. You could escort me back there, though." She grinned.

"I can do that," I said, "assuming we come to an agreement on the fee."

"I'm sure that will be no problem." Agatha Pepper sat back and beamed at us as if we were her favorite library patrons. It appeared that our client was going to have a really great time with this investigation, whether we did or not.

CHAPTER THREE

I returned a little after ten from escorting Ms. Pepper to her hotel. We'd gotten the rest of the standard background information, which included no hint of a murder suspect or motive—except possibly money. Our client had apparently lived a frugal life and accumulated a substantial nest egg, on the order of a half-million dollars, that she intended to leave to the Friends of the Portland Public Library.

That amount of money would serve nicely as a motive, Malone and I agreed, though it was pretty much unheard of for a Friends group to accelerate the collection of a bequest by means of murder.

"Still," my partner said as she peered at her computer screen, "we should take a look at the membership list. There might be something there."

"I'll put Eleanor on it."

Our accountant down the hall was also our resident researcher and hacker, one of the many advantages of our location. In addition to Eleanor Ivory Accounting, we shared this floor with the legal firm of Bitterly and Barclay (our attorneys), and the Witkowsky Insurance Agency (our insurance agent). At the far end of the corridor was a small telephone survey operation that we'd never needed.

"I'll get the police report on the hit and run," Malone went on. "You want to track down the arson investigator and see why he or she ruled it an accident?"

"Sure. And there's the emergency room visit for the food poisoning." I looked at the check still sitting in the middle of the desk. "I think we shouldn't cash this until we've done some of this preliminary. Agatha seemed a bit too thrilled about hiring a couple of private detectives."

"You think she might be buying herself some excitement?"

"That seems as likely as someone determined to kill a retired librarian."

"Hmm. Could be. We'll know soon enough. Did you mail the package to Martha Mondragon while you were out?"

"I did."

Malone smiled a little grimly. "I hope she and hubby are on good terms by the time she has that gun in hand again."

"Thank goodness it's not our problem."

I looked up the main number for Portland Fire and Rescue and began my inquiry into Agatha Pepper's house fire—an inquiry that took a grand total of ten minutes. Arson investigator Natalie Takahara had determined that the fire began in leaves left piled against the house since last fall. She found no evidence to indicate it was anything other than spontaneous combustion and she so ruled it. She conceded that arson was theoretically possible, but without any evidence she wasn't willing to go there.

Malone had ended her call a little before mine and was typing away on her keyboard, probably recording notes.

"Anything?" I asked.

She stopped typing and swiveled toward me. "Not much. Agatha was walking Morty near her house and got knocked down when a passing car jumped the curb. She wasn't seriously injured because it was a glancing blow and she couldn't say much about the vehicle except that it was a dark-colored sedan. The driver was either male or a short-haired female. She sustained cuts, bruises, and a cracked bone in the leg that she's currently limping on. Morty was unhurt. There were no security cameras since it was a residential neighborhood and no witnesses that the investigating officers could find. It's already gone cold."

"Huh. Two down, one to go." Just then there was a quick knock on the door and it began to open. "Come in," I said to Eleanor Ivory, who by then already was.

Eleanor was a long-time friend and fellow black belt besides being our accountant and resident hacker. Forty years old, she was five-nine with long blond hair and the body of a fitness magazine model. Her lips were slightly too full and nose slightly too small for classic beauty but they worked well enough together with the wide violet eyes.

Today she was wearing a simple blouse and skirt outfit in summer pastel colors. Also, a somewhat exasperated expression as she paused between the door and the desk, surveying the two of us with arms akimbo.

"You already missed your first estimated tax payment last month," she announced. "You're going to owe the feds a penalty next year if you don't keep up with those. I told you, you're making too much money now for the deductions you have. Hell, you hardly have any deductions since everything is expensed to the clients. I know it's a new routine, but you've got to keep up with those payments."

I looked at Malone. Malone looked at me. "I thought you were doing that," we said in unison.

"Get your act together." Having issued her admonition, Eleanor turned to leave.

"Wait a minute," I called out. "Besides our promise to get the check in the mail, we have something else for you." Her arrival had reminded me that technically, as far as possible avenues of investigation went, there were two rather than one to go.

She turned back. "What?"

"It's pretty simple. We need the membership list of the Portland Friends of the Library, the officers of the organization...oh, and phone numbers and addresses if available."

"And any associated criminal records you can find," Malone added.

Eleanor resumed her exasperated look. "That just stopped being pretty simple."

"The tax check will be in the mail today."

Sigh. "I'll see what I can do." With a slight flounce, Eleanor went on her way.

"Just to clarify responsibility this time," I said after she shut the door behind her, "you will be mailing that check today?"

"I will. And you'll talk to Ms. Pepper's doctor about the food poisoning?"

"I will. I'll bet she's already called him with permission to share her information."

I was just reaching for the office handset when the upper right-hand drawer of my desk began to buzz. It had to be my cell phone, which I generally store in there with my Smith and Wesson—and carry with me a lot less frequently than I do the weapon.

I opened the drawer, grabbed the phone, and flipped it open. Yes, it flips open. At least the little screen shows the calling number, so I knew it was my daughter.

"Hey, Colleen, what's up?" Which is sometimes a fraught question given that my twenty-five-year-old offspring is a perpetual seeker of both enlightenment and a job she actually wants to keep. Both she and her boyfriend Hoke Moseley seemed to be still in the work-when-you-have-to-at-whatever's-available stage of life despite being in their mid-twenties. They were currently both unemployed, which did not make me happy.

"Hi, Dad." Pause. "I think we might have a stalker."

That wasn't very happy news, either. "What's going on?"

"Well, there's this woman that we keep seeing."

A woman. That was unexpected. I grabbed a pad of paper and a pen. "What's she look like? How many times and where have you actually seen her?"

"She's a brunette, average size, curvy, probably early to mid-thirties. We've seen her at least three times, twice when we were out and about, once in front of the apartment building."

"What's she doing when you see her?"

"Watching us."

"You sure she's focused on you guys? Maybe she's just a neighbor who happens to be around."

"I'm pretty sure she's following us. We saw her in Powell's Books and in Vancouver Mall. Not exactly the same neighborhood."

"Okay. But she hasn't done anything threatening."

"Nothing but showing up and watching us. Which is creepy if not threatening."

I had to ask: "Is there any chance this is related to what happened in Vegas?"

Colleen paused again, then muffled the phone as she exchanged a few words with someone nearby, probably Hoke. "Neither one of us remember seeing her in Las Vegas," she said when she came back, "so I doubt it's related."

"Hmm. Well, I can't think of much we could do besides follow you around ourselves until we see her—and that's not in the cards. Tell you what: You keep an eye out and call me the minute you see her again. We'll try to get there while she's still in sight."

"Okay. I hate to even bother you with this, but...creepy."

"I understand. Make that call if you see her again."

"Will do. Thanks, Dad. Love you."

"Love you too." I punched off the phone.

"Well, crap," I said to Malone, "now I guess I'm going to have to carry my cell all the time."

CHAPTER FOUR

Being married involves trade-offs, which I already knew having been married once before. Devon was still learning.

"I can't believe we're arguing about whether the toilet lid should be up or down," she pouted after taking a good swig of the red wine we were having with our steak and salad dinner. We'd left the office early and were at my—now our—house in the Hawthorne District.

"We aren't arguing about it. We're discussing it."

"Okay, then I can't believe we're discussing it." She forked up another substantial bite of steak and chewed it at me.

"What's wrong with leaving the lid down?"

"I like to leave it up. It's more convenient if it's already up."

I took my own, somewhat more modest, bite of the beef. "I guess I can see that, but it looks better with the lid down—and it's safer for the cats."

I—now we—had two cats named Stella and Maxine. They were currently done with their dinners and probably asleep on the couch in the living room. Thankfully, they had never voiced an opinion about the toilet lid.

"How is it safer for the cats? You think they might jump in and drown?"

I shrugged. "Well...yes, I have worried about that. I know it isn't likely, but it could happen."

Another, even larger, swig of the wine. "Any fucking thing could happen...but, all right. Jesus. We've spent, what, five minutes now on the toilet in the middle of dinner? I concede. I'll put the fucking lid down. God knows I should do my part to protect the cats from drowning."

I swallowed my last bite of steak. "We appreciate it."

"And the toilet paper should roll *away* from the wall, not toward it."

"Done." I saluted her with my wine glass. "A successful marriage is all about compromise."

She clinked hers against mine. "Fuck you," she said pleasantly.

I knew that one reason we were debating toilet lids over dinner was to avoid worrying aloud about Colleen and Hoke. I didn't know about Devon, but I was doing plenty of silent worrying nevertheless.

The kids, as I still think of them, had recently returned early from a short trip to Las Vegas convinced that someone there had been out to harm them. They claimed to have no clue who or why. I was concerned enough that I set them up with bodyguards for a week or so. It was the last formal assignment before permanent retirement for Johnny Crew and Hap Harbaugh, my two old mentors, and I also used Reuben Keys, well-known Portland pimp and sometimes backup for me and Malone. There was no sign of any trouble, so we let the protection lapse.

But now they had a stalker. Maybe. A curvy woman in her thirties. What the hell?

"How about tomorrow we check out the restaurant where Agatha Pepper got poisoned?" asked Devon as we cleared the table, interrupting my reverie.

"You think they might confess?" I inquired as I dumped my dishes in the sink. Tomorrow morning one of us would load the dishwasher. That was the routine so far.

"Probably not. Probably we won't learn anything useful. But we've got the case and that's a box that needs to be checked. And, speaking of checks, you should deposit hers."

"Agreed. What is the restaurant? Harold's something?"

"Harold's Family Dining, on Sandy near Glisan."

We were just headed back to the living room to displace the cats from the couch when I heard my cell phone buzzing on the coffee table. I trotted ahead of Devon to get it before the caller disconnected.

I glanced at the calling number and punched it on. "What is it, Colleen?"

"She's out front. I'm sure it's her."

"You're home?"

"Yes."

"Hoke's with you?"

"Yes."

"Is the woman in a car or standing in the open?"

"Standing next to a car, actually. It's a little green sports car. I don't know what kind, exactly. She's staring right at the house."

"Okay. Hunker down. Don't go trying to confront the woman. We're on our way."

"Okay."

By the time I had disconnected and stuffed the phone in my pocket, Malone had already retrieved our guns and jackets from the bedroom. She handed me mine. "My Jeep's parked behind you, so I'll drive," she said.

"Fine with me."

The cats didn't even stir as we headed for the door.

CHAPTER FIVE

Malone got us there in less than ten minutes, 39th to Sandy to the corner of Tillamook and 50th. Colleen and Hoke were renting, way below market, a little tree-shaded house that belonged to a friend of his. The house and traveling seemed to be the main reasons that they worked at all. Well, eating was in there somewhere as well.

It was early evening, with plenty of daylight remaining. I could see four cars parked on the block as we came around the corner. None of them were little and green, definitely no sports cars, nor was anyone standing beside a vehicle. I was out of the Jeep before it came to a full stop at the curb and headed up the walk to the front door of Colleen's rental.

It opened just as I stepped onto the little porch, Malone right on my heels. I was relieved to see Colleen and Hoke standing in the doorway, apparently unharmed. They had their arms around each other's waist, clearly a unit.

"Come on in," my daughter said, sounding a little shaky. "She left almost as soon as I hung up the phone. Do you think she knew you were coming? Is she tapping our phone?"

"I seriously doubt that," I said as we accepted her invitation and entered directly into a small but comfortably furnished living room. It was not our first time visiting, so I knew the kitchen was off to the right with the bedrooms and single bath through the doorway ahead of us.

The two young people stepped a little apart so I could hug Colleen and shake hands with Hoke. He and I were nowhere near the hugging stage as yet.

Colleen gestured to the couch. "Sit down, sit down. You guys want some coffee or something?" My daughter, the hostess.

I exchanged a glance with Malone as we sat down. "No, we're fine. Tell us again exactly what you saw out there. Did you get a better look at the woman? Anything you can add to her description?"

Colleen and Hoke settled on a love seat opposite the couch. They made an interesting looking couple. My daughter is five-two, slim, with punk-cut blond hair capping her head. Today she was wearing a sweatshirt, faded jeans, and the granny glasses that she favored. Hoke is nearly six feet with reddish-blond hair and a lanky, well-muscled body that carried several prison tats. I often think of them as The Librarian and The Thug. If it sounds like I'm not entirely happy about their relationship, that could have something to do with the fact that Hoke at one time was planning to kill me. Long story.

There was a small, low coffee table between the couch and loveseat, bare except for a dish of wrapped candy. Chocolates, knowing my daughter.

"What did I tell you already?" she asked.

"That she's a curvy brunette probably in her thirties."

"Okay. Well, she's pretty attractive. Hair is shoulder length.... She looks tough."

"Tough? You mean like a fighter?"

"Like she can handle herself." Colleen nodded at my partner. "She reminds me of Devon."

Malone and I looked at each other. "So, maybe a cop, now or in the past," she said. She looked at Colleen. "How is this woman dressed? Is it the same every time you've seen her?"

"About the same. Casual, I guess you'd say. Nice denim pants, tennis shoes or maybe running shoes, plain top with what looks like a lightweight linen jacket over it."

Again I exchanged a glance with Malone, knowing that she'd registered the same thing I did. Why did we both wear lightweight jackets on a warm July day? To cover our guns.

"There's no reason a cop would be watching us. We haven't done anything."

"This is all speculation right now," I said to my daughter. "We'll figure it out."

Hoke finally spoke up. "I think the car was a late-model Miata. I'm not sure."

"Okay," I said. "A green, late-model Miata. That's good. Light green or dark green?"

"Bright green, I guess. Like Christmas green."

Malone had stood up during this exchange and now was kind of wandering idly around the room. I didn't know if she was bored or what, but I wasn't going to ask right now because I wanted to refocus on Las Vegas. "So you guys never saw this woman or the green Miata in Vegas."

"Not that we noticed," Hoke responded and glanced at Colleen for confirmation.

"We were on the strip almost the whole time we were there," she said. "We rented a car for a few hours to drive out into the desert because we'd never seen a desert in person. Otherwise we were surrounded by lots of people and cars, lots of sports cars. All I can say for sure is that she doesn't look familiar."

"And nothing seemed threatening besides the black Hummer trying to run you off the road during your desert drive." I focused on Hoke. "You thought you'd seen that car before."

Hoke nodded. "Yes, I'm certain of it. And it was definitely a Hummer, not a sports car. Still, we were followed there and now we're followed here. It's weird, if nothing else."

I was about to agree when we were interrupted by an "Ah ha!" from my partner. I turned to see that she was standing by the front picture window.

"Is she out there again?" I asked as I sprang to my feet. Then I realized that Malone was looking downward rather than outward.

She glanced up, then down again. "I'm betting that in a sense she never left. Maybe the phone isn't tapped but I think the window is."

She pointed down at the lower left-hand corner of the glass as I stepped up beside her. I could see a small...something, black, maybe an inch square, that seemed to be attached to the outside of the window.

"Listening device?"

"That would be my guess," she said as she moved toward the front door. "I'll go retrieve it and confirm."

As I watched Malone exit, Colleen came up beside me and put her hand on my arm. She looked about as pale as I'd ever seen her. "What's going on, Dad? What does this woman want? You think it has to do with one of your cases?"

I could understand why she would ask that. She'd found herself in jeopardy several times before and it usually did have to do with me rather than her. I couldn't see it this time, though.

"I don't think so," I said. "We don't have anything complicated going on. Well, we just yesterday got a case that might get complicated but it's too new to have anything to do with you guys being surveilled—and I can't think of any old cases that would be coming back on us right now."

"Still, are we in danger? Do we need protection again? I hate that."

I put my hand on hers. "If the woman wanted to hurt you guys, she's had plenty of chances. No question we have to figure out what's going on and put a stop to it, but I don't think we need to involve bodyguards quite yet."

"Good."

Malone returned from popping the device off the front window. "Could I have a glass of water"? she asked Colleen while she held her hand out so the three of us could see the little plastic gizmo resting on her palm. My daughter looked puzzled by the request, but headed off for the kitchen.

"It's exactly what I thought it was," my partner announced. "I saw one just like it on a joint police-FBI operation when I was with the Tigard department. It translates the vibrations of the glass into sound and transmits them to a receiver—located within a half-mile, if my memory serves me."

Colleen returned with the glass of water. "Do you think they're listening right now?" she asked.

"Could be," Malone said as she took the glass of water from her and dropped the device into it. "But now they aren't."

CHAPTER SIX

"At least the kids had a quiet night," I said to my partner as I drove us to Harold's Family Dining the next morning. I'd rousted Colleen out of bed with a call first thing, to confirm that they were okay.

"You didn't have one," Devon noted. "You tossed and turned all damned night. Not that I blame you. If we get another call that they've seen the woman and we miss her again, we should probably reconsider bodyguards."

I glanced over at her. "I agree—and I appreciate the fact that you worry about them, too."

"Well, she's my daughter now. Step-daughter."

That left me smiling, despite the potential seriousness of the situation, as I negotiated the mid-morning traffic on Sandy.

The restaurant turned out to be a green one-story box with blue awnings, located between a car lot and jewelry dealer. Since they apparently had been in business at this location for some years, I had to assume their food was more appealing than their façade. At least one poisoning notwithstanding.

The interior was pleasant enough and larger than it looked from outside, though still only about the same size as the Pen and Pastry, the coffee shop/café owned by our friend Veronica Fortune. There looked to be about two dozen four-top tables and a half-dozen booths along the far side. The color scheme was continued with muted blues and greens, the rest of the décor leaning toward brass trim and impressionist paintings. There were only a few mid-morning customers. One young woman stood behind the host station and I could see one waiter, who was currently pouring water for an elderly couple.

"Table for two?" inquired the woman as she picked up two menus.

I held out my state-issued private investigator ID, which at a glance could be mistaken as police investigator. I think she took it as the latter, since she paled slightly when I asked to speak to the manager.

"Just a moment," she said, and replaced the menus before hurrying off toward the back.

She returned in less than a minute with a middle-aged, balding gentleman dressed in dark khakis and white short-sleeved shirt, no tie. His round and slightly puffy face carried a grim expression and he spoke in practically a whisper.

"I'm Carl Cortez, the manager. What can I do for the police today?" He motioned for us to step away from the host station.

We gathered at a nearby table, minus the young woman who remained where we'd found her. This time we both showed our ID. "We're private, not Portland Police Bureau," I said. He tossed a quick frown over his shoulder at his employee and turned back to us.

"Well, what can I do for you?"

"Are you familiar with a customer named Agatha Pepper?" asked Malone.

His face went from grim to smiling just that fast. "The peppery Ms. Pepper? Sure, I know her. She has dinner here two or three times a week. She was in here just a couple of days ago. Why? Is there a problem? Is she okay?"

"She's fine. Do you remember the evening she got food poisoning here?"

That took care of the smile again. "It wasn't our food. I swear to God. I don't know what happened. But, yes, I sure remember it. The poor woman wasn't feeling well at all and we had to call 911 for her."

"And you don't think it was the food." I said.

"I'm sure it wasn't. It was a busy evening and a number of customers had exactly what Ms. Pepper was having—the roast beef and salad, her usual. Nobody else got sick. She's an old lady. It was probably just a stomach upset." Apparently at this point it occurred to him that two private detectives probably wouldn't be investigating indigestion. "Wasn't it?"

"Ms. Pepper doesn't think so, especially given some other problems that she's had recently. Which is why she hired us to look into it. Do you remember anything odd, even slightly unusual, about the evening at all, anything that attracted your attention to her and her table?"

"Well, now that you put it that way, I do remember one thing."

"What?" asked Malone.

"I saw this young guy at her unoccupied table. I figured she'd left, but she must have gone to the restroom. Anyway, for a moment I thought it was one of our waiters there to clear the table. He was about the right age, but then I realized that, one, I didn't recognize him and, two, he wasn't wearing the right outfit."

I again surveyed the visible staff people, currently numbering three now that another waiter was taking an order. "There's an outfit?"

"It's kind of subtle, but all our staff wear dark pants, anything but denim, and short-sleeved light-colored shirts or tops. We're all wearing our own clothes, but there's a consistency to it. It's an outfit."

Really subtle, as far as I could see. "Okay."

"Anyway, this young man was wearing dark pants but they were denim and what at first looked like a short-sleeved shirt was long-sleeved, rolled all the way up to his biceps. Who does that?"

"What was he doing at the table?" asked Malone.

"I don't know. He saw me looking at him and took off. I walked over to the table and checked it out, but I didn't see anything missing—and, as I said, I thought Ms. Pepper was gone. I guess I'd forgotten the guy by the time I later noticed she was back at the table, finishing her meal. It was a busy evening. You think he did something and I missed it?"

"No way to know," I said, "not at this point. Can you give us any further description of this young man?"

His brow furrowed. "Well, he was stocky, not tall, a little

29

shorter than me, maybe, dark hair, kind of shaggy, like just over his ears. Good-looking young guy. Oh, and he was wearing an earring or something like that."

"You saw that from across the room?" asked Malone.

He nodded. "I saw it glint, like it was a diamond or polished metal. I couldn't say what it looked like beyond that. It was something on his ear, his left ear."

And that was all he could tell us. We thanked him for his time, reassured him that we wouldn't go around bad-mouthing his food, and took our leave.

"So," my partner said as we hit the sidewalk, "now we've got a stud with a possible stud. It's not much, but more than we had."

"Time to go see the peppery Ms. Pepper," I replied.

CHAPTER SEVEN

The Dunhill Plaza on Taylor Street was a medium-sized, medium-priced hotel with barely adequate parking. It was also apparently pet-friendly, since our knock on the door of room 415 was greeted by the faint sound of barking from within.

I waited about thirty seconds, picturing Ms. Pepper making her way toward us with her cane, and was about to knock again when the door opened. And there she was, in all her little old lady glory. This time she wore a vivid maroon robe and her white hair was hanging down her back rather than beribboned into a ponytail. I was grateful she wasn't carrying the bright green purse. That against the maroon might have caused severe dizziness.

Peering around the bottom hem of said robe, thankfully no longer barking, was a seriously overweight beagle with a white muzzle hinting at a lot of years to go with his pounds.

Agatha Pepper's expression went from inquiring to that big smile in a heartbeat. "Ah, it's the detectives! Come in, come in."

It was a standard hotel room, small bathroom to our left and open closet space to our right as we entered, with bed, two chairs, small desk, dresser and TV ahead. The colors were predominantly brown and beige. The colors provided by management, that is. The colors provided by Agatha Pepper included not only the maroon robe but a whole set of vividly patterned dresses hanging in the closet space, the green purse resting on one of the chairs, and several pieces of bright yellow luggage stacked to one side. A large doggy bed sat on our side of the human bed. It was deep cerulean blue with orange padding.

Clearly, we had an extremely colorful client in Ms. Pepper.

She stood aside and indicated the lightly upholstered little armchairs. "Sit down! Do you want some tea? I could call down for some tea."

"No, we're fine," I said, and sat on the edge of the bed. "You and Devon can have the chairs."

We all settled ourselves accordingly, including the beagle flopping down beside his mistress.

"I assume that's Morty," I said.

She beamed down at him and then back up at me. "Yes, that's my boy." She sat up very alertly in the chair, again reminding me of some exotic bird. "What have you learned?"

"Not a lot, as yet," I said, "but we do have a description of a young man seen near your table when you got the food poisoning. We're hoping you will recognize him."

If anything, she sat up even straighter and grinned more broadly. "A suspect! Well, let's hear it."

"According to the restaurant manager," Malone began, "he was a stocky young man, average height, with shaggy dark hair and wearing an earring or stud in his left ear. Something shiny. He had on dark pants and a white shirt with the sleeves rolled up."

Agatha Pepper had followed the description avidly, but then frowned when Malone stopped. "An earring? No, I didn't see anyone like that at the restaurant. What was I doing when he was near my table? Did the manager say?"

"That's the point," I said. "You were away from the table at the time. Probably in the restroom. Which would give this person the opportunity to put something in your food—although the owner didn't see him do anything like that. The question is, does the description sound like anyone in your life currently? Anyone you know or have seen hanging around?"

"No, I'm sorry." She sat back, looking a little discouraged. "No one I can think of."

"The shiny earring or stud in his left ear is the one distinctive feature," Malone pointed out. "Think. Does that ring any bells at all?"

Ms. Pepper took another minute, thinking hard, but finally shook her head. "I'm afraid not." She looked from Malone to me and back again. "So. What now?"

"Well, honestly," I responded, "that's a good question.

We've talked to the restaurant, the arson investigator, and the officers who investigated the hit and run. They all believe what happened to be an accident. We haven't looked at the hospital records, but food poisoning is food poisoning. Have you heard or seen, or thought of, anything new since we saw you yesterday?"

She shook her head. "Other than taking Morty for a couple of walks, I haven't left the hotel—and nothing happened on the walks. I haven't thought of anything. You're not giving up, are you?"

Malone sat forward. "Not at all. We will pursue it as long as there are avenues available. As Clint said, we haven't talked to the hospital yet. That's something we can do."

She caught my eye with a look that cautioned me not to make any pessimistic noises. I didn't.

"Can you remember the name of the doctor who treated you? Maybe he or she will have some thoughts that didn't make it into the records."

Our client squinted with the effort to recollect. "It was a she, a young black woman actually. It was a pretty name...that I'm afraid I can't recall. But it was 'doctor' something; she wasn't a nurse or a physician's assistant."

"A young black female emergency room doctor should be easy to track down. The main Providence hospital on Glisan, right?"

"Yes, that's correct." She perked up. "I would recognize her, of course. Maybe I could come along. I'd love to see you guys in action." Morty apparently picked up on her excitement, as he stirred and gave a little yip of agreement. She looked down and then up at us with a sly grin. "Could Morty come along, too?"

I offered a smile of my own at that, though it worried me a little. "Neither of you can come along," I responded gently. "You're seeing us in action right now, Ms. Pepper. We'll talk to the doctor just as we've been talking to you. It's not that exciting."

My partner cocked an eye at me as we stood in the

descending elevator. "You might have been onto something when you speculated that the old lady is buying herself some entertainment."

I sighed. "Yeah, I haven't abandoned that possibility yet, but we do have a hint her concerns are legit. We'll talk to the doctor and then see where we're at."

"Us guys in action," agreed Malone.

CHAPTER EIGHT

After getting permission from Agatha Pepper to talk to us, Dr. Latisha Morningside was of little immediate help. The petite and pert emergency room doc reported that there had appeared to be no symptoms beyond weakness, nausea, and vomiting. Those were consistent with food poisoning, though she'd been slightly suspicious because the symptoms had come on during the meal. Food poisoning usually took at least several hours to manifest.

Her suspicions had risen nowhere near the level that would have required notifying law enforcement, but they were enough to draw and store a blood sample—upon which she agreed to run a few more tests after hearing the full story of Ms. Pepper's recent experiences.

Even though we'd tracked her down just before lunchtime, we didn't expect to hear about any lab results today.

So now we were at the Home Run Sports Bar, across Third Avenue from the office, finishing our usual hamburgers and fries.

The ambience of the Home Run is casual, the color scheme warm golden yellow rather than fast-food orange. Malone and I were in one of the booths that ran along three walls; the bar occupied the fourth. Tables of various sizes from two- to ten-top spread across the open floor space, with at least one big flat-screen high-def TV visible from every seat. All of the TVs were tuned to one sports channel or another.

Our food hadn't even been delivered yet and we'd temporarily—I hoped it was temporary—run out of ideas about what to do next on Ms. Pepper or my daughter. The conversation during the meal had been desultory at best. I was currently watching a tennis match over Malone's left shoulder as I took my last big bite of burger.

"I've been wanting to ask you about your Zen stuff,"

Malone said out of nowhere as she dipped one of her fries in ketchup.

"My Zen stuff?"

"Before we got married, you spent a lot of evenings with your friends doing Taekwondo and you used to meditate every morning, didn't you? Now you only go to the dojang maybe once a week and quite often we start the morning with...activities that wouldn't exactly count as meditation."

I had to smile at the reminder of our morning activities, but Malone looked serious. "All that's true," I said. "So?"

"So, do you miss it? Any of it?"

Devon Malone, expressing even a hint of insecurity? This was serious indeed. I reached across the table, to put my hand on hers. "You're asking me if I'd prefer getting beat up to spending an evening with you? If I'd rather sit on the floor in the corner with Maxine than make love to you? Well, gee, let me think...."

That had her grinning again, which was my intent. She waved her last french fry at me. "I was just wondering. I'm still new at this wife business and I don't want to stand in the way of your enlightenment or whatever."

"You are all the enlightenment I need, Devon."

She popped that last fry into her mouth, I left the money including tip on the table, and we hiked across the street to the office. Where I heard the phone ringing before I even got the door open. I hurried over to the desk and picked it up.

"McCall-Malone Detective Agency. This is Clint McCall."

"Mr. McCall, this is Martha Mondragon."

"What can I do for you, Mrs. Mondragon? If you haven't received your gun back, it should arrive any time."

"I don't care about the gun. I want my husband back."

"Pardon me?"

Malone gave me a look as she settled on her side of the partners desk.

"My husband. He's missing."

"Well, we don't have him."

She made an exasperated noise. "I didn't think you did, but

I want to rehire you to find him. He swore that he wouldn't go catting around anymore. I'm worried."

I gave that about two seconds of thought. "I'm sorry, Mrs. Mondragon, but we're booked solid right now. I'm sure your husband will turn up." Actually, I was pretty sure she shouldn't have believed his swearing. "Maybe he just needed some time alone, you know, to repent."

"Repent?"

Okay, admittedly that was a little lame. "Whatever the explanation, we can't take on another case right now. I'm really sorry. I can recommend another agency here in town, if you'd like."

Silence. And then the click of her hanging up. Either too disappointed or too pissed off to even say goodbye.

"What was that all about?" Malone asked as I replaced the handset in its cradle.

"Bernie Mondragon is apparently straying again."

"That didn't take long. What did she want us to do about it?"

"Find him."

"He's actually missing? For how long?"

"I didn't even ask. It couldn't be long. It was just two days ago that we saw him ourselves. Whatever's going on, we've already got Colleen and Agatha Pepper to worry about, plus two or three minor matters to wrap up."

"Huh."

"You don't agree?"

"You were the one talking to her, so it was your call." Malone turned to her monitor that had been booting up as we spoke.

She didn't agree.

CHAPTER NINE

The rest of the afternoon was devoted to reviewing a client's surveillance footage and identifying the employee who'd been pilfering cosmetics. I wrote up the report while Malone prepared the billing. We'd leave it to the client whether to involve the police or not.

Colleen didn't call. Latisha Morningside didn't call. We didn't have any new ideas. We probably could have tracked down Bernie Mondragon for his wife and picked up another day's pay. Oh well.

I spent part of the evening at the dojang (taekwondo workout space) that I rented along with several other black belts and then sat zazen this morning. I'm not sure if I was responding to the mild tension that I felt between us or just wanted to prove our marriage wasn't standing in the way of anything.

Maxine, at least, was happy about my morning choice, settling down beside my cushion to vigorously purr away while I meditated. Stella was probably off in the kitchen having more breakfast, as usual.

Malone and I were just settling ourselves in the office around eight-thirty when Dr. Morningside called. I put her on speaker as soon as she identified herself.

We all exchanged good mornings and I thanked her for getting back to us so quickly.

"I'm afraid there's nothing conclusive to report," she said. "There are indications of possible digitoxin poisoning but they're very slight and could result from certain medications or even be false positives from liver or renal disease. I would have to know much more about Ms. Pepper's medical history and even then I couldn't say for sure that she was purposefully poisoned with some form of digitalis."

"But there is that possibility," Malone confirmed.

"Yes, given these results it is possible."

We all agreed that in that case there was no point in pursuing further medical background on our client, at which point we thanked the good doctor and hung up.

"So," my partner said as she swiveled back and forth in her chair, "we have a food poisoning that might be on purpose, a fire that might be arson, and a hit and run that might not be an accident." She snorted. "Which means we have fuck-all."

"We have one possible suspect: the stud with the stud."

Which brought forth another snort. "Yeah, let's have Eleanor run that description through all her databases and see who she comes up with."

My partner was still swiveling back and forth. "Are we okay?" I asked her.

She stopped abruptly and sat forward. "Of course we're okay. I'm just feeling frustrated. I'm sure that Agatha Pepper has someone trying to kill her and Colleen has a stalker. Meanwhile, we don't have any serious leads on either one."

"And you think we should help Martha Mondragon as well."

She sat a moment and then shook her head. "No, I think you're right about that. She should deal with her husband herself. And we may be twiddling our thumbs right this second, but either or both these cases could get critical at any time. We need to be ready—and keep looking for leads."

I was taking a moment to contemplate the apparent hopelessness of that when my cell phone buzzed. This time it was my daughter's number. I picked it up and punched it on.

"Hey, Colleen."

"I think that woman is following us again."

"Where are you?"

"We're grocery shopping at the Fred Meyer on Glisan. I'm pretty sure I saw her pulling into the parking lot as we entered the store. This is getting more weird all the time."

"The Fred Meyer nearest your house?" Glisan is a very long street and there are a couple of Fred Meyers on it.

"Yes."

"Keep shopping. We're on our way."

Malone had already retrieved her gun and was on her feet by the time I ended the call. "Talk about timing. The stalker's back?"

"A green Miata anyway."

I joined her and we headed for the door.

We took my Subaru, so I was the one frustrated by the heavy Thursday morning Portland traffic. It took about twenty minutes to get to the Fred Meyer just past 60th on Glisan. The lot was almost full and I had to take a spot that was a long city block from the main entrance. We hadn't seen a green Miata as we searched for a place to park, but there were hundreds of cars we hadn't yet seen.

What I did see as I was closing the car door, in the distance, was my daughter and her boyfriend exiting the store pushing two full grocery carts.

I pointed them out to Malone as we hurried in that direction. "Damn it, I told them to stay inside."

"Actually, you told her to keep shopping. I guess they finished."

"Well, I meant they should stay inside." We were still five rows of parked cars away from them at that point. I couldn't see where they were parked, though they were moving at an angle away from us. Still no green Miata in sight. It could all be a false alarm. I hoped it was.

"Check that out." Malone pointed off to the right, where a large black limousine had just turned into the lane where Colleen and Hoke were pushing their carts.

I started feeling uneasy and began walking faster. You don't normally see fancy limousines in the Fred Meyer parking lot. Plus the windows were tinted—all the windows, including the driver's side and windshield, which was illegal.

The uneasiness was just transitioning to serious concern when the limousine abruptly stopped next to my daughter and her boyfriend. I could see the passenger door open on our side and a very large man emerging. At the same time two more men exited the other side to confront Colleen and Hoke. If that wasn't enough to go from concern to panic, I became aware that sprinting from the left toward the kids and limousine was a woman who fit the description of their stalker. She had a gun in her hand.

Malone and I drew our weapons and broke into a dead run of our own, as best we could with five rows of cars between us and them. We were way too far away.

CHAPTER TEN

It took us a frustrating and frightening thirty or forty seconds to weave our way through what seemed like hundreds of vehicles and reach the scene of the confrontation. It was over before we got there.

The frustration stemmed from being unable to keep my eye on what was happening since there were so many cars to avoid along the way. I knew that the woman running from the left had shouted something and I heard Colleen scream. By the time I looked up again, the three men were not in sight and the limousine was peeling out.

My heart peeled right with it until I saw that Colleen and Hoke had been left behind. They were still there with their shopping carts, my daughter held tightly by her boyfriend. Then I realized that the armed stalker-woman was standing beside them and I kept moving as fast as I could.

The woman held up her hands to show that she'd put her gun away as we dodged through the last row of cars. We pulled up in front with our guns trained on the woman. I had no fucking idea what was going on and wasn't going to give her a chance to draw her weapon again.

My first words, once I'd caught my breath for a moment, were for my daughter. "Colleen, are you all right?"

She pulled back from Hoke just a little, looking as pale and breathless as I felt. "Yes, we're okay. Who were those men?"

"I have no idea who they were," I said and then focused on our unidentified third party. "Or who you are."

She lowered her right hand slightly. "My name is Sonny Sampson. I'm a private investigator from Las Vegas. I'm going to reach into my pocket for identification, if that's okay with you."

"Very slowly," I said as I tried to process her words. Another PI? That fit with our speculation. From Las Vegas?

That was sure as hell no coincidence. And she was, as Colleen had said, a little reminiscent of my partner: shorter but equally lean and fit. Lighter brunette hair, with sharp blue eyes and sharper cheekbones. Wearing blue jeans, white t-shirt, light jacket, and low-heeled boots. She radiated competence and potential menace, just like Devon Malone.

And assuming she came up with valid ID, this was getting more interesting by the moment. I cocked an eye back at Colleen. "I meant for you guys to stay safely inside until we got here."

Hoke, looking almost as shaken as my daughter, spoke up. "Colleen didn't tell me that or I would have kept us inside. We were nearly done in the store before she called you because we were debating whether to bother you with it, so we just finished up and headed for the car."

"You didn't say to stay inside," Colleen chimed in. "You said to keep shopping. We kept shopping."

"Okay, okay." Meanwhile the woman had come up with a leather wallet that she held out and open.

Malone stepped over to examine it, then lowered her gun and stepped back. "The ID looks legit," she said.

I holstered my own gun. "Why have you been following my daughter?" I asked Sonny Sampson. "And who were those men? What the hell is going on?"

"I can answer some of your questions, but not nearly all of them. Not yet. And not here." She glanced around and only then it occurred to me that we'd all been running around a Fred Meyer parking lot with guns drawn and apparently no one called the cops. People should pay more attention.

I looked at the two full shopping carts. "Might as well talk at Colleen and Hoke's. They've got to get this stuff home, anyway."

Sonny Sampson nodded. "Okay. Meet you there." She started to turn. Of course she knew where it was.

Malone, who was nearest to her, put an arm out to stop her. "You ride with us. We can bring you back to pick up your car after the questions are answered."

Sampson had to tilt her head back a bit to look Malone in the eye but she did a good job of it. "You don't trust me?"

"Not yet."

Long pause, then she nodded. "Fair enough. Let's go."

CHAPTER ELEVEN

It took about a half-hour to get everybody back to my daughter's house, the groceries put away, and the five of us settled in the living room with coffee. Colleen and Hoke again sat together on the couch, while I sat in one armchair with Malone perched on its left arm while Sonny Sampson occupied the other armchair.

"Okay," I started it off, "why is a Las Vegas PI following my daughter around Portland and who were those men in the limousine?"

Colleen spoke up before Sampson could even open her mouth. "It was Hoke," she said.

"Pardon?"

"Those guys were looking at Hoke when they got out of the car. They weren't paying any attention to me." She focused on Sampson. "Were you following me? Or Hoke?"

The Las Vegas detective nodded agreement. "You're perceptive. I was following your boyfriend." She paused to survey all of us. "And I think this might somehow be all my fault—or at least related to what I've been doing. I recognized one of the men from the limousine. He's muscle who works for Antonio Sabado."

Finally, some answers. I sat forward. "Who the hell is Antonio Sabado?"

"He's a Las Vegas gangster, more popularly known as Tony Saturday--and he's my client, who claims that Mr. Moseley here might be responsible for the disappearance of his daughter."

That provoked a variety of exclamations from the four of us, from my "What?" to Colleen's "That's crazy!" Hoke grunted like he'd been hit with a two-by-four.

"I don't understand," he said.

I stayed focused on our guest. "None of us do, Hoke, but Miss Sampson here is going to explain. Right, Miss Sampson?"

"As best I can. I'll give you the story so far and then we can try to figure out what's really going on." She paused, apparently gathering her thoughts. "About a week ago, I was hired by Antonio Sabado to find a young man, a tourist apparently, who was seen with his daughter shortly before her disappearance. He thought she might have gone with this young man voluntarily but he wasn't sure."

I interrupted. "And you say this Sabado is a gangster? Is that typically your clientele in Las Vegas?"

"It's typically everybody's clientele in Las Vegas, at least everybody who charges as much as I do. They're the people doing the high dollar business, the people with money. I don't do anything illegal for Sabado or anyone else; they have plenty of employees already for that. But they don't have the resources that I do for tracking someone down. Admittedly, the police or FBI could do even better, but guys like Sabado are not going to turn to law enforcement, not even to find a missing kid."

"How old is the girl, by the way?" asked Malone.

"Sixteen, supposedly."

Malone's eyes narrowed. "I'm getting the impression that you've begun to doubt your client's story."

Sampson offered a remarkably Malone-like snort. "As of today, I've finished doubting my client's story. It's complete bullshit. And I feel like a fucking idiot."

"Because?"

"I'm sure you noticed that I was busy with my phone on the way over here. Normally, if someone hires you to find their daughter, you don't check to confirm that they have a daughter. After the incident in the parking lot, it occurred to me that I should do that. According to the great god Google, at least, Sabado does not have children of any gender."

"Well," I said, "so what do you think is going on?"

"I don't know yet. All I know for sure is that Sabado wanted the identity and whereabouts of Mr. Moseley."

"How in the world did you find me?" Hoke asked. "And please call me Hoke. Mr. Moseley sounds like my father."

"Okay, Hoke. Sabado told me that his daughter was last seen talking to a young man in the lobby of Circus, Circus and he gave me a description. Which fits you to a tee. I checked with the registration and they matched your name to the description. Right then I started thinking something might be off because they told me you were part of a couple who'd been staying there, clearly on holiday. Which is why I didn't report the info to Sabado at that time. I tracked you here to Portland and started following you around to see what I could see. As far as I could tell, you have no sixteen-year-olds around, voluntarily or otherwise, so the day before yesterday I called my client to tell him it was probably a bust."

I interrupted. "But you did identify Hoke by name and location at that time, right?"

Sampson grimaced a little. "Unfortunately—as it turns out—I did, yes."

"And you kept following him. Why?"

"Because Sabado wouldn't take 'probably' for an answer. He wanted me to stay on the job. He's paying a very hefty daily fee, so I stayed on the job. And kept him posted about Hoke's apparent innocence."

"Then today three goons, all of whom likely work for Sabado, show up to...what? Kidnap Hoke?" I looked at the young man in question. "What the hell did you do in Las Vegas that you haven't told us?"

He threw up his hands. "Nothing! I swear! I've never heard of this Sabado guy and I didn't do anything to piss off a gangster. Colleen and I were together the whole time. She can tell you."

"It's true," my daughter agreed, looking every bit as mystified as I felt.

"Every second?" asked Sonny Sampson. "Sabado had to get onto you somehow. He had a time, a location, a description. Was there ever a time you were in that hotel lobby without your girlfriend here and had any kind of interaction with a younger woman? You remember anything at all like that?"

Hoke went absolutely still for a moment. "Yes."

Colleen's head snapped around. "What? What do you mean, you remember? Remember what?"

"I didn't think anything of it at the time, but I was approached by a young girl when I was waiting for you in the lobby—the first day we were there, before we'd even checked out the strip. She asked me where I was from and said she'd like to go to Portland sometime but couldn't because somebody— maybe she said Tony; I don't remember for sure—wouldn't let her. She wanted to know if I was traveling alone, but right then this kind of big ugly guy came up and took her by the arm. He told me he was her father and apologized for her bothering me. Then they left."

"What did the girl look like?" Sampson wanted to know.

"She was a teenager, could have been sixteen, small, thin, brunette I guess you'd say, nothing special about her. I thought for a moment she might be trying to pick me up and that was kind of shocking, but then her dad showed up and I forgot about it."

"Description of the father?"

"Oh, he was a big guy, kind of scary actually, looked like he worked out a lot, hair cut so short I couldn't tell you the color for sure, dressed nicely though—suit, white shirt, tie...."

"Anything distinctive like tattoos, birthmark, scars, a limp?"

Hoke squinted as he thought about that. "Yes, he had quite a scar now that you mention it, from the corner of his eye almost down to his mouth. Left side of his face."

Sampson sat back. "And that's what Tony calls him. Scarface. He's Sabado's right-hand man, a stone killer and nobody you want to mess with."

"Shit." I think we may have all said it in unison.

CHAPTER TWELVE

It took more than two hours to retrieve Sonny Sampson's car from the Fred Meyer parking lot and get her settled with the two kids at Veronica Fortune's Pen and Pastry. The green Miata was currently parked in our driveway around the corner from the coffee shop—which was not something I could have anticipated when I woke up that morning.

Devon and I, meanwhile, were back in the office after having a quick lunch. I didn't know about my partner, but I was feeling more than a little overwhelmed.

We'd eaten at Veronica's place after deciding that Hoke and Colleen would be safest there for the afternoon, given that Veronica and crew could keep an eye on Sampson as well. As far as any of us could tell, our little caravan hadn't been followed, so none of Sabado's people should know where they were.

Also, while we were still there I'd called Mike Whitehall—good friend, fellow black belt, and Portland Police Bureau homicide detective—to clue him in about Sabado's people and the apparent threat to my daughter and her boyfriend. In return, he promised to make a couple of calls and increase patrols past the restaurant for the afternoon.

So Colleen and Hoke were as secure as they could be, for the moment.

"She come up with anything interesting?" Malone inquired as I returned from a visit down the hall to Eleanor Ivory's office. Another call I'd made from the Pen and Pastry had been a request that Eleanor do a deep background on Sabado.

"Surprisingly, no," I said as I sat down on my side of the partners desk. "She confirmed what Sonny Sampson told us. Antonio Sabado, AKA Tony Saturday, is a major player in Las Vegas with his fingers in the standard array of pots—gambling, prostitution, money laundering.... But apparently he's quite adept at avoiding prosecution. Very little criminal record, per se."

"Crap. What the fuck could Hoke have done to bring a big-time gangster down on his head? You think he's telling the whole truth? It was kind of convenient, I thought, that he suddenly remembered the young woman who spoke to him and the scar-faced guy who claimed to be her father."

I sat back and thought about it as I watched the traffic on Stark. "I don't know," I finally said. "Normally I would trust him. Colleen's a good judge of character and I haven't had any reason to doubt that Hoke's left his troubled past behind...but...."

"Exactly. But. Now we have him meeting a known killer in a hotel lobby and Sabado's muscle showing up in a Fred Meyer parking lot. There sure as hell is something going on beyond an innocent exchange of words with a young girl."

"I'll get Colleen alone and find out just how long Hoke was waiting for her in that lobby and if there were other times he was off on his own while they were there."

"Good plan."

"Speaking of plans, I do have one idea. I'm going to give Reuben a call. Who better to have information about the newest thugs in town?"

Malone shook her head as she turned to her computer. "That's one of the things I first loved about you," she muttered, "that you had your very own pimp slash drug dealer as backup."

She's never been a big fan of Reuben Keys—and it was certainly true that he and I had developed an unusual relationship, going all the way back to when he was Veronica Fortune's pimp and she was my first client. There was no getting around the facts that Reuben ran prostitutes on the streets of Portland and that he also dealt drugs on those streets. At least he didn't abuse his "girls" and he didn't permit johns to abuse them; he even made sure they didn't use drugs, which was eccentric for a drug dealer to say the least.

What I learned way back when he helped me with Veronica's case was that, while nowhere near the straight and narrow, Reuben could be trusted to back you up if he liked and respected you. Also, it didn't hurt that he knew how to fight, how to use a gun, and what almost all the other bad guys in Portland were doing.

It was early afternoon, so he was probably already out on the streets with his ladies. I called his cell phone, which he answered on the first ring.

"Yo, McCall. You back from your honeymoon already?"

"We didn't go on one. We're still in the office, working cases—and one of the cases is a threat to Colleen."

"Well, shit. What can I do?"

"You ever heard of a Las Vegas kingpin named Antonio Sabado, or maybe Tony Saturday?"

"Tony Saturday. Sure, I know who that is—as of yesterday. You calling because he's in town? Don't tell me your kid got on his bad side somehow. I hear he's really bad news...."

I caught up with what he was saying and interrupted. "He's in Portland?" I registered Malone turning back toward me from her monitor.

"Yeah," said Reuben in my ear, "Isn't that why you want to know about him?"

"Let's start over," I said. "I'm going to put you on speaker, so Devon can hear this." I set my cell phone on the desk, took a deep breath, and pushed speaker. "Still there?"

"I'm here. Hey, Malone, your hubby treatin' you right?"

"Fuck you, Reuben. What were you saying about Sabado?"

"If that's the same as Tony Saturday, I was sayin' he's here in town. Has been for a couple of days, as far as I know. What's the deal with him and Colleen, for fuck's sake?"

"It might be Hoke who's actually in trouble with him, though we don't know why. Something that happened when he and Colleen took that trip to Vegas. And, of course, any threat to Hoke...."

"Is a threat to Colleen. Yeah, I get it."

"Good, because I don't want to take the time to lay it all out for you right now. What I want is for you to tell us what you know about Sabado being in town."

"Not a lot. I don't play in his league. He's been in town a couple of days and brought some muscle with him. I didn't hear anything about him going after a local. I heard he was in town on business—or maybe to set up some business."

"What business?" Malone asked.

"Don't know. Probably not gambling and I hope not women because I don't need the competition. Maybe washing money? I'll ask around and see if I can pin it down more. Right now, that's all I got."

"Okay," I said, "thanks for that. Let us know if you hear any more."

"I will, and you take care of your kid."

"She's covered for now. Talk to you soon." I ended the call.

My partner swiveled her chair back and forth as she looked meditatively out the window. "I hate to do it but maybe I'll give Carl Gunther a call. If anybody knows what Sabado is doing here, it would be Portland's very own crime boss. In fact, protocol would require Sabado to touch base with him."

"That's a last resort," I cautioned. "Let's see what Reuben comes up with first."

Malone had opened her mouth to reply when our main agency phone rang. I got to it first. "McCall-Malone Detective Agency."

"This is Agatha Pepper, Mr. McCall." It sounded like she was on a cell phone outside somewhere.

"Ms. Pepper. What can I do for you? Everything all right?"

"Well, I'm not sure. I think I have a tail."

"A tail?"

"Yes, I'm giving Morty his afternoon walkies and when we left the hotel I noticed a young man standing out front on the sidewalk. He seems to be following me, about a half-block back."

"Does he match the description of the young man in the restaurant?"

"Right down to the shiny earring."

I stood and motioned to Malone that we needed to get moving. "Where are you right now?"

"Morty and I are just arriving at Pioneer Courthouse Square. Perhaps if I sit down and appear to be taking a break, the young man will stay nearby until you can arrive."

"Sounds like a plan," I said as I retrieved my Smith and Wesson from the desk drawer. I ended the call and we left the office on the run.

CHAPTER THIRTEEN

We didn't bother to drive; getting through the sunny Thursday afternoon traffic and finding another parking place would have taken us twice the eight minutes required to rapidly walk the six blocks to the Square.

We stopped on the Morrison Street side, Nordstrom to our right, the Pioneer Courthouse itself to our left, and surveyed the colorful array of citizens and tourists strolling, sitting, and snacking throughout the space known affectionately as "Portland's Living Room." The center of the large square was arranged like an amphitheater with a semicircle of approximately two dozen steps that also served as seats.

Malone tapped my arm and pointed toward the bottom tiers almost directly below us. There sat Agatha Pepper, arrayed in purple and gold and looking like she didn't have a care in the world, with Morty splayed out and apparently snoozing beside her bright green purse.

Using the pair as a center, I slowly panned my gaze outward looking for anyone who appeared to be particularly interested in them. It took probably less than five seconds to identify a young man sitting alone, third step up on the Nordstrom side, and staring at our client. I could tell from Malone's grunt that she'd seen him too.

"So how do you want to do this?" she asked.

"Well, he has no reason to pick us out from this crowd, so why don't you wander around the corner and ease behind him while I casually head diagonally down to position myself in front of him? Then you make your move and I'm there if he tries to run."

"Sounds good to me. See you on the other side." She moved off to our right.

I waited until she was in position above him and then we simultaneously started moving in. He was wearing a white polo shirt, jeans, and sneakers with no place to conceal a weapon; he did match the description of the man in the restaurant, though that didn't mean much since half the young men on the street came close enough. But there was that glint in his left ear and his laser focus on our client, not to mention her claim that a man who looked like this had followed her from the hotel.

I was fairly confident we'd have an interesting conversation once we'd corralled him—which wouldn't be difficult since he was totally oblivious to our approach.

I sped up a little so that Malone and I reached him at the same time. We casually sat down, me to his left and she to his right.

I looked over at him. He still wasn't paying any attention to us even though we were practically snugged up against him. "Nice day, isn't it?"

He jerked as if I'd poked him. His head swiveled from me to my partner. "Who are you? What do you want?"

I didn't see any reason to pull punches. "My name's Clint McCall and that's my partner Devon Malone. We're private detectives. We want to talk to you."

He visibly paled in the bright sunlight. "Detectives? I didn't do anything wrong. What do you want to talk about?"

I pointed down toward Agatha Pepper. "You see that older lady, with the dog, sitting on the lowest tier over there?"

He looked, nodded reluctantly. "Yeah."

"We want to talk about her."

"And," interjected Malone, "you might want to revise your statement that you haven't done anything wrong."

I swear the guy started to tremble. "Oh crap. Oh God. This can't be happening."

Meanwhile, Ms. Pepper had risen in response to my pointing and all of us staring at her. I guess she figured there was no more point in pretending she was unaware of what was going on. She and Morty started slowly working their way up toward the three of us.

We all waited silently for her to arrive. She stopped right in front of the young man and frowned down at him as Morty huffed.

"Who are you and why are you trying to kill me?"

A couple of kids sitting nearby snapped to attention and I quickly stood, hauling our captive to his feet as well. He hadn't made a sound since Agatha confronted him. "This is not a discussion for the middle of a crowded square," I said to her. "I suggest that we all walk back to the office together and have our chat there."

Malone also stood. "Excellent idea. Agatha and I will be right behind you two." She opened her jacket just enough that we could all see her Glock. "You'll come along quietly, right?"

He nodded, still mute.

Agatha apparently wasn't feeling so cooperative. She stood fast, arms crossed, glaring. "I'll wait on the explanation," she said, "but I want to know who you are. Right here. Right now."

Maybe she saw something in him, sensed that the answer was important, but clearly she didn't expect the reply she got when he finally looked up from his shoes and met her glare.

"My name's Rodney Pepper. I'm your nephew."

CHAPTER FOURTEEN

Malone, Agatha Pepper, and I escorted her purported nephew back to the office, he and I walking in front of the two women and the dog with an explicit caution that Malone would shoot him in the leg if he tried to escape.

Beyond that, none of us said a word during the twenty-minute walk, taking our time since Ms. Pepper had to use her cane. I couldn't imagine what our client could be thinking about the young man's claim and I was having a hard time focusing my own thoughts away from Colleen's jeopardy.

Once we were finally settled in the office, however, I did my best to set our other problems aside. This was a possible attempted murderer in the visitor's chair nearest me. I gave him a good hard look as his own eyes darted wildly around the office.

"Can you prove that you're Ms. Pepper's nephew?"

"I...well, my father said I am."

"Your father is Ms. Pepper's brother?" I looked over at her. "I assume you have a brother or you probably would have mentioned by now that you don't."

Agatha Pepper was still looking, as the British might say, gobsmacked. "Well, I had a brother, a long time ago. He disappeared when he was seventeen and I was twelve. I've hardly thought of him in years."

She hadn't taken her eyes off the young man as she spoke. I'm not sure she had since he introduced himself. "You're Conrad's son? But you're too young. Conrad would be in his early eighties now."

"He was in his late fifties when I was born."

"Why did he go away? Why has he never contacted me? Where is he now?"

"He died six months ago."

Ms. Pepper took a long moment to absorb that. "Oh."

"I'm sorry."

"I have so many questions."

"You think I don't? All I have is a letter he left me that I found after he died—and some of it doesn't make much sense because he was on a lot of meds at the end. The cancer had gotten into his spine. Anyway, I got out of it that he had a sister he'd never told me about. He knew your name and where you were, so he must have been keeping track of you somehow. He knew you were a librarian and that you had a lot of money. That was about it."

"He told you I have a lot of money?"

"Yes. Isn't that true?"

The old woman frowned at him. "Well, yes, but how would he know? And why would he tell you about it?"

"I don't know how he knew. He was really good at finding things out, before he got so sick, and he did still have days when he was sharp. I'm sure he told me because we *didn't* have a lot of money."

Malone spoke up. "What was he? Some kind of investigator?"

Rodney Pepper shook his head. "Not exactly. He was a con man. No other way to put it. In and out of jail all my life." He looked at Agatha. "That's probably why he disappeared so young. He went off to con somebody. I don't think he ever cared about anything but money."

Agatha finally looked away from him, first to me and then to Malone. "I don't believe this." I noticed Morty stirring and gazing up at her as if he sensed her distress.

"None of us know whether he's lying or not," I said, and then focused on the young man. "Enough family stories. Let's cut to the chase. If all this *is* true and you just learned a few months ago that Ms. Pepper here is your aunt, why have you been trying to kill her?"

He shifted uncomfortably in his seat. "That wasn't me."

I decided this would be a good time to lie. There's no law against it and a guilty conscience is easily misled. "It was you, asshole. There were witnesses. We have descriptions of you in the restaurant, driving the car, setting the leaves on fire.... They all match you, right down to the earring. You might as well explain yourself."

Rodney Pepper slumped back in his chair. "Shit. I just thought.... We never had any money and all of a sudden I'm the only living relative of this rich old lady...."

Malone sat forward. "You were trying to kill your aunt because you wanted to inherit her money? That wasn't going to happen, anyway."

That got young Rodney's attention. "Why not?"

"Because she has a will, dum-dum. And you couldn't be in it because she didn't even know you existed."

"Crap. She had a will?"

"Yes, you know, one of those legal documents that specifies who will inherit your money?"

He was frowning now, like my partner was speaking a foreign language. "I know what a will is, but I didn't think of her having one."

"Probably be more accurate to just say you didn't think."

"Who inherits?"

"The Portland Friends of the Library."

"You're shitting me."

"Nope."

"Then why was I trying to kill her?"

"An excellent question."

At this point, Agatha Pepper threw up her hands. "I don't believe it!"

"Ms. Pepper," I responded, figuring it was time she had the floor, "what is it you don't believe? That's he's your nephew or that he was trying to kill you?"

"That he's so darned stupid!" she exploded as Morty offered a little bark in support. "That my brother was a sleazy criminal! That I have the same genes as him and this moron!"

Rodney jerked back and held up a hand. "Now, wait a minute, I'm still your only family...."

"Ha!" she interrupted his appeal. "That is hardly a blessing." She gave me a hard look. "Mr. McCall, please contact the police. I want to charge this little shit."

CHAPTER FIFTEEN

A very unhappy Rodney Pepper was booked by Mike Whitehall on three charges of attempted murder. Malone and I returned to the office after leaving Ms. Pepper in the lobby of her hotel where she planned to immediately retrieve Morty, check out, and return to her home in Lake Oswego just south of Portland proper.

"I'll write up the final report," Malone said as we settled on opposite sides of the partners desk. "You wrote the last one." She swiveled to her keyboard. "Everything's covered by the retainer, right?"

"Definitely. We probably should refund part of it since Rodney basically caught himself and then confessed."

"I don't think I'll include that option," she said dryly, and commenced typing.

Grateful that there was one fewer distraction from taking care of my daughter, I decided to call the Pen and Pastry to see how Colleen and company were doing. I didn't even try her cell phone; she wasn't any better than me at keeping it with her—a technology Luddite just like her father.

The waitress who picked up the phone knew Colleen and went to get her. Even though she'd given no indication of there being anything wrong, I think I held my breath for the thirty or forty seconds it took for my daughter to pick up.

"Hey, Dad, what's going on?"

"Just checking on you and Hoke. Everything okay? Is Sonny Sampson still there with you?"

"We're fine. The four of us are sitting at a table near the kitchen and Sonny's keeping an eye on the entrance."

"The four of you?"

"Veronica is sitting with us."

"You're sure everything's okay."

There was just the slightest hesitation. "Yes, it's okay. Getting kind of interesting, but we're perfectly safe."

"What's interesting?"

"Oh, you know.... Stuff. Interpersonal relations."

This was becoming a very odd conversation, not the first I'd had with Colleen. "You and Hoke having a problem?"

"No, we're fine."

"Then what the hell are you talking about?"

"I really need to get back to the table. Talk to you later, Dad."

She ended the call. What the fuck?

Malone gave me the eye as I in turn hung up. "What was that all about? She's okay?"

"So she says, but something's going on." I opened the drawer where I'd stashed my Smith and Wesson just minutes before. "I think we should take a little ride to our favorite coffee shop, see what's so interesting."

Malone saved her document and went for her Glock. "How do you know something's interesting?"

"Because Colleen said so, but she wouldn't tell me what it was."

"Okey dokey."

It took us almost ten minutes to get out of downtown through the late afternoon traffic. Then it was a straight shot down Hawthorne to the Pen and Pastry—or, more accurately, to my house where I parked behind the green Miata. Then just a minute more to walk around the corner to Veronica's place.

It was packed, as usual. The Pen and Pastry is open and airy with glass picture windows looking out on Hawthorne and a first-class kitchen. It has twenty-plus tables that each seat four patrons but can be moved together for bigger groups. No booths. It's a very successful business equally because of the excellent pastry selection, simple all-day luncheon fare, and Veronica Fortune herself.

It's the only café in Portland, perhaps in the world, that is owned and operated by a former prostitute who's a best-selling author. Considering that every staff member is also a former prostitute, no surprise that the customer demographic tilts strongly toward young males.

At a table in the far corner near the kitchen, however, the balance was reversed: three females and a young male.

None of the four had noted our entrance and I could see why, even from clear across the room. Hoke had his back to us and Colleen was sitting to his right. Sonny Sampson was in the best position to watch the entrance, but she wasn't. She was instead intently focused on Veronica Fortune, leaning in to her very intimately I thought, and very close to holding hands. No, not very close. They were holding hands.

Malone obviously saw the same thing.

"Well," she said, "that *is* interesting."

CHAPTER SIXTEEN

We were about halfway across the room before anyone at the table noticed us, and it was my daughter rather than the woman who was supposed to be watching out for her. Sonny Sampson was still intent on our friend Veronica, looking downright smitten in fact.

They did make a striking pair: the small, tough-looking Sonny with her cap of brunette hair, probably mid-thirties, wearing jeans and sleeveless top, next to the voluptuous Veronica, still a knockout at forty-nine and wearing a bright orange caftan that somehow did not conflict with the red hair flowing loosely down her back.

The Las Vegas PI finally saw us, did a double take, sat up straight, and let go of her new friend's hand.

Colleen, meanwhile, was looking concerned. "Hey, Dad. We just hung up. Has something happened?"

"No, we decided to drop by and see what's going on." I gave Veronica Fortune a good hard look as I finished that sentence and was rewarded with cheeks almost as red as her hair.

She abruptly stood. "My break's over. I'd better get back to managing this place." She did a quick survey of the room. "It looks like the ladies could use my help." Quick glance down at Sonny Sampson. "It was nice meeting you."

Looking back up at her, Sonny failed utterly to keep a straight face and the rest of us began to chuckle. "I'm sure we'll see each other again," she said as solemnly as she could—which wasn't very.

Veronica fled toward the pastry counter and Malone took her place at the table. "I guess you're used to things moving pretty fast in Vegas," she said to Sampson.

"They do," Sonny agreed, and took a big swallow of whatever she was drinking. It looked like 7-Up.

I was already making a mental list of what I wanted to accomplish as long as we were here. First was to have a little chat with Sonny Sampson about keeping her eye on my daughter rather than potential girlfriends. The second was to get said daughter aside to have that talk about what might have gone on with Hoke in Las Vegas. The third....

"Incoming," Malone suddenly said. "And you won't believe it."

I looked at her and then followed her amused gaze toward the entrance...where I observed Agatha Pepper and Morty making their way across the room toward us. She walked up to us with a big smile as if we'd all arranged the meeting.

"Ms. Pepper," I greeted her. "How did you get here?"

"When my driver came to pick me up, I saw the two of you drive by as we were leaving the hotel. I told him to follow you."

"You have a driver?" Malone asked.

"Of course, dear. The motor vehicle people took my license some time ago—over my vehement protests, I might add."

"Okay," I said, "better question. Why did you follow us?"

"Oh, I thought you should know that I changed my mind. I've decided to provide a lawyer for my nephew and he'll probably walk."

"You're hiring him a lawyer? You were the one who wanted him charged."

"Exactly. It's a very good lawyer, hired by the victim. He'll probably get off." She offered a bird-like shrug. "He may be abysmally stupid, but he is family. My only family, actually, and I want a chance to get to know him."

"And possibly get killed by him," Malone said.

"Oh, no, there's really very little chance of that. I'm ever so much smarter than he is."

My partner and I looked at each other. "Go figure," she said.

It was about then that I remembered all this was being witnessed by Colleen, Hoke, and Sonny. I gestured at the table. "Ms. Pepper, I should introduce...."

She stopped me with a hand lightly resting on my arm. "Perhaps we should wait on that."

"Why?"

"Because Morty and I passed a man sitting at a table back there, about halfway to the entrance, who seemed very interested in your group here. He looks like a very bad man." She leaned in to whisper in my ear. "And I think he's packing."

Sometimes you can't help doing the dumb thing. We all looked in the direction from which she'd come, trying to see who she was talking about. In a split second, I found myself making eye contact with a big man seated alone at a table about twenty feet away, glowering back at us. He looked to be maybe in his fifties, stocky and very fit, classic fireplug guy, wearing a lightweight tan sport coat over a grey t-shirt that matched his closely trimmed hair. His broad and grizzled face had a scar on the left side, running from the corner of his eye almost down to his mouth. He must have come in right behind us because we certainly hadn't walked past him.

Sabado's Scarface. In the Pen and Pastry, twenty feet from my daughter, with a gun.

CHAPTER SEVENTEEN

Behind me I heard an "oh my God" coming from Hoke. I knew without turning that he had recognized the man and we, along with everyone else in the Pen and Pastry, were potentially in big trouble.

"Everybody sit still," Malone said just loudly enough to be heard by the four behind us at our table. "Let's see what he does."

I was sure that she had her hand on her weapon just like I did, just as Sonny Sampson probably did. If I had been a praying person, I'd have been offering a big one that none of us would have to draw. A gun fight in this crowded café would be a disaster no matter who won.

While I doubted that Antonio Sabado's main man gave a shit about the welfare of Pen and Pastry customers, he apparently did give a shit about the possibility of three guns versus his one. At least I assumed he knew we were armed because after a moment more of glaring, he slowly stood and pulled his sport coat open just enough for us to see the large handgun he had holstered there. Yeah, he knew who we were, all right.

My brain finally caught up to the fact that I was looking past Agatha Pepper at Scarface. She didn't resist as I quickly moved her to the side and back so she wouldn't be directly in the line of fire if there was one.

At about the same time, Sabado's man started backing toward the entrance. That was attracting some attention from nearby patrons, but no one was panicking yet. He'd covered his gun again and they were probably just mildly curious about why this big ugly idiot was walking backward.

When he was within five feet of the door, he turned to make his exit. Malone and I stepped off to follow him the second his eyes left ours. I didn't want a gunfight, but I sure did want a conversation if possible.

I realized as we quickly crossed the distance to the front entrance that Sonny Sampson was right behind us. That made me a little uneasy even though we'd tentatively decided to trust her. Tentative doesn't count for much when armed people you don't know well are in front *and* behind you.

The three of us spilled out onto the sidewalk and I immediately saw that Scarface was standing about fifteen feet to our left, next to a big black sedan. He wasn't actually looking at us at that moment; he was watching a Portland patrol car drive slowly by. Good for you, Mike Whitehall.

Then he glared at us and moved to go around the front of the sedan to the driver's side. We were maybe ten feet from him and I held up both hands as I kept going. "We just want to talk," I said. "No guns, no problem."

He stopped. We stopped. Now we were about six feet apart. He looked to either side of me as his right hand eased his jacket open again. "Tell that to the cunts," he said. His voice sounded like it was emanating from the bottom of a rusty barrel.

I glanced to either side, keeping my hands up, and saw that both Malone and Sampson still had their hands on their weapons—and my partner looked like she was about to draw hers. "No guns, no problem," I repeated, focusing particularly on Malone. After a moment, she and Sampson both lifted their hands to match mine and Scarface relaxed slightly, moving his own hand away from his gun.

Okay. I took a deep breath. Maybe now we could learn something without anyone getting killed.

No point in starting with small talk. "We know who you are. Why are you following Hoke Moseley?"

He sneered. "I don't know who the fuck you are and I'm not following anybody."

"Why are you here?" asked Malone.

For a moment it looked like he was going to ignore her question but then he shrugged. "Here at a coffee shop? Getting coffee. Here in Portland? I'm here with my boss because he fucking has business here. Why do you want to know, bitch?"

"Just wanted to confirm that besides being ugly, you're a liar."

"Like I said," I quickly interjected before Scarface could attack my always-discreet partner, "we know who you are, who you work for, and that you're focused on the young man back in the café for some reason. If you don't want to tell us the reason, if you want to deny the whole thing, we can't do much about that right now, but I would strongly advise you to let your boss know that harming the young man would not be a good idea. Harming his girlfriend would be an even worse idea. She's my daughter."

The son of a bitch smirked at me. "I'll be sure to tell Tony what you said—and you should tell your daughter to be careful about the company she keeps."

With that he again headed for the driver's side of the vehicle. I wanted to stop him, to warn him again, to punch his lights out...but I knew well enough there was no point in continuing or escalating the confrontation.

We watched him get in the car and pull away from the curb. As the three of us turned back to the restaurant, it occurred to me that Sonny Sampson had not said a word during all this, even though she was the one who knew the most about Scarface and Sabado. I would have to think about that.

In fact, my first three priorities now were to get Colleen and Hoke somewhere safer than the Pen and Pastry, have that talk with Colleen about Hoke's veracity, and do some serious checking on Sampson. If she was going to be at my back, I wanted to make sure she had my back.

CHAPTER EIGHTEEN

We all walked around the corner to my house—"all" including Agatha Pepper, who'd dismissed her driver for the day, apparently having decided that she was part of our team, and Morty, who didn't have anywhere else to go.

I unlocked my front door and stepped inside to the traditional greetings of Stella and Maxine, but they hadn't even made it the length of the living room before they were stopped by the crowd of strangers piling in behind me.

Then they saw Morty, at about the same time that Agatha Pepper saw them. "Oh, they're adorable!" She launched herself in their direction, whereupon my two cats disappeared, probably never to be seen again. The dog plus the onrushing elderly kaleidoscope of color was too much for them.

"Leave the cats alone," I cautioned our client. "Everybody find a seat. We need to clarify a few things and then decide what to do next."

"But they're so cute," she pouted as she settled in one of the armchairs.

Sonny Sampson took the other armchair while Colleen and Hoke settled on the couch. Malone and I stayed on our feet for the time being.

"What *are* we going to do?" asked my daughter, somewhat plaintively. "Where are we going to be safe?"

"Clarification first," I responded, having decided that getting her off alone was too much trouble. "How long was Hoke in that hotel lobby without you and were there other times when he was off on his own?"

Hoke stiffened and stared at me. "Hey!"

"I'm sorry, Hoke, but this has become a critical situation and I have to be sure there's nothing you are neglecting to tell us. Is there?"

"No!"

Colleen meanwhile had put her hand comfortingly on his arm. "Pops, I thought you trusted Hoke by now. He was in the lobby for maybe five minutes before I came down and, no, there was no other time that he was out and about without me." Now they were both giving me the evil eye.

I held up my hands in surrender. "I apologize again. Something happened in Vegas that brought a big-time gangster down on you guys—and it had to be more than exchanging a few words with a young woman in a hotel lobby."

"Maybe not." That was Sampson, the first words she'd spoken since we were all in the Pen and Pastry together.

"Yeah?" I noted her grim expression.

"I've made some calls since we last talked and I've started getting hints that some of Sabado's prostitutes might have been underage."

"What?" That was Malone.

Sampson grimaced. "Just hints so far, but if it's true...."

I focused again on Hoke. "Did the girl in the lobby say anything like that to you? Any hint along those lines? Could she have been propositioning you?"

"No, I don't think so. She just said she'd like to visit Portland but that she couldn't because Tony wouldn't let her...then she started to say something else, but that's when the guy came along and said he was her father. I figured he was Tony. There was nothing about her being a prostitute. She didn't seem like that."

"It would help a lot if I could identify her," Sampson said. "The girl didn't tell you her name?"

"No."

"Was there anything distinctive about her appearance?"

"No, nothing. She was a teenaged girl, five feet tall or a little less, brunette, really thin, like maybe she'd been sick."

"Or brutalized," Sampson said.

This was getting more worrisome all the time. I focused on Sampson. "Okay, you keep checking to see what else you can find out. Even if the girl was an underage prostitute, that doesn't explain why Sabado would be interested in Hoke, much less a threat to him. There's got to be more."

She nodded in agreement. "There could be. You know that prostitution is legal in Nevada—but only in counties with a population below 700,000. Clark County, in which Las Vegas is located, has more than 700,000. That's a problem for the folks who see how much money could be made if it were legal within the city limits. It may be that could happen if enough money reaches the right hands. Again, I just have hints. But a big scandal about underage prostitution could put a stop to such a project real quick. The infamous Tony Saturday would not want to be blamed for that. It would make him very, very unpopular with a bunch of people who have hired killers on their payroll."

That washed some chills down my spine. "That would do it, all right. Well, like I said, keep checking." I focused on Colleen and Hoke. "Meanwhile, we need to get serious about keeping you two safe. You can stay here until I think of something better, but not by yourselves." I cocked an eye back at Sonny Sampson, realizing that, for better or worse, I needed to trust her. At this point, it seemed like a good bet.

"I'd rather not stay here with them," she said. "I need to be out and about, you know, investigating. I want to see if I can discover who Hoke's mysterious teenager was and of course keep an eye out for Sabado or any of his people. We need to know what they're doing here, if anything, besides stalking this young man."

"I might have a source for that," Malone said. I knew she was again talking about local crime boss Carl Gunther, Sr.

I still had the problem of finding more protection for my daughter and her boyfriend. It couldn't be any of my fellow black belts; they enjoyed occasionally playing detective, but I wasn't going to put amateurs up against professional killers. Reuben was capable, but wouldn't want to take that much time away from his business....

My train of thought was interrupted by Agatha Pepper,

whom I'd practically forgotten was still with us. "I can stay and protect them," she announced gleefully. "I'm all set."

Whereupon she stood up, reached into her massive bright green purse, and pulled out a handgun.

Everybody gasped, me right along with the others.

"You are fucking kidding me," said my partner.

CHAPTER NINETEEN

Our suddenly well-armed client seemed surprised that we were surprised. She looked appraisingly at the gun in her hand. It was small, compact, and deadly looking. She held it out to me, finger very near the trigger, as if it were her most prized possession. Given that this was Agatha Pepper, it might have been.

First things first. "Is the safety on?"

She looked down at the weapon again and lost a shade of her prideful glow. "I think so," she said at last. "The clerk showed me how to do it, but I think I forgot."

Malone bravely rose and approached the old lady, gently easing the gun out of Ms. Pepper's hand. Everyone else was choosing to stay put and hold their breath. My partner hefted the weapon and looked over at me. "It's a Walther, a PK380. Good firearm." A closer look. "And the safety is on."

Agatha Pepper, meanwhile, looked absolutely delighted. "It's a Walter? I love that. A gun named Walter!"

"Wal-ther," I said. "That's the name of the company that makes the gun."

"Oh, well, I shall call it Walter anyway. You can give it back now," she said to Malone, who complied somewhat reluctantly. "And would you show me how to take off that safety."

Malone stepped back. "No, Agatha, I don't think I will."

Ms. Pepper casually stowed the gun back in her purse. "Oh well. I'll figure it out."

My partner gave me a look. "I think we should put a stipulation in our contract that the client is not allowed to buy a gun while we're working for them."

"Couldn't agree more," I responded.

"So," Agatha announced, "now that that's settled...."

"Whoa," I quickly interrupted. "Nothing is settled. You're

not qualified to be a bodyguard for Colleen and Hoke." I felt ridiculous even having to say it.

She sat firmly back down in her chair, the purse solidly in the center of her lap. Morty snorted his support. Maybe he was spending too much time around Malone.

I tried being reasonable. "Agatha, it's not your responsibility to put your life on the line for my daughter and her boyfriend. You don't even know them. And you may have a gun, but right now you don't even remember how to put the safety on and take it off again. You really think you could outshoot a professional?"

It wasn't working. She was sitting like an elderly stone, tight-lipped and grimly determined, clutching the bright green purse and no doubt trying to recall how to deal with the safety.

"And I can't have Morty here." I was getting desperate. "I have two cats and you saw how they reacted. They wouldn't be able to eat or sleep or anything."

"My driver can take care of Morty while I'm here. He's done it plenty of times when I go to the spa."

I was considering simply ordering the woman out of my house when Colleen spoke up. "I think you ought to let her stay."

I couldn't believe it. I had to bite my lip to keep from blurting, *Are you fucking insane?* That's just not the sort of thing you say to your daughter in front of strangers. After taking a good, deep breath, I said, as calmly as I could, "I don't think it would be a good idea, Colleen."

"I don't mean that she should do it by herself, but I don't see why she couldn't stay with us if she wanted to. She's got somebody to take care of the dog and..." She smiled fondly at Agatha. "...it would be like having the grandmother I never had." Then she grinned at me. "I like her."

Oh great. Just great. Everybody was looking at me now, Malone with a grin even bigger than Colleen's; she was enjoying this. Hoke and Sonny Sampson, looking as neutral as they could, had clearly decided to stay out of it. Agatha had relaxed as if it were already settled. Apparently it was.

Well, okay. I'd already eliminated the black belts and Reuben. Johnny and Hap seemed determined to make a go of their retirement this time...but then I had a thought that brought a grin to my own face.

"I'm going to call Reuben to see if he knows where Big Avenue is."

CHAPTER TWENTY

"What kind of name is Big Avenue?" Agatha Pepper asked me the next morning, comfortably ensconced at the kitchen table while I microwaved bacon to go with the eggs that Devon was scrambling.

"It's a nickname, I guess because he's big and works the street."

"Works the street?"

"Don't ask," my partner said.

"His given name is Na'hahu Kemaoutu," I offered. "He's Samoan."

"Can't wait to meet him."

When I finally talked to Big last night, we'd agreed he would show up this morning. It had been, meanwhile, quite a night in the McCall-Malone household and I was feeling half-woozy from lack of sleep.

Sonny Sampson and Morty both left, separately, soon after I had reluctantly conceded that Agatha could stay, which still left us with five people to feed and house overnight. It was somewhat chaotic. Stella and Maxine didn't emerge from wherever they'd been hiding until everyone but Devon and I were bedded down and quiet. They joined us as we were having a very late-night snack in the kitchen and finally ate their own dinners.

Neither the cats nor the kids had yet appeared this morning and I envied their ability to sleep in.

Malone, Agatha, and I were just finishing breakfast when we heard a loud knock on the front door. I hurried through the living room and opened the door to reveal the six-foot-six four-hundred-pound Big Avenue.

I heard a gasp behind me and realized that Agatha Pepper had followed from the kitchen.

"Oh my goodness," she almost whispered, "you are quite large."

Big cocked his massive bald head to the side and looked down past me at the elderly librarian, breaking into a big grin. "That I is," he said.

I shook his hand and introduced him to the bird-like Agatha who gazed up at him in wonder as he gently took her hand between his thumb and forefinger to shake. He nodded over Agatha's head at Malone, who was watching with a bemused expression from the kitchen doorway.

Then he focused on me. "So your kid's in trouble again. Needs watching."

"Her boyfriend's apparently the actual target, but that puts her in danger, too."

"They both here?"

"Yeah, still in bed as far as I know."

He slid a side-eye at the elderly librarian. "And...?"

I had to clear my throat before I could say it. "Ms. Pepper is here to help you guard them. She's armed, by the way, a handgun in her purse."

The big grin returned as he looked down at her. "So you my backup? You ever shot anybody?"

Her spine stiffened and she hit him with the perfect librarian glare. "I was here first, young man, so you're my backup. Have you ever shot anyone?"

His laugh was loud, long, and deep. "Yes, lady, I've shot people."

"Well, I guess that's good then." She looked at me. "We'll be fine."

I spent a few minutes bringing Big Avenue up to speed on what he needed to do, what he'd be paid for it, and why it needed doing. Meanwhile Colleen and Hoke came out to say hello, probably awakened by his laugh. I cautioned everyone to not open the door to any strangers, under any circumstances.

I knew the big man probably didn't get all of it, but enough. Big Avenue was not one of the brighter lights on the street, but immensely tough and loyal, a good man to have at your back or protecting your daughter. Among friends he could be a gentle giant, but nobody hostile was getting past him without automatic weapons, explosives, and a small army.

Plus, of course, he had Agatha Pepper and Walter as backup.

CHAPTER TWENTY-ONE

Devon Malone took in the new-car smell of the elevator was trimmed in leather as she stepped inside. Very luxurious, as you'd expect in a building owned by Carl Gunther. It even included a comfortable bench in case you were too tired to remain standing on the way up.

She was anything but tired, brimming with apprehension and anticipation, ready for her first confrontation with Gunther in over a year.

Portland, Oregon, has a long history of corruption; cronyism, bootlegging, rackets, and white supremacy are all ingrained in the city's psyche. Powerful organized crime bosses from other places including Las Vegas have tried to move in on the city, but none have been successful. They might develop loose associations and friendly social relations with the local bad guys but they've never owned Portland.

Currently, Carl Gunther owned Portland.

Malone wondered if he was still interested in owning her. Still out of luck, if he was. She smiled to herself as the elevator doors opened.

The offices of Gunther Global Import/Export were on the twenty-second floor of one of the newer downtown Portland office buildings, just off Pioneer Square, a building that was all pink-tinted glass and glimmer and a very snazzy business address indeed.

She stepped from the elevator into a spotlessly clean carpeted hallway that extended some distance in both directions. There was a small metal directory on the wall in front of her. The arrow for Gunther Global pointed to the right.

Framed works of modern art were hung on the glowing off-white walls of the wide corridor. They were originals, or so Gunther claimed. She made no more noise walking on the thick carpet than the elevator had made getting her here. The air was fresh as the outdoors.

She arrived at the properly labeled door, which opened into a simple but tastefully decorated reception area. The plush carpet from the hallway continued inside, as did the fresh-smelling air. What appeared to be reproductions of old maps were hung, one on each of the walls. There was one other door, which she knew led into Gunther's office. A medium-size leather couch sat against the wall to her left and directly before her was a highly polished wooden desk. Behind it sat an older woman who—despite her standard office attire—looked like Central Casting's idea of everybody's favorite grandmother: white hair, a round, cheery face with pink cheeks, half-glasses over which she gazed at Devon Malone in surprise. A little free-standing nameplate sitting toward the front edge of her desk said she was Mrs. Agnes Pinkerton. Malone knew that she kept a fully loaded handgun in the middle drawer of the desk.

Central Casting would have been wrong about her.

"Well, Ms. Malone. Long time no see. Mr. Gunther didn't tell me you were dropping by."

"I didn't call ahead. Is he free?"

"Quite expensive, actually, but there's no one in there with him right now." She reached for her phone. "I'll tell him you're here and see what he wants me to do."

Malone sincerely hoped it didn't involve that middle drawer, but mentally rehearsed quick-drawing her own weapon just in case. She and Carl Gunther were not friends, mostly because at one point he'd wanted to be much more than friends and wasn't used to being told no.

And of course there had been her partner's run-in with Gunther's son, but that was another, long story.

The door to Gunther's office opened before Mrs. Pinkerton even had a chance to hang up her phone.

"Devon."

"Carl."

Carl Gunther was expensively dressed in a gray pinstripe suit with dark red tie and shiny black shoes. Early fifties with a full head of dark brown hair and craggy features, a little over six feet tall with a broad chest and thick legs, much more muscle than fat. He looked like a man used to getting his way and capable of hurting people who didn't cooperate.

Maintaining a neutral expression, Gunther told Mrs. Pinkerton to hold his calls and stepped back to allow Malone entry into his office proper.

And proper it was indeed, just as classically executive as he was classically gangster: the highly polished power desk with the plush leather chair behind it, the matching bronze desk set with no miscellaneous files or paper marring the immaculate desk surface, the leather couch along one wall, two visitor chairs in front of the desk and two more chairs on this side of a large coffee table in front of the couch.

Gunther chose to take his seat behind the desk, so Malone settled into one of the very comfortable visitor chairs.

"To what do I owe the pleasure, Mrs. McCall?"

Malone snorted. "You heard that I got married."

"I did. But you're still Devon Malone?"

"Yep, still me."

"No surprise there. But you could have done better, you know."

"I have a rule against marrying crime bosses. Sorry."

The big man clasped his hands on the desktop, ignoring Malone's sarcasm. "So, what can I do for you? I know you aren't here just to say hello."

"Antonio Sabado, aka Tony Saturday, is in town."

Carl Gunther sat back and gave that a moment's thought, then nodded.

"I heard."

"I'm sure you heard straight from him. It would be a major insult if he didn't pay proper respect. What I want to know is, what did he say about *why* he's here?"

Gunther appeared to be fully on alert by now. "If indeed we met and he shared anything about the purpose of his visit, why should I tell you?"

Malone grinned. "For old time's sake?"

"Yes, you're still you, all right."

"Come on, Carl. Lives could be on the line here, including my step-daughter's."

"McCall's daughter? What's she got to do with Tony Saturday?"

"It's her boyfriend actually, something that happened in Vegas we haven't pinned down yet, but she could easily be collateral damage."

"I see."

"So? What did the guy tell you?"

Gunther sat forward and rested both elbows on his desk, his expression grim. "When we met, he said he was here to check on some business interests. Laundromats, I believe. Nothing I needed to worry about."

"Laundromats that clean money rather than clothes?"

"Could be."

"Okay. Good."

"But then, just this morning, he called to give me an update."

Now it was Malone's turn to frown.

"Why would he do that?"

Gunther met her frown with a faint smile. "Because I need to know if somebody like Tony Saturday is going to come into my town and start killing people. Otherwise there might be some misunderstanding."

Malone in turn leaned forward intently. "He called you this morning to tell you he's going to kill somebody in Portland?"

"Have them killed, anyway. One, at least. He thought there could be one or two beyond that. Definitely something he needed to give me a heads up about."

"He didn't say who?"

"Just assured me that they were none of mine."

Malone sat back, looking grim. "Which means they might be some of mine."

CHAPTER TWENTY-TWO

I was puttering around the office, worrying about Colleen and waiting for Malone to return, when I heard my cell phone buzzing. It was in fact my partner calling.

"What's up?" I asked. "You on your way back?" She'd walked over to Gunther's building and I could hear the sounds of traffic in the background.

"I'm nearly there and will meet you in the parking lot. We need to get back to your place. Call Big Avenue in the meantime and tell him to be on his guard."

Adrenaline shot through my system. "What's happening?"

"Nothing yet. I hope. But Gunther just told me that Sabado is planning to kill one or more people here in Portland."

I was already on my feet and holstering my Smith and Wesson. "Oh shit. And the only person we know he's interested in is Hoke."

"Yeah. Warn Big Avenue."

She disconnected and I was calling my house as I headed for the office door.

By the time I'd gotten downstairs to the sidewalk and crossed with the light, Malone was in sight walking quickly down Stark Street. We met at my Subaru.

"You talked to Big?" she asked as soon as we were both in the car. I was already pulling out into the traffic on Stark.

"Yeah, he says everything has been quiet, but he's going to be on alert until we get there."

Malone caught me up on everything Gunther had said as I bullied my way through the late morning traffic and cut the usual drive time to the Hawthorne District by nearly a third. I pulled into our driveway and we both bailed out. Big Avenue opened the front door before we got there. I could see Agatha

Pepper peering around his left arm, which was about the size of her torso.

Ah yes, something else had to be done about Ms. Pepper.

"Ain't nothin' happenin' yet," Big announced as we entered the house. Hoke and Colleen were standing together in the doorway to the kitchen. The cats were not in sight.

I went first to give my daughter a hug and shake hands with her boyfriend. "I'm sorry this is happening."

Colleen held on for a moment. "It's not your fault."

"Or yours, either," I said as we parted. I looked at Hoke. "Or yours, as far as I can tell. We'll figure it out and meanwhile we'll keep the two of you safe."

I turned back to the others in the room. "First things first. You need to go home, Agatha. We're going to move the kids and Big Avenue to a safer place and there's no reason for you to come along. You'll be safer in your own house."

I expected her to object, but instead she smiled and nodded. "I was hoping to be relieved of duty because Rodney is going to be released in a few hours."

"Really?" Malone beat me to it.

"Yes, they're dropping the charges."

"The guy tried to kill you three times."

"We've already talked about this. I'm smarter than he is and I'm not worried."

"So, what now?" I asked.

"I have to give him a chance, even if he is dumb as rocks. He's the only family I've got—and I didn't think I had any. You understand."

Not really, I thought but didn't say.

"Okay," I did say. "Can you have your driver pick you up?"

"He and Morty are already on the way. I called him when Biggie told me you were coming back."

"Biggie?"

She smiled fondly up at the massive black man beside her. "Well, it didn't seem right to call him Big, though he is."

Big Avenue carefully reached down and very gently hugged the little old lady that he could have easily crumpled like a tissue. "We friends now," he said to me.

"Driver's here," Malone called as she looked out the front window.

"Well, good," I said to Big. "Why don't you escort your new buddy out to her car and then get back in here so we can make a plan?"

He nodded. "Let's go, Aggie."

Biggie and Aggie. Give me strength.

"God, I'm glad she's on her way," I said to Malone as soon as the door closed behind them.

"I wondered why you caved on Ms. Pepper and her gun staying at the house," my partner replied. "Seemed like a terrible idea to me."

"You didn't say anything."

"I was trying to be a good wife."

"Ha. A role for which you are really not cut out."

Malone snorted.

I put my hand on her shoulder. "Just be yourself next time and tell me if I'm being an idiot."

"Will do. And ditto." She leaned in close to my ear. "And if those two get it on I'm resigning from the human race."

I jerked back a little. "I will never forgive you for that visual."

She chuckled.

I noted that Colleen and Hoke had not moved from the kitchen doorway but seemed to be amused by our exchange. I pointed at the couch. "Why don't you guys make yourselves comfortable. We'll decide where you're going next when Big comes back inside."

"This is no fun, you know," Colleen said as she settled beside Hoke. "Hoke and I both have lives."

"I do know that. It's not fun for us, either. We'll get it resolved and you'll be able to get back to your lives, hopefully pretty soon." Malone cocked an eye at me. "Somehow."

Big Avenue lumbered back inside at that point. "Aggie's gone," he announced. "She's funny."

"I'm glad you enjoyed her company," I responded. "You're sure it's been secure here today? You haven't seen anything that looked like a problem?"

He thought, hard; I could see the wheels turning. Slowly, very slowly. "Well, there was that limo."

Oh, shit. "What limo?"

"Big limo with tinted windows parked outside for a while earlier today. Couple of houses down. Couldn't see who was inside, but we thought it looked suspicious, so Aggie went out to talk to them."

I could feel my partner practically vibrating. "You let Ms. Pepper go out, by herself, to talk to people in a mysterious limo?" And she sounded every bit as outraged as I was.

Big Avenue looked a little bewildered at our reaction. "She wanted to go and she took her gun." He squinted from one of us to the other, trying to figure out what he'd done wrong. "She was my backup...right?"

Malone ignored that. "Who was in the limo and what did they say to her? Did she tell you?"

"Well, yeah, sure. She said there were three men, two big ugly guys in the front and a slick-looking guy in the back. The guy in back did the talking, I guess. Said they were here to visit his mother but she wasn't home."

"Any names?"

"Uh, let's see, yeah, she said she traded names with the guy in back. He was Tony something." Big looked from one of us to the other. "We didn't think nothin' of it. Did I fuck up?"

There was no point in giving him a hard time, but this complicated matters even further. Of course it was Sabado. It had to have been Sabado—and now he knew that Agatha Pepper was somehow associated with Hoke.

He also knew where we all were.

CHAPTER TWENTY-THREE

I immediately called to leave Ms. Pepper a message that she should keep her driver around and not open her door to any strangers. I had no idea what she planned to do with nephew Rodney, but I certainly wasn't counting on him—or a gun named Walter—to protect her.

We were still sitting around my living room, except for Big Avenue who was standing off in one corner unsuccessfully trying to be invisible, when we heard a knock on the front door. I was on the phone with Mike Whitehall, arranging to use a Portland police safe house and wondering if I should include Ms. Pepper and Morty. I paused what I was saying to Mike and watched Malone approach the door with her gun drawn. She looked through the spy hole, holstered her Glock, and opened the door to admit Sonny Sampson.

Sampson took one look at all our faces and asked Malone what had happened. I left it to my partner to explain as I finished my conversation with Mike. He and I agreed that a former crack house on 99th just off Prescott would do the trick. By the time I hung up, I'd already decided that if Ms. Pepper was willing to relocate one more time, I would include her and whoever came along with her in the package. The more the safer, probably.

Sampson was settled in one of the armchairs and gave me a concerned look. "So Sabado was out front earlier today?"

"That's my supposition. As soon as we're done talking here, Colleen, Hoke, and Big Avenue are heading for a safe house that a friend of mine is setting up. Probably they'll be joined by Ms. Pepper and her dog. And possibly her nephew. And God knows who else before this is over."

"I hope it's a big house."

Malone spoke up, addressing Sampson. "You said you have news."

The Vegas P.I. nodded. "I do. After calling in some more favors, I think I can tell you what your daughter's boyfriend here stepped in. At least a very good guess."

Malone frowned. "Your big news is that you have a guess?"

Sampson frowned right back at her. "It turns out that a day or two after Hoke had his encounter in the hotel lobby a young woman's body was found in a shallow grave outside Vegas city limits. She was initially a Jane Doe, but has since been identified as Jacqueline Hudson, fifteen years old." She focused on Hoke. "She matches the description of the girl you talked to and word is that she'd been seen in the company of Sabado's people. There's no way to be sure she's the girl you encountered, but that is my guess."

Hoke meanwhile had gone dead pale. "The girl's dead? Is it because I talked to her? How can that be? We really didn't say anything." Colleen put a comforting hand on his arm but didn't speak.

"I'm not saying it's because she spoke to you, if she's even the same girl, but I have a theory based on some other information that I've gotten." She paused, her lips forming a tight line. "It's information that I really wish I hadn't gotten because it makes me look very bad—and puts you in a lot of danger."

"What is it?" asked Malone.

"Well, apparently my client Mr. Sabado is not just a run-of-the-mill Las Vegas crime boss with a few underage prostitutes on the street. It looks like he may be sex trafficking underage girls, from where and to where I don't know yet." She paused as we all took that in. "It's a very closely held operation, whatever it is, and I'm not sure about it yet. I can tell you I would not have had him as a client if I'd known something like that might be true. If it is, I'm quite sure he doesn't want anyone outside his inner circle to know about it. It would be an even bigger threat to the efforts of his compatriots to get prostitution legalized in the city."

She grimaced. "I'm going to give the LVMPD organized crime guys a heads up, of course, but they can't do much without evidence or access to my sources, who are not going to talk to cops. And, yes, I'm going to vet my gangster clients a lot more thoroughly from now on. Anyway, all that brings me to my theory."

"He thinks," I said, "that the girl might have told Hoke about the sex trafficking operation in an effort to escape."

Sampson almost smiled. "Very good. That's exactly my theory."

I looked at Hoke. "You told us she said something about going to Portland and she mentioned a man named Tony. She could have been about to tell you everything, but Scarface—or whatever his name is—caught up with her before she could."

"Only he didn't know that he was in time," said Colleen, looking as pale as her boyfriend by now. "He wouldn't have believed any of her denials. Or maybe she even said she did tell Hoke, to try to protect herself."

"Which obviously didn't work, if she was the girl in the grave," Sampson responded.

Hoke was sitting stiff and grim. "He killed her for maybe telling me and now he wants to kill me, just in case she did. I should have...."

I stood abruptly. "There was nothing you should have done. A young woman stopped to chat with you and then her father showed up. You had no reason to think otherwise. Enough talk. There's a lot of speculation involved here but, just in case, we need to get these folks to the safe house and round up Ms. Pepper, too."

Big Avenue finally stepped out of the corner and spoke. "I'm gonna need more guns."

CHAPTER TWENTY-FOUR

It was three in the afternoon before we got everyone settled in the safe house: Colleen, Hoke, Agatha Pepper, her nephew Rodney, Morty, and Big Avenue. The latter had his requested arsenal and Mike Whitehall had ordered frequent patrol drive-bys.

The rundown but relatively large clapboard former crack house was probably about as obscure—and thus safe—as we could manage for the moment. Still, I was finding it hard to believe that my daughter and her boyfriend were hiding out with an elderly ex-client, her dog, her murderous nephew, and a heavily armed Samoan pimp.

I said as much to my wife and partner as she enthusiastically tackled her second hamburger in our booth at the Home Run Sports Bar.

"We do have an interesting life, don't we?" she opined as she started on her second order of fries. We hadn't eaten since breakfast and she would normally have had at least two more meals by now, so she was making up for missed calories.

"Any regrets?"

She shook her head as she swallowed. "No. Any insecurities?"

I laughed and popped the last bite of my one and only hamburger in my mouth. She was right. I should accept the fact that she was okay with marrying me.

She leaned a little forward and lowered her voice. "More to the point, do we have any ideas about what to do next?"

I suddenly found it a little difficult to swallow that last bite. "I haven't come up with much. I think all the possible targets are safe for now, which gives us some time—but it's not like we can prove Sabado is breaking the law, at least not right now, not here in Portland. Maybe Sonny will come up with something closer to home. She's out trolling for more information."

Malone snorted. "Or trolling for a date with Veronica."

I sighed. "Either way, it's probably not going to be any help. I'm actually thinking that maybe the best thing would be to rattle Sabado's cage."

That shot her eyebrows up. "Go confront him? Tell him to leave town? That would be great if it worked, but what leverage do we have?"

"We're theorizing he's worried that girl blew the whistle on him, that Hoke has his secret. What's the point of killing Hoke if everybody has his secret? So far it's just five or six of us, admittedly, but it could be a lot more if he didn't leave."

"And then we'd keep it ourselves?"

"Of course not, but once he realizes that he can't kill fast enough to keep up with the growing number of people who know, maybe he'll decide it's a good idea to go home and make some changes to cover his ass."

She chewed her last french fry thoughtfully. "It could work, if we can find him over the weekend. This is Friday afternoon, you know." She looked at her plate as if hoping to see another french fry and then looked up at me. "Or he could decide to kill us all just because he's so pissed."

I stood and tossed enough cash on the table to cover our meals and the tip. "We'll give it some more thought," I said.

Malone was grinning a little as we headed back to the office. I unlocked the door and our main agency line started ringing before we made it to the desk. "No new cases right now," I muttered as I reached for the handset.

"That I can agree with," my partner said as I picked it up. "McCall-Malone Detective...."

"Mr. McCall!" It was Martha Mondragon again. Irritation surged. No way. Not right now.

"Mrs. Mondragon...."

"You have to help me! The police are here and they're saying I murdered Bernie!" She was half sobbing and half shrieking.

I was flummoxed for a moment. "Bernie's dead?"

She started to answer, but then I heard a cop voice behind her. "Is that your lawyer on the phone, ma'am?"

"No, it's my detective," she whimpered.

"Then you need to hang up and come with us."

"Mrs. Mondragon," I started again, but the phone was indeed hung up. My bet was that the cop took it out of her hand. I wished I had recognized his voice.

Malone meanwhile was staring at me like I had two heads. "Did you just say that Bernie Mondragon is dead?" she asked as I set the handset back in its cradle.

"And his wife is being arrested for his murder. That was her on the phone."

"So I gathered. Is she rehiring us?"

"She asked for our help...but we've got Sabado to deal with. We can't...."

"I know. I agreed with you just a minute ago, but I think we should at least find out a little more about the situation. Maybe Mike knows what's happening?"

I knew she was right. We couldn't ignore Bernie Mondragon's death and the accusation against his wife. I nodded my acquiescence, sat down and punched on the speaker phone, then hit the speed dial for Mike Whitehall.

He got it on the first ring. "Whitehall."

"Hey, Mike, it's Clint and Devon. We just got a call from a former client saying she's been arrested for murdering her husband."

"Would that be Mrs. Martha Mondragon, by chance? Are they bringing her in?"

"Yes it would and yes they are. She was on the phone with me when they were arresting her. So you already know about it?"

"I sent the officers to bring her in."

"What's the deal?"

"Bernie Mondragon's body was found in an alley

downtown, multiple GSW. After just a little research, I concluded that his wife was a likely suspect."

"Research?"

"A photo she has posted on Facebook. Take a look. She's on there under her own name and it must be public since I can see it."

Malone was already tapping away on her keyboard and I watched her expression change from curious to grim as she was tracking the results on her screen. "Are you fucking kidding me?" she muttered as she turned the monitor so that I could see it.

And there was my partner's photo of Martha Mondragon, gun in hand, outside the motel room door, in full living color. Better yet, above the photo were the words, "My husband is inside with another woman. Guess what happens next?"

CHAPTER TWENTY-FIVE

It took us about sixty seconds to conclude that we had, to say the least, some responsibility for Mrs. Mondragon's arrest. We didn't go charging down to the Justice Center because there would be nothing we could do there until after Whitehall finished interrogating our erstwhile, and apparently current, client.

Then if she were charged and booked, we would be in line somewhere behind whatever lawyer she obtained and probably further interrogation by the authorities.

I called Whitehall back and informed his voicemail that his suspect was again a client of ours and that we wished to speak to her as soon as possible.

Then I checked in with Colleen to be sure she was all right. She reported that Big Avenue was keeping an eye on the front door while Agatha Pepper and Morty watched the back. She and Hoke were half watching TV and half keeping an eye on Ms. Pepper. Planning ahead, I asked to speak to Big and told him I was going to see if Sonny Sampson could provide additional backup overnight. I didn't tell him or Colleen that we had yet another distraction from solving Hoke's problem, though that was certainly weighing heavily on my mind.

So my next call was to Sonny Sampson's cell phone. The background noise as she answered was a giveaway.

"You're back at the Pen and Pastry, aren't you?"

"Well, uh, yes. I can do research and make phone calls from here. And the food is good."

"As is the company, right?"

I could hear her grinning. "Yes, that too." Veronica said hello from somewhere very nearby.

"Has your research and phone calling resulted in any new or helpful information?"

"Not yet. I'm learning more about the scale of Sabado's sex

trafficking operation; we're talking girls as young as twelve here, and I'm amazed that he's managed to keep it so totally off the LVMPD radar, but I don't see how any of that helps us right now."

"Let me make a suggestion about how you could help. If you can tear yourself away from the...food...at the Pen and Pastry, head on out to that safe house and provide backup for Big Avenue overnight. I've already cleared you in if you can do that."

"You and Devon going to be there tonight?"

I sighed. "I don't know. We have another client in bad trouble and we have to deal with that. I'm not sure what it will do to our evening and night."

"It must be bad if it's going to take priority over your kid and her boyfriend."

"Can you back up Big Avenue or not?"

"I'll head over there right away."

"Thank you."

Malone and I spent the next two hours sitting around the office, basically driving each other nuts speculating about Bernie Mondragon, Antonio Sabado, and what the hell we might do concerning either one.

Around five-thirty we heard from Whitehall that Martha Mondragon was not being charged. Yet. Apparently they'd been unable to find the gun in her house, so they didn't have hard evidence that she was the shooter. That didn't let her off the hook but did put her back on the street. Mike went on to say she'd been released only about ten minutes ago and he had no idea where she was now.

I had a hunch that I knew, a hunch that proved correct when we heard a knock on the office door only about two minutes after I hung up.

The door opened before we had a chance to respond and Martha Mondragon burst into the room.

No PTA Special Ops outfit this time. She wore a plain gray

housedress with sandals, her hair looking more like straw than straw-colored; her face was pale and complexion mottled. She came to a dead stop after she closed the door behind her, noticeably trembling, as if there were some kind of frightening barrier between her and us. She looked about ten years older than when I'd last seen her.

I quickly jumped up and went to her, taking her by the arm and escorting her to the visitor's chair nearest Malone. As soon as she was seated, Devon reached out and put a hand on the woman's bare arm.

"We're sorry for your loss," she said, and in that moment I saw the police sergeant I first met several years ago.

"Also, I'm sorry I took that stupid fucking photo," she continued, bringing me back to my partner and wife.

At least that elicited a response from Mrs. Mondragon, who covered Malone's hand with her own. "It's not your fault. I didn't have to post it on Facebook. I thought it was funny." Her eyes followed me as I took my own chair again. "It wasn't."

I leaned a little toward her, trying to be as gentle as possible. "Can you tell us what happened?"

"Are you willing to help me? Am I your client again?"

One more eye contact with Malone, to confirm. "Yes, we will do what we can."

That seemed to relax our client slightly. "Good. As for what happened, I don't know! The police showed up at my door, told me Bernie had been murdered and that I had to go with them. I asked them what happened, but they wouldn't tell me. They just said there was a detective who needed to talk to me. I was in total shock, numb. I didn't know what to think. I asked *them* if I could see the...body. Maybe it wasn't Bernie, maybe it was a mistake. But, no, they said, it was no mistake, and I had to come downtown right now. Then one of them—there were three uniformed officers—said she would stay behind and 'look for the gun.' That's when I knew I was in serious trouble and I called you."

"Did they have a warrant?" I asked.

"I have no idea. I didn't think to ask."

"Well, that's a legal question that may or may not be important later. Why didn't they find the gun? Had you disposed of it?"

"Well, I did think better of keeping it. I sold it to a gun shop. The police said they'd track it down. It won't be the gun that shot Bernie. At least, I sure hope it isn't."

"Do you have any idea who might want to murder your husband?" asked Malone. "Or why he was in that alley at that time?"

"No! Bernie was a real estate agent, for God's sake. He sold houses, sometimes office buildings or warehouses. People don't kill you for doing that. He didn't have an enemy in the world, as far as I know."

"But there were a lot of things you didn't know."

Our client teared up again at that. "Oh, God, yes, that's true."

"Bernie was in the habit of seeing other women and one or more of those women could have been married. That would provide a motive for a pissed off husband."

"I thought Bernie saw prostitutes."

"We don't know that those are the only women he ever spent time with. You need to provide us with a list of your married friends."

"Oh God."

"And," I added, "give us access to his business records. There could be something there."

"I'll make the list this evening and I can email you the files and links for the business stuff; it's all on his computer."

"Better do that as soon as you get home," I said. "The cops may want that computer sooner rather than later."

"Fine. You guys can have all the lists and records and whatever else that you need. Do you think you can prove I didn't do it?"

"Do you have an alibi?" asked Malone.

"No. I was home alone during the time they say Bernie was killed."

"Then, no, even if they find the gun and it's not the murder weapon, that doesn't prove you are innocent and we probably can't prove you didn't do it, either. We'll have to find out who did."

CHAPTER TWENTY-SIX

We staggered into the office about eight thirty the next morning, after stopping at home again for showers, clean clothes, and cat care. We'd eaten a simple and not very savory breakfast of oatmeal and toast at the safe house.

"I feel like shit," Malone muttered as we settled at the partners desk and booted up our computers. "And I'm already hungry again."

"You're always hungry," I noted.

The evening before, soon after Martha Mondragon finally headed home, we'd followed suit—just to take care of the cats and make sure everything was secure before adding ourselves to the crowd at the safe house.

It was an even bigger crowd than we anticipated since Veronica Fortune had come with Sonny Sampson. At least they took only one of the bedrooms. Colleen and Hoke also took one, of course, leaving the last for Agatha and Morty. Big Avenue either didn't sleep or could do so sitting up and staring at a door, while Malone and I took the two couches in the living room and Rodney got a sleeping bag on the floor. At that, the homicidal but extremely repentant nephew may have been more comfortable than we were since the couches were both lumpy and smelly.

So here we were in the office on a Saturday morning, tired and grumpy, and—in my wife's case—still hungry.

My PC finished booting up and I saw that we already had two emails from Martha Mondragon. Apparently she hadn't slept much either. One was a list of married couples; I printed that one. The other had several attachments, large files of business records and links to cloud storage where I assumed there were still more business records. I forwarded that one to Eleanor with an additional note of my own, hoping she would have time to get started on them Monday morning.

Malone retrieved the list from the printer and held it up. "So. We have"—she glanced at the list—"six couples we can talk to. It's the weekend, so we might even catch some of them at home. The murder scene is downtown here. We could check that out." She gave me a moment to respond and, when I didn't.... "What do you want to do, Clint?"

"I want to find Antonio Sabado and beat on him until he agrees to leave the kids alone, get out of town, and never return."

"Ookay. I don't think that's doable right this second. For one thing, we have no idea where he is."

"I know."

"But I do have an idea how we could find out."

She was looking at me like I should know what she was talking about and, after a few seconds of confusion, I thought I did. "Gunther. Carl Gunther would know where Sabado is staying."

"Might know. Probably knows. The only number I have is for his office and it's unlikely he's there on a Saturday morning, especially this early, but I can leave a message. He'll call me back."

That brought a transient grin to my face. "I'm sure he will." But then reality crashed in on me again. "We'll do what we can for Mrs. Mondragon until we hear from Gunther, but then we have to focus on Sabado again. They already tried to kidnap Hoke. They may have had at least one young girl killed...."

"I agree completely. Let me make the call. Maybe he is in the office and we can get to it."

But he wasn't. The message that Malone left made it clear that she urgently needed to talk to Gunther, so I was hoping he'd get back to her quickly. In the meantime, we had an obligation to do what we could for Martha Mondragon.

Bernie's crime scene was only about five blocks away, between Washington and Alder near the transit mall. There was no point in driving; it would have taken longer to find a place to park than it would to walk there and back. We didn't really expect to find anything that the police had missed, but my partner and I had long since agreed that when we were investigating a violent crime it helped to see the scene. And it was something to do.

Portland is not an early rising city on the weekend. At a little after nine on a Saturday morning in August, we had the sidewalk entirely to ourselves on some blocks even though we were right downtown. The sun was out in a cloudless sky, but it wasn't really warm yet. It was supposed to be before the day was over.

We walked in silence. I was listening for her cell phone to signal an incoming call. It didn't.

It turned out that the "alley" was more like a pristine delivery corridor between the rear entrances of businesses on either side. The name of each business was nicely stenciled on the delivery door. There were a few trash receptacles but no trash visible outside their confines, nothing to mar the pavement except the fading red patch approximately halfway down. There was no dramatic body outline—they don't do that anymore—and it looked like someone had already taken a swipe at cleaning it up.

But it was clear enough where Bernie Mondragon had breathed his last.

We stood looking down at the now-faded pink splatters.

"It was really stupid to take that photo," Malone muttered, "and even more stupid to give it to Martha."

I gave her a quick hug, but didn't say anything. There was no point and any reassurance would have just earned me a snort, anyway.

Malone looked around. "No cameras back here," She cocked an eye at me. "You picking up on anything?"

I sighed. "No."

"Okay, so much for examining the scene." She turned and took a step back toward the street, then stopped abruptly as her cell phone trilled. She grabbed it from her jacket pocket and put it to her ear.

"Malone." She listened, then nodded. "Yeah, I'm surprised you're even up."

I moved closer and she gave me an okay sign with her free hand. It had to be Gunther.

"We need to meet with Sabado," she said, "and I'll bet you know where he's staying." She listened for almost a full minute. "I understand. I'll be waiting."

She ended the call and stuffed the phone back in her pocket. "He thinks that Sabado was staying downtown, at the Hotel deLuxe, but isn't sure he's still in town. He's going to check and get back to us. Meanwhile, I have an idea we need to talk about."

"Okay. What?"

She grinned, just a little. "We bring Carl Gunther along when we meet with Sabado."

I frowned, more than a little. "Oh, wow. Well, assuming he'd even agree, you're right that we need to talk about that."

CHAPTER TWENTY-SEVEN

We debated the idea of using one crime boss as backup for confronting another crime boss as we walked back to the office.

Malone argued that Gunther would provide a lot of leverage and that it was a better idea than telling Sabado we're onto his sex trafficking operation—which could just get us killed.

I argued simply that Gunther couldn't be trusted, that he was Portland's version of Antonio Sabado and not somebody we wanted at our backs in a confrontation.

We were still arguing while I unlocked the office door.

"And, on top of all that," I continued as we crossed to our opposite sides of the desk, "it would mean we owed Gunther a favor. Do you really want to owe Portland's crime boss a favor?"

"Why not?" My partner stored her Glock in the usual desk drawer and sat down. "He isn't going to ask us to snuff somebody for him."

"That's not a sure bet," I muttered. "Let's let it rest for a while," I suggested in a more normal tone of voice. "Check our messages, make a few calls, see what Gunther has to say when he calls back. If he calls back."

"That's fine." Malone turned to her PC as it was booting up. "But we need some weight. You know we do."

Plus your daughter's life could depend on it, she didn't say.

"I'll think about it."

I focused on the phone system to see if we had any messages. Remarkably, there were none on the main agency line or my private line. I saw that Malone was doing the same. "I've got nothing here," I said. "You?"

She put the phone down. "Not a thing. It is the weekend." She looked at her screen. "No emails of interest, either."

I pulled out the list we'd gotten from Martha Mondragon. "Which reminds me that I might as well see if any of these folks are available to be interviewed. Maybe we could get a couple in before hearing from Gunther."

Those calls turned out to be about as fruitful as everything else we'd been doing lately. Four of the numbers didn't answer, so I left messages identifying myself and asking them to call back. The other two were busy for the weekend and dubious about whether they wanted to talk to a couple of private detectives, although they both agreed to tentative appointments on Monday.

It was close to eleven by the time I got all that settled and there had still been no incoming calls, from Gunther or anyone else. We decided to grab an early lunch across the street and, if we'd still not heard from Malone's criminal buddy, we'd go check on the safe house again.

The Home Run wasn't busy, so we settled at our favorite table and soon tackled our usual burger and fries combos.

I couldn't help picking up our argument one last time. "I wish we didn't have to involve Gunther in all this," I offered after my first couple of bites. "We've got enough problems."

"Several of which we wouldn't even know about for sure if I hadn't talked to him."

"True, but still, I don't like him."

Malone broke off a sustained attack on her fries to give me a look. "Of course you don't like him. He's a vicious criminal, has a dangerous asshole for a son—and the hots for me."

"Still? You didn't mention that."

"He made a point of telling me I could have done better, but it was not a compelling argument."

"Son of a bitch."

Malone put down the remains of her burger. "Look. We already agreed to see what he has to say when he calls back, if he does, and we'll go from there. You're not going to let jealousy get in the way of protecting Colleen. We both know that."

We both did, so we spent the remainder of the meal on more quotidian subjects and then, since there was still no word from Gunther, headed for the safe house.

I was able to park right in front and we were only about halfway up the crumbling brick walkway when the front door opened, the frame filled by Big Avenue with an appropriately large gun held low against his leg.

"Everything good?" he asked as we stepped onto the rickety porch.

"So far," I said.

"Here, too," he said as he stood aside to let us enter.

It was, as I've mentioned, a big house and the living room was commensurately large with the two couches, four overstuffed chairs, three coffee tables, a variety of lamps, and a number of side tables. Small TV and no free wifi, which was probably one of many reasons I found myself confronting the grumpy faces of my daughter and her boyfriend. Colleen was sitting in one of the chairs with Hoke standing beside her.

"Colleen. Hoke. You guys okay?"

"We've been better," replied my daughter. "Do you have any news?"

I shook my head. "Nothing that will let you out of here yet. The threat is still very real. We did hear that Sabado has a money laundering operation here in Portland." I looked over my shoulder at Big Avenue. "You know anything about that?"

"Nah, that's way above me. I know the street. Ain't no clean money on the street."

At that moment Sonny Sampson swept into the room, looking well-rested and intense. She was wearing simple brown slacks, tee shirt, and light jacket to cover her shoulder holster.

"Hey guys," she greeted us. "I was just on my way out."

I held up a hand to slow her down. "You're leaving? Who's covering the back door?" I was afraid I knew the answer.

"Agatha, Rodney, Morty, and Walter."

"And you're leaving it to them?"

"You're the one who said she could serve as backup. The big man here has given me some tips on places to go and people to talk to. I want to see if I can identify a trafficking operation here in Portland, find out if there's any reason Sabado's here besides Hoke."

"We've learned that he apparently has a local money laundering operation."

"Okay. I'll check that out, too. If the big guy knows what he's talking about, these are good connections. I've got to get out of here. If I stay any longer, I'm going to start talking to that old lady's gun just like she does."

I had my doubts about the value of Big Avenue's connections, but I let it go. "Is Veronica still here?"

"No, she's gone to work. Just like I'm about to do. I'll call you as soon as I learn anything."

There was no way to make her stay and we needed all the info we could get. "All right. Take care."

As soon as Sampson was out the front, Malone and I headed for the back door. Oddly, the kitchen, which let out into the back yard, was at the end of a hallway leading from the living room past two of the three bedrooms.

Agatha Pepper and her nephew were sitting at the kitchen table. Rodney had a cup of coffee in front of him and Ms. Pepper had Walter. Morty was snoozing next to a food dish off to our left. Ms. Pepper was staring so intently at the back door that she didn't even glance at our entrance.

Rodney, on the other hand, paled as if he expected us to apprehend him again.

"Everything quiet back here?" Malone inquired.

At that, Ms. Pepper relaxed slightly and turned to give us a big smile. "All is well," she announced. "In fact, I don't know if I've ever had so much fun."

Rodney took a nervous sip of coffee and eyed the Walther PK380. "Aunt Aggie, you're sitting in an abandoned crack house staring at a door. How much fun could that be?"

She reached over and patted his hand. "You have so much to learn, Rodney. But never fear. I'm up to the task."

I heard Malone's cell phone and she grabbed it out of her pocket. "Yeah?"

She listened for a long minute. "Thanks. I may be back in touch shortly. You going to be available?"

After another moment, she ended the call. "Sabado is

staying at the Hotel deLuxe and Gunther has eyes on him. It's decision time."

CHAPTER TWENTY-EIGHT

It was more than a year since I'd been in Gunther's office building with its fancy lobby and fancier elevator. I could have waited another year or more, but Malone had convinced me that talking with the man about working together was a good idea.

Gunther Global Import/Export's receptionist was absent, it being a Saturday. That was a relief since I did not feel the need for another gun-toting grandmotherly type in my life right now.

The door to Gunther's office was open and he apparently heard us enter. We had just paused in front of Mrs. Pinkerton's desk when he appeared in his doorway, dressed as always in an expensive pinstripe suit and highly shined shoes. He nodded at Malone and frowned at me.

"Devon. McCall. Come on in."

He moved behind his massive desk as we entered his fancy office and sat in his fancy visitor chairs. He did not offer to shake hands.

"Devon tells me you need my help," he said, his flat gaze directed at me.

She shifted a little. "I said we might need your help. That's what we're here to talk about."

I hadn't said a word yet, but it seemed like the time. "What is your relationship with Antonio Sabado?"

"I don't have a relationship with him. He's a businessman visiting from Las Vegas and he paid me the proper respect. Nothing more."

"According to my wife, he also told you he planned to kill one or more people here. That's a little something."

"Letting me know *is* the proper respect."

"Did he give you any indication who?"

"No, but Devon seems to think it might be your daughter's boyfriend. Is that not so?"

"It is."

"While I'm sorry to hear that, why should I back your play trying to prevent it?"

Malone spoke up and I was willing to let her take the lead on this. I was focused on not shooting the son of a bitch.

"We've worked together successfully once before," she said. "Perhaps we could again."

"Perhaps. What's in it for me?"

I did *not* like the way he was looking at Malone as he asked that. Not at all, but I kept quiet.

"The satisfaction of doing the right thing," Malone responded.

Gunther laughed. "We might have a slightly different view of the right thing, you and I."

She leaned a little forward. "Well, how about this? Have you ever trafficked underage girls? Is your view of that different from mine?"

Gunther's expression went absolutely grim and his body tensed. I edged my hand a little closer to the Smith and Wesson under my jacket. "Who said that I did?"

Malone held up her hands, palms out. "Nobody. I just wondered what you thought of the practice, because our understanding is that your respectful visiting businessman is a sex trafficker of young girls in Las Vegas."

"How good is your information? He told me his business here was laundering money."

"That may be all he's doing here, but we have very reliable information that he has other business in Vegas. And maybe he chose not to mention similar business he might have here."

Our host swiveled in his fancy leather chair, a deep frown creasing his broad forehead. "That could be. Young girls? You're sure? That's not on in my city. I don't like it anywhere, or anybody who would do it." He stopped and focused on Malone. "So. What are you thinking? That we flatline this asshole? That could cause more problems than it solves, at least for me."

I felt the need to step in at this point. For all I knew, my partner was about to agree with him. "We don't want to kill him, Carl. We just need him to forget whatever he has against my daughter's boyfriend and leave town."

"You gonna let him off on everything else?"

"We're working on doing something about that, legally, but first things first."

"Speaking of legal, why are you sitting here in my office instead of down at the Glass Palace?"

"There's not that much, yet, the folks at the Justice Center could do. We have no overt threat, no evidence. We have what we know and what we speculate. The cops aren't going to try to chase him out of town on my say-so and they probably couldn't anyway."

"So we go talk to him," Malone said. "The three of us, with whatever muscle you want to bring along to match his, and maybe you suggest that as a gesture of goodwill he leave the innocent kids alone and wrap up his business in Portland."

"Would that work?" I asked. "Would he leave just because you told him to?"

Gunther shrugged. "I'd leave Las Vegas if he told me to. Unless my life depended on staying and I had a small army with me."

"Well, let's hope that's not the case with Sabado."

CHAPTER TWENTY-NINE

Carl Gunther arranged for us to meet with Antonio Sabado in his hotel lobby at ten o'clock the next morning, Sunday. We first gathered in the open-air beer garden across the street—and, by "gathered," I mean me, Malone, Gunther, two very large goons who accompanied him, and a third thug who lumbered across 15th from the hotel to join us. Not a small army but it would have to do.

The morning was sunny and the day looked to be hot. There were only a few pedestrians in sight, though I was sure that Pioneer Square, a couple of blocks over, was already well-populated.

"He's in there?" Gunther asked thug three.

"Yeah."

"Downstairs yet? How many with him, all four?"

"He was just headed down when I left. Five now."

"Shit," Malone muttered in my ear. No kidding. It was not good news that he was apparently bringing in reinforcements.

I looked at my watch. "It's two minutes til," I announced. "Showtime." We all headed across the street.

I'd never been inside the Hotel deLuxe. The centerpiece of the spacious lobby was an immense framed poster, a scene from an old black-and-white Cary Grant movie, probably twelve feet tall and framed in what I guessed was heavy plastic that was supposed to look like crystal. The whole place had a Hollywood veneer. Everything was immaculate, almost glowing. The predominant color scheme was warm beige with a half dozen crystal chandeliers far above our heads and seating for at least fifty people.

Currently it was seating one. With five more in attendance.

He was sitting on a couch in the far corner and stood as we registered his presence and headed his way. His five men were already on their feet. One was at each end of the couch,

Scarface on the right. The other three were spaced along our approach. Apparently the desk clerk and concierge had been banished for the moment.

Antonio Sabado looked like a distorted reflection of Carl Gunther: about the same age, same full head of dark hair, same I'm-in-charge-and-I'll-kill-your-ass-if-you-cross-me demeanor, but a full foot shorter, six inches wider, and at least fifty pounds heavier.

He was wearing a dark gray suit that had to be bespoke because you couldn't buy something off a rack that would fit that body.

Crossing the lobby felt like walking a gauntlet. At least we were six to six. I wondered if Sabado had added a man because he somehow knew we were going to be six. No telling how far and deep the reach of a man like that might be.

Initially, he didn't look at any of us except Carl Gunther, who was just a step ahead of Malone and me and stopped our forward progress about eight feet in front of Sabado.

The voice that emanated from the fat man was high-pitched, almost feminine. "So. Carl. You brought private cops to see me. This had better be good."

Gunther nodded, somewhat regally I thought, and stepped to the side. "This is Clint McCall and Devon Malone. I agreed to facilitate this meeting." He stopped there, clearly conveying that was all he had agreed to, and took another step to the side. Malone and I were left in the center of a circle of bad guys. Up close and personal now, I could see that Sabado's eyes were those of a classic psychopath, devoid of any feeling, just as his face was utterly without expression.

Did I mention that I had been dubious about doing this?

Nevertheless, I took a deep breath and went for it. "We're hoping to come to an understanding, Mr. Sabado."

"About what?"

"Well, just suppose that part of your business here had to do with a young man who was seen, by this gentleman over here..."--I nodded toward Scarface--"...talking to a young woman in a hotel lobby. Suppose that this gentleman reported his concern that the young girl could have shared something she shouldn't have with the young man. We are here to tell you that she didn't, that the young man knows nothing about your business, and that you can safely leave him alone."

"That's a lot of supposing. A lot of very good supposing. If the girl didn't say anything, how did you put all that together?"

Malone held up her hand as if in class. "Detectives here."

The dead eyes moved from me to her. "You got a smart mouth."

"Brain's even smarter."

I resisted the urge to punch my partner in the arm, or possibly even clap my hand over her mouth.

"I hope we can reach an understanding," I said again.

Sabado focused back on me. "Why should I give a shit what you hope?"

"Because," came a rumble from off my left shoulder and I realized that Carl Gunther had stepped back into the conversation, "you can take my word that these two are telling you truth. You got no reason to pursue the boy. You got other business here, finish it, and head home." He paused, as he and Sabado attempted to glare each other to death. "You'll take my word, won't you?"

You could have powered a small town off the nervous energy in the lobby at that moment. Everybody on both sides knew that the answer had better be yes. I didn't dare twitch, but I was mentally rehearsing the move for my Smith and Wesson.

As everybody held their breath, Sabado's face slowly transitioned from the glower to expressionless to a tight smile that didn't come within a lightyear of his eyes.

"Of course, Carl. I would never doubt your word. As it happens, we are done with our business here in Portland and will be leaving this afternoon."

I took a breath, but not because I believed him.

CHAPTER THIRTY

I'm not sure I ever took a longer walk than the one that got us out of that lobby and back on the sidewalk in front of the Hotel deLuxe.

It was sunny and hot already with a few late Sunday morning pedestrians in sight—all of whom chose the opposite sidewalk when they saw our little group of three obvious thugs, two slightly scruffy private detectives, and one crime boss wearing a three-thousand-dollar suit.

I wasn't sure what I was feeling at the moment, besides relieved to be alive and uninjured. My big idea of confronting Sabado would have been a complete bust if Gunther hadn't stepped in and offered his combo of reassurances and subtle threat. One thing I was certain of: I did *not* like the idea of being rescued by Carl Gunther.

"Why did you do that?" I asked him as soon as we had all taken a breath. "You don't know that we're telling the truth, you don't owe us anything, so why put your reputation on the line?"

He gave me a look with one eyebrow raised. "I'm fond of your wife and there were about to be shots fired." He shrugged. "Unfortunately, I had to save you both."

I felt Malone's hand on my arm, which saved me from tackling the son of a bitch right there on the sidewalk.

"We appreciate it, Carl," she said. "I don't care why you did it, but are you certain Sabado believed you and what do you want in return?"

"I'm certain he believes that there will be a serious problem if he goes after someone I've vouched for. I'll keep eyes on him to make sure he leaves and I'll let you know when he does." He switched his attention to me. "You should suggest to your daughter and her boyfriend that there are better places to vacation in the future than Las Vegas. I have no influence there."

"You still haven't told us what you want in return," insisted Malone.

The smile that Gunther directed at my wife was, in my opinion, smarmy; and it was a good thing she was still firmly holding onto my arm. "Devon, I'd like to say that your gratitude is all I need. But that's not the way business is done, is it? Let's say you owe me a favor to be collected later. I don't happen to need anything right now."

"*We*," I responded with great emphasis, "will consider your request when it comes. That's how our business is done."

No smile, smarmy or otherwise. "It will sort itself out, one way or the other, won't it? Devon, have a good day. Let's go, men."

Malone and I stood there as Gunther led his thugs away, though one of the men peeled off before they reached their vehicles; I assumed he was the "eyes" Gunther referred to. I glanced over my shoulder. It appeared that the lobby was now empty, except a clerk who had reappeared behind the desk. Nothing to see right now. My partner's hand was still resting on my arm.

"I was wrong," she said, "and I'm sorry."

It took me a moment to get focused. I was having a few too many different reactions to what had just happened, a whole spectrum of anger, irritation, embarrassment, doubt.... It must have shown on my face, that I wasn't quite taking in her words.

"About Gunther," she clarified. "I did ask him to step in— not literally, not right that second, but I asked him for his help. It was a mistake."

I felt shitty about it, too, but.... "I couldn't think of anything else. And it did end up with Sabado saying he's going to leave town."

"Do you believe him?"

"I don't know."

She slumped a little, dropped her hand, and let out a sigh. "I don't, either, which leaves us right back where we started.

Except that now we owe Portland's crime boss a big favor. What a total fuck-up."

It was my turn to take her by the arms. "We didn't have anything else. It was worth a shot and, who knows, maybe it even worked. Let's go back to the safe house and regroup, decide what to do next."

I released her and she looked around, almost as if she were just realizing that we were still standing in the middle of the sidewalk in front of the hotel. "Yeah, that feels like the right plan. I want to know everybody's okay and what we're all going to do next. Let's go."

CHAPTER THIRTY-ONE

It was a long drive out to 99th Street and I was more than a little worried about my partner's mental and emotional health by the time we parked in front of the old crack house where so many people we cared about were hiding out. It was past noon by now and she'd said nothing about stopping to eat.

Not that I had much of an appetite myself. We were here to make a new plan and I still had no idea what it would be.

No one reacted to our approaching the front door, which was locked. We both had our hands on our holstered weapons as I knocked.

I heard the lock click open and was greatly relieved to see my daughter opening the door. After a quick greeting, we stepped inside and locked the door again behind us. There was no one besides Colleen in sight.

"Where is everybody?" I asked her.

"In the kitchen, having lunch. Everybody but Veronica, anyway. She's only here at night." She reached out and gripped my arm. "I know you're doing what you think is necessary to protect us and I don't want to sound ungrateful, but how much longer do we have to stay here, Dad? Everybody's going nuts. Even Big Avenue is grumpy. I guess he's getting worried about whoever is covering for him on the street. Do you have any news?"

"We do. Let's join the others and talk it over."

"Great!" She let me go and practically pranced down the hallway toward the kitchen.

It was almost like we'd never left: Agatha Pepper, Rodney, and Big Avenue sitting at the table, this time joined by Hoke and Sonny Sampson, with Morty snoozing nearby. Several large bags of potato chips were open and spilling among the paper plates on the off-white tablecloth and my nose told me that the hamburger buns held fried bologna rather than beef.

Not a vegetable or a fruit in sight. Everybody except Morty was drinking beer.

We really needed to get the kids out of here.

Our appearance was greeted with a variety of exclamations, all of which amounted to demands for information about when they could go home or, in Big Avenue's case, back to pimping.

"One of you can take my chair if you want," Colleen announced as she indicated the one empty seat, "but there are no more chairs. We're out of almost everything, in fact."

"Including toilet paper," Rodney Pepper contributed.

"Hush, Rodney," said Ms. Pepper with a fond smile.

Sonny Sampson gave us a little wave but said nothing, instead digging into one of the potato chip bags for further lack of nourishment.

Malone and I stayed on our feet, so my daughter took the chair and then Hoke's hand. "You said you had news."

"We do," I said. "The good news is that we met with Sabado and he says he's leaving town right away."

Big Avenue frowned at that. "He's goin' away. Just like that?"

"We had a little help in persuading him," Malone responded. "Carl Gunther."

"Well, fuck," said Big Avenue.

Sonny Sampson finally spoke up. "What's the bad news?"

"We don't necessarily believe Sabado," I said.

Sonny nodded. "It does sound like it was too easy."

Big Avenue turned to her. "Carl Gunther tell you to go, you go."

"Unless you're another Carl Gunther," Malone said. "If Sabado was telling the truth, you all will be able to get out of here pretty soon. But we need to wait and see. Carl will let us know when Sabado makes a move."

Big Avenue was looking at Malone with something like awe. "You friends with Carl Gunther?"

"Not exactly."

"Basically," I interjected, "he has the hots for her."

Big Avenue sat back. "Well, fuck."

We spent maybe another ten minutes trying to reassure everyone, which wasn't easy given our own lack of assurance. I'd realized by this point that there simply wasn't a plan to make beyond waiting and hoping, so we said we'd take our leave and let everybody know as soon as we heard anything.

Surprisingly, after having offered up only a few words since we arrived, Sonny Sampson said she'd walk us to the front door because she had something to discuss. She escorted us through the front door, out onto the small porch, and closed the door behind us.

"Do you trust this Carl Gunther guy?" she asked.

I tossed that one to my partner with a glance. "No, I don't trust him," she said carefully, "but I know him pretty well. He is essentially boss of the city and we did witness him getting Sabado's commitment to leave town today. Let's say it would be surprising if Sabado crossed him."

Sampson nodded. "Okay. That's good. But from what I know of Tony Sabado I doubt his own mother would trust him. I have to doubt that your big city boss friend can, either."

"What do you suggest?" I asked.

"I don't have any earthshaking ideas, but I think I'll stick around for at least twenty-four hours after Sabado supposedly leaves and keep an eye on Colleen and Hoke—from a distance. I think they've had it with the protective detail. I know you guys must have things to do besides sit around just in case."

"And you don't?" interjected Malone.

Sampson shook her head, looking grim. "Really, I don't. My whole focus when I get back to Vegas is going to be taking down Sabado's sex trafficking operation. You didn't hear all the details that I did, or see the crime scene photos—though I do want to meet with you guys one more time before I leave to go over some more information I've got. It's not important right this minute. Meanwhile, if there's any chance of taking him on here, outside his own turf, I'm willing to spend another day waiting for the chance."

"And it's another day with your new friend," noted Malone.

I punched my partner in the arm. "Enough."

Sonny chuckled. "It's okay. I don't mind—the snark or the extra time. I'll be back to visit after I deal with Sabado." She grinned. "I think Portland's a very attractive city."

"I appreciate the extra day," I said. "We do have one other case we should be paying attention to and we're available to back you up if you need anything."

She held out her hand to shake. "I'll keep you posted."

"And we'll call if we learn anything," Malone repeated as she reached to also shake hands. "We can have that meeting when we're sure it's all clear."

"Sounds good," Sampson said, and went back in the house.

My partner gave me a look. "What now? Keeping in mind that it's Sunday afternoon."

"I guess we go home and wait to hear from Gunther."

"I guess you're right."

CHAPTER THIRTY-TWO

By mid-afternoon, we'd managed to feed ourselves (herb roasted chicken, straight from the microwave) and the cats (ocean whitefish and tuna, straight from the can), though only Maxine and Stella seemed to have good appetites. And energy. Lots of energy. Apparently they were thrilled to have us to themselves again.

We were sitting together on the couch, Maxine trying to get Malone to throw her mousie and Stella licking chicken odor off my fingers, when my home phone rang. It hardly ever rings and then it's almost always a sales call or scam.

Malone reached over and punched me in the shoulder. "You going to answer that?"

"It's your phone, too. You going to answer it?"

She tossed Maxine's mousie. "Shit. One of us better. It might be news."

"More likely somebody calling from Sudan to tell us we need to renew our Microsoft subscription," I said as she rose and stepped over to the side table that held the phone.

"This is Devon Malone. Oh, Mrs. Mondragon." I got an I-told-you-so look. "No, it's okay. I understand. We don't have anything yet. I'm sorry. Yes, it's a priority. Oh, really? That's good news. I'm glad to hear it. I understand. You'll hear from us as soon as we have something. We won't let you down. Thanks, you too."

She hung up and returned to meet Maxine and mousie at the couch. She tossed it again and sat down. "Our client wants us to know that the police have tracked down the gun and confirmed that it isn't the murder weapon. So she's off the hook for now—but she still wants us to find out who killed her husband. Doesn't entirely trust the cops, I guess."

"Well, at least we don't have to prove her innocence. That takes the pressure off."

My partner didn't have a chance to agree because right then her cell phone vibrated.

She checked the display. "It's Gunther." She punched a button and set the phone on the coffee table in front of us. "You're on speaker, Carl. What's going on?"

"Sabado kept his word. He and his crew have left town."

Malone leaned forward. "Are you absolutely sure?"

"My guy followed them from the hotel to the airport where they all boarded a private jet. They were all accounted for and they all got on board. He watched it take off and then confirmed with a contact of ours that the flight plan was a straight shot to Las Vegas. Sabado's gone home. Your step-daughter should be fine."

We exchanged a look and then Malone nodded. "Okay. That's good. Thanks, Carl. We owe you one."

"I'll collect in due time." He hung up.

I let out a breath that I'd apparently been holding. "Okay. So now we have a plan. We have that meeting with Sonny and then we let the others know they're free to leave the safe house."

That got me a frown from my partner. "Why meet with Sonny first?"

"So she can keep an eye on the kids from the moment they're loose. I believe Gunther's man saw Sabado and his thugs fly away, but I'll feel better if Sonny puts in that whole twenty-four hours she was planning on. Planes fly in both directions."

"You really think Sabado might fake giving up and then come back to try to get to Hoke? As far as Sabado's concerned, Hoke has told everybody what he knows by now. There would be no point."

"Unless he comes back after everybody."

Malone snorted. "That would be a pretty fucking big job."

"Yeah, well, my brain agrees with you but my gut still has doubts. At least Sonny's plan will give us a chance to do what we can for Martha Mondragon without having to worry so much about Colleen and Hoke." I grinned. "We can make it the priority you already claimed it is."

"I'm permitted a slight exaggeration. Let's have that meeting and get this show on the road."

CHAPTER THIRTY-THREE

Sonny Sampson pulled into our driveway exactly a half-hour later. As she strode up the short walkway to the door I was already holding open, I was struck again by how much she reminded me of my partner. Another couple of inches of height and hair, they could be sisters or at least cousins.

"I've been dying to know why I couldn't tell the others that Sabado has left town," she said after we settled in the living room.

"I wanted you to keep it quiet because we want you back at the house before they know they're free to leave," I replied. "You are still planning to stick around a while, right?"

"Yep. I will keep an eye on your daughter and her boyfriend for another twenty-four hours, at least."

"Excellent. The reason we wanted to meet with you first is that this new information you have might affect how willing we are to trust Sabado's gone for good. So. What do you have?"

She took a moment, apparently choosing her words. "I was wrong about Sabado running a normal sex trafficking operation. It's even worse than that. He's not moving young women in or out of the country. His men specifically target underage runaways in Las Vegas itself. They recruit them off incoming buses and trains just like prostitutes are normally recruited, by initially offering to help them, but then instead of turning them out on the street they groom them as sex slaves and sell them to extremely wealthy clients right here in the U.S."

Malone and I both sat back. "Well, that's fucked," she said.

"It is. We're talking all-American child sex slavery. If *that* were exposed, I guarantee you Sabado would be a dead man."

"Wow."

"Any hint that this is going on here in Portland," I asked, "or that he's thinking of starting up here?"

"No, no evidence at all that he's thinking of a Portland operation. I'll get him in Vegas. Or see to it that someone gets him."

"Huh," I said. "Best of luck. I almost wish there were something here because I'd like to be in on taking it down."

Malone punched me in the arm. "Really? You wish there were underage sex slaves in Portland?"

"Ouch. I said almost." I ignored the bruise and focused again on Sonny Sampson. "What about the money laundering? That is a Portland operation?"

She nodded. "That, I can confirm. He's really quite creative about it, from what I've been able to learn, using several different kinds of companies. I've identified at least one construction company and a mortgage lender for sure; there are almost certainly others. The most interesting thing, though, is that apparently there was some kind of trouble after Sabado hit town. I can't pin down exactly what, but some sort of crisis in the money laundering chain. Had people running scared."

"That could be when Sabado called Gunther to give him the heads up about possible killings," Malone said. "That would be good. For Hoke, anyway." She frowned in thought. "Let me ask you something: Given that you've been in town less than a week, how exactly are you learning all this?"

Sampson grinned. "It turns out your friend BA knows a lot of people on the lower side of town."

"BA? You mean...?"

"Big Avenue."

That brought a frown from me. "I'm sure Big knows a lot of people, but are they reliable sources of information?"

"Some of them were pretty flakey, no question, but there were enough solid ones that I trust what I'm telling you. Maybe you should give the big guy more credit."

"We give him plenty of credit for being able to stop somebody at the front door, but I'm surprised he was able to steer you in the right directions. Good for him. Anything else?"

She shook her head. "No, that's everything I've learned. I'll head back to the house. You want me to tell them that they're free to leave?"

"No, we'll follow you over there so we know for sure what everybody's plans are. I'm glad you're sticking around awhile, especially given your newest information."

"No problem. I want Sabado, here or in Vegas, I don't care which."

Malone held up a hand. "Be careful. You realize that he might well consider *you* to be the threat now."

"I'm aware. And he would be right."

"Okay," I said, "let's go give everybody the good news."

CHAPTER THIRTY-FOUR

As soon as we settled in the office the next morning, I headed down the hall to knock on Eleanor Ivory's door.

Given that it was only a few minutes after eight-thirty, I was a little surprised to hear her respond with a "Come in."

I opened the door and stepped inside. "Good. You're here early." My initial smile dropped away as I realized my friend wasn't looking quite herself. In fact, her normally somewhat seductive good grooming had gone completely to hell. Her long blond tresses were all over the place and she was wearing ratty jeans and t-shirt rather than her normal business attire.

She was on her feet behind her desk frowning down at a veritable mountain of papers and files. She looked up and gave me a gimlet eye. "Welcome to my really crappy Monday morning."

"I would never have guessed," I said as I edged carefully into one of her guest chairs. "What the hell is all of that?" Then a possibility struck me. "Did you print out those business records I sent you the other day?"

Somewhat to my disappointment, she shook her head. "No," she said mournfully as she sank into her own chair, "what you're looking at here is the last decade of my wealthiest and unfortunately dumbest client." She waved a hand over the mess as if in hope it would disappear. "It turns out he hasn't been sharing quite everything he should have with yours truly. Or the IRS. They caught it before I did and now I'm trying to keep him out of prison."

"You look like you've been at it for a while."

She snorted very much in the spirit of my partner. "He called me just past midnight in a total panic. That was when he finally got home and read the letter from the IRS. They want to see him—us—on Wednesday with all his records and an explanation of how he failed to report income and how he's going to pay the incredibly massive penalty. Which he can't afford right now, apparently. Thus the possibility of prison."

"Huh."

"Since they're giving us so little time, I came straight down here to try to get a handle on it."

I surveyed the mess on her desk. "And how's that going?"

Deep sigh. "Not as bad as it looks. I think I have sorted it out in the last hour or so and I'm optimistic that I can put a settlement proposal together, probably this afternoon, for him to review. It will be painful for him, but if he approves it I think we'll be good on Wednesday."

"Glad to hear it. So does that mean you can look at the files I sent you pretty soon?"

"Not this afternoon or this evening. I'm going to need to catch up on my sleep first. But if my client is satisfied with what I'm doing here, I should get right on your problem in the morning. I didn't look too closely, but it appeared to be a lot of material."

"It is."

"And what am I looking for?"

"The usual. Anything hinky. Anything that could get a real estate agent killed."

"Ah. Of course. Okay. That sounds relatively easy compared to this crap."

I stood up. "Well, I'll leave you to it."

I walked back down the hall to the agency and opened the door to find Malone halfway out of her seat, focused on me with her hand in the drawer where she stashes her Glock.

I held up my own hands. "Whoa! Sorry I didn't knock! Somebody's feeling the tension."

She eased back down into the chair and closed the drawer. "Just got off the phone with Sonny Sampson and I was thinking about Sabado."

That stopped me halfway to my side of the partners desk. "Why? Is there a problem?"

"No, but apparently Colleen and Hoke are enjoying their freedom to the max. Taking walks. Hanging out in public places. Dining al fresco. If someone did have them targeted, there wouldn't be much Sonny could do besides report that they'd been hit."

I moved on to my chair. "Maybe we have her sit on them closer whether they like it or not."

"She said the same thing. She's going to move in close if she gets any hint of a problem, so you might be hearing from your daughter before the day is over."

"So be it. Maybe there won't be any hints."

"That would be good."

We sat looking at one another for a moment. "We haven't heard of any developments from Mike, so I guess we focus on the Mondragon case," I said, and looked at my watch. "Our first interview from that list of friends she gave us is in about an hour. Meanwhile...."

My thought was interrupted when an email popped up on my computer screen labeled "urgent." It was from Martha Mondragon. "Hold on," I said as I clicked on it. "This is weird."

"What?"

"Talk about timing. It's an email from Mrs. Mondragon urgently requesting that we come to her house right away. Says it's a life or death emergency."

"That's it?" Malone kind of squinted at me and got up to come around the desk and look at my screen. "That *is* weird," she agreed after scanning the brief message. "You've got a life or death emergency and you send an email rather than making a call?"

I picked up the phone. "Let me make the call." I punched in Mondragon's home number and let it ring. It went to voicemail.

"She didn't answer?" Malone asked as I hung up.

"No."

"And you didn't leave a message, tell her we're on our way?"

I looked up at my partner as I opened the desk drawer to retrieve my Smith and Wesson. "Call me crazy, but I think an unexpected arrival might be better."

Malone stepped back around the desk to get her own gun. "I would never call you crazy."

CHAPTER THIRTY-FIVE

We didn't have a choice. We couldn't ignore a client possibly in trouble, we didn't have time to get backup, and we had no reason to call the cops. So off we went.

All our meetings with Mrs. Mondragon had been in our office, the Justice Center, or her husband's motel, so first of all we had to find her house.

Our information had it in the 6000 block of 28th, so I figured the quickest way was to pick up Interstate 5 north to the exit nearest Concordia University. Then it should be more or less a straight shot east. I reminded Malone to postpone our upcoming interview on the way, just in case.

The drive took about fifteen minutes and once I took the exit I found it with no difficulty. I parked right in front of the two-story light beige house with full front porch featuring white columns to either side. It looked to be one of the newer and better houses in a nice middle-class neighborhood. About what you'd expect for a reasonably successful real estate agent.

We sat in the car for a minute, looking it over. No reaction from within the house.

"Apparently she's not keeping an eye out for us," Malone observed.

"I don't see any sign of trouble," I said.

"I don't see any sign of life. Probably we should go see what's up."

"Let's do it."

We bailed out of the Subaru and followed the walkway, then up the concrete steps. The wooden porch creaked as we approached the front door. Anyone inside had to know they had visitors, but there was still no movement or sound other than our own.

I knocked as Malone stepped to the side to peer in a

window. No response to my knock. "Anything?" I asked Malone.

"Nobody in sight. Nothing looks out of order." She rejoined me at the door where I was knocking yet again. After a moment, she reached down and tried the knob. "It's open," she announced as she reached for her Glock.

I drew my Smith and Wesson as she very slowly pushed the door open to reveal a shadowed entryway. Still no sound, no movement.

"You think we should identify ourselves?" she whispered.

"Better not. Don't shoot Martha if we surprise her."

"Got it."

There was a wide archway ahead of us that appeared to open into the living room. I could see a couch and coffee table against the far wall. Apparently all the shades in this part of the house were closed. The light was not good and that made me even more uneasy. Somehow I did not expect to see Martha Mondragon pop around a corner and ask what we were doing in her house.

"I'm left and low," I muttered at Malone.

"Got it."

I swung left through the archway in a crouch as my partner stepped through to the right. Nothing. Just a normal living room lit only by the summer sun through heavy curtains. Besides the couch and table, there was the standard array of floor lamps and armchairs, a small flat screen TV, and some kind of curio cabinet.

There was another archway, this one regular-door size, beyond the far end of the couch; it led to a hallway. I stood up and glanced back past Malone. She was looking at a combination kitchen dining room separated by a half-counter. Nobody there unless they were hiding behind the counter.

She gestured that she was going to check that out and I tried to keep an eye on both her and the hallway as she did so. She indicated it was clear and I pointed at the archway ahead of us. She nodded and stepped up beside me as we approached it, both our guns held at the ready.

It was a hallway, a rather long one with three doors to the right, two to the left, and stairs leading upward at the far end. We stood for a moment, looking it over.

"Four bedrooms and a bath?" Malone speculated softly. "Down here? Then what the hell's upstairs?"

"Let's check these first," I whispered back as I moved slowly to the nearest door, on the right. It was unlocked and we made our usual entrance, me low and left, Malone high and right. An empty bedroom.

It took almost five minutes to work our way to the end of the hall, one room at a time. Two bedrooms, a bath, a home office, and a storage room as it turned out. There was also a large walk-in closet under the stairway, between the two bedrooms. No evidence in any of the spaces that they'd been searched or were the scene of violence.

We still didn't know what we were dealing with. Could Mrs. Mondragon have gone somewhere, leaving the front door unlocked? After emailing us that she urgently needed to see us? Unlikely. If there was nothing of interest upstairs, though, we would have to leave and start looking for our client.

We headed slowly and quietly up the stairs to find out.

The stairway was wide enough for us to move shoulder to shoulder. The layout of the stairway appeared to be an odd design. It looked like we were approaching a small landing, maybe four feet deep, that was right up against the back of the house. If we proceeded up the stairs normally, the entire second floor would be behind us as we stepped onto the landing.

We both paused at that realization, looking up at a large display case against the otherwise blank wall beyond the landing. It appeared to hold a remarkable number of bowling trophies. The case had a glass front and it looked from the reflection as if most of the second floor was well-lit open space in contrast to the first floor.

We didn't have to say a word. I nodded at my partner and we both turned to carefully back up the last few steps.

When our eyes cleared floor level, we stopped. Martha Mondragon sat bound and gagged in a chair at the far end of the room. She appeared to be both conscious and alone, but we stayed put for the moment anyway.

As I'd anticipated from the reflection in the trophy case, the second floor was one big open space, amounting to the biggest damned family room I'd ever seen. One wall, to our left, was all glass with what looked like theater curtains to either side that I presumed would close.

To our right was a truly massive flat screen TV, at least ten feet by six with a whole array of comfortable looking chairs oriented toward it. Otherwise there was a pool table and a ping pong table, a corner of the room with floor to ceiling shelves that looked like a reading nook, another corner that looked like it held a tanning machine—or maybe it was a hyperbaric chamber, for all the hell I knew.

The Mondragons were seriously into toys.

There was no sign of life besides our client, who had seen us by now and was making moaning sounds and pulling vigorously against her bindings.

"Why," muttered Malone out of the corner of her mouth, "is she struggling like that when she can see rescue is at hand?"

"Maybe," I muttered back, "because that isn't all she sees."

There were places throughout the room that could conceal someone from our viewpoint at the head of the stairs. At least three oversized armchairs that would work. The pool table that had some kind of heavy fabric skirt down to the floor. A cabinet-type thing that sat near the center of the TV viewing chairs.

Malone was still sotto voce. "Pull back and call 911 or forge ahead?"

I had to think about that for a moment. "I don't like our client's chances if we leave her up here. I say forge ahead. Very slowly and carefully."

"Okey dokey. I couldn't go fast up these stairs backwards anyway."

Moving in tandem, as quietly as we could, we mounted the few remaining steps and paused on the landing. No movement or sounds besides Martha Mondragon, who was struggling even more violently. I motioned that I would move around the stairwell to the left while Malone took the right.

The second we stepped apart, all hell broke loose.

Two men rose up, firing steadily, one from behind an armchair on my side and one from behind the pool table on Malone's. Before I could even react, I felt a bullet go past my head and heard Malone grunt. Then I was diving forward as I fired back as fast as my finger could pull the trigger. Cacophony reigned for about five seconds.

And then everything was quiet again.

I was on my hands and knees crawling over to where my wife had landed before the sound of the last shot died away. To my great relief, she was shoving herself up onto her own hands and knees before I got there.

"Devon! You okay? You hit?"

She surveyed the room before replying. "Are *they* both hit?"

I surveyed with her. "They're both down." Then I focused on Martha Mondragon. She wasn't wriggling anymore but her eyes were wide open, very wide open, and she didn't appear to be wounded. So far so good. That was when I turned back to my wife and saw the blood on her left sleeve.

"You are hit," I said. "How bad is it?"

She pulled up the sleeve and flexed her fingers. "Just took some skin off. I've gotten worse from rose bushes. You okay? Nothing missing?"

I did a quick check. You never know when your system is flooded with adrenaline. Couldn't see any damage. "I'm fine. I'll go free Martha while you call 9-1-1 and restrain those two—if they need it."

We both got to our feet and I hurried over to Martha Mondragon, removing her gag first in case she was having trouble breathing, and then going to work on her restraints.

"Oh my God, who are those men?" she gasped as soon as she was able to speak. "What did they want?"

"I was going to ask you that," I replied as I got her hands free and came around to untie her feet.

I was about to follow up when Malone called out from

where the second shooter was down. "These guys are both dead. Are we good or what?"

"Good," I responded, leaving it to her to decide if it was an agreement or an affirmation.

She headed for the stairwell. "I'll meet the cops downstairs. Mondragon okay?"

"Appears to be." I focused back on getting the final knots untied. "What did the men say to you?" I asked Martha.

"Nothing! Well, they told me to be quiet and go up the stairs and sit in this chair...but that's all. Not another word. Once I was tied up, one of them went back downstairs for a few minutes; I don't know what he was doing. Then they kind of checked out the room, deciding where they were going to hide, I guess, and after that they just stood around, not saying anything. They must have been waiting for you two. Did you know they were here?"

"No. We got an email from you saying it was urgently important that we come to your house. Did they make you send that?" I helped her stand up and lent my support as she took a few steps to get the circulation going again.

She gave me a totally bewildered look. "They didn't make me do anything but come up here and sit down. I didn't send you an email. Are you sure it was from me?"

"Well, it certainly appeared to be. We'll take a look at your computer, or the police will, and figure it out."

"What in the world is happening?" she asked me plaintively as we heard the first sirens in the distance.

I didn't answer, because I didn't have one. That was going to take a little longer to figure out.

CHAPTER THIRTY-SIX

"It doesn't make any fucking sense." Malone irritably swiveled her chair back and forth.

"I know," I agreed.

We were finally back in the office after being swarmed by uniforms at the scene, stopping at Providence Emergency to get Malone's arm treated, joining our client at the Justice Center in giving lengthy statements, and having a very, very late lunch at the Home Run Sports Bar. Martha Mondragon was temporarily holed up in a hotel nearby.

"And don't look so fucking concerned," she grumped further. "I'm fine."

"I know."

I also knew, because I'd had flesh wounds like hers before, that she was hurting like hell...but she wanted us both to pretend otherwise. I'd do my best. The good news was that it shouldn't inhibit her range of motion much.

"Why would two local lowlifes want to kill us? And how would they know to set us up at Martha Mondragon's house?" She grimaced and slammed the fist of her uninjured arm on the desk. "How would they know *how* to set us up at her house? What the fuck?"

"I don't know."

At least we'd learned the identities of our attackers from Mike Whitehall before we left the Justice Center. Gavin Holt and Stuart Morgenthal were well known to the Portland police as muscle for a local loan sharking operation.

Which only added to the mystery. Attempting to assassinate two private detectives was way above their normal pay grade and neither of us could recall ever investigating a loan sharking operation. Somebody was very seriously pissed and we had no idea who or why.

"Bernie Mondragon must have been involved in something

we don't know about yet," I said. "I hope Eleanor has a chance to go over those files in the morning. Maybe she'll come up with a lead, or at least a hint."

"Saved by Eleanor Ivory. Great."

"Well, that's what we pay her for. One of the things."

Malone had just opened her mouth to respond, probably with another sour comment about our resident hacker/accountant, when we heard a knock on the door.

"Gee, maybe that's her," I said. "Come in!"

I noticed that my partner had her hand in the top drawer that housed her Glock as the door opened. I didn't know if it was healthy paranoia or a desire to shoot Eleanor, but she eased off immediately as we saw—to my surprise—that Mike Whitehall was in the doorway.

Until he showed up at the latest crime scene, I hadn't seen him since I was last in the dojang. And now here he was again, six-three of solid muscle with close-cropped brown hair, having added a sport coat to his khaki and white shirt outfit.

"Weren't we just talking to you?" I greeted him.

He grinned and shut the door behind him before crossing over to the visitor chair nearest my side of the desk.

"I thought it would be good to have a talk outside of the formal statement process. You guys have had quite the time of it, lately. Just in the last few days, I've booked—and then released—your client's nephew for attempted murder, arranged extra drive-bys for both the Pen and Pastry and the safe house because somebody might be after Colleen's boyfriend, and now you get ambushed by Holt and Morgenthal...for no reason that I can determine. Could it have to do with the Las Vegas people threatening the boyfriend?"

I exchanged a glance with Malone and shook my head. "I don't see how. They were a whole different problem and supposedly they've left town anyway. You haven't found any connection between the two shooters and Bernie Mondragon?"

"Not a one, but it's only been a couple of hours. There almost has to be one, because somehow they knew they could use his wife to lure you. Oh, and they had written instructions about how to hack her computer and send the email."

"What? Written instructions?" That was hard to believe.

"Crime scene found them downstairs near the machine. They had Holt's fingerprints all over them. I couldn't share that with you in front of my colleagues, of course. Ongoing investigation, you know."

"What the hell?" Malone jumped up and started pacing the office. "This is extremely weird. They had written instructions on how to set us up for the ambush but no clue how to actually pull off an ambush?" She stopped and looked at Mike. "You heard our statements. These idiots hid behind pieces of furniture and then stood up to start shooting. They might as well have both had a big SHOOT ME sign on their foreheads."

"I agree that it's very strange. In the first place, they were not killers; they were knee-cappers. You're sure that neither of you has crossed paths with Holt or Morgenthal before? How about the loan sharking operation run by Stuffy Smithers?"

"That's a great name but, no, I've never heard of any of them." I cocked an eye at Malone, who had sat down again. "You should check with your buddy Carl. Maybe he knows something interesting about Stuffy or his goons."

"I'll do that."

Mike gave her a look. "Carl Gunther?"

"Yeah."

"Well, he probably has a finger if not a whole hand in Stuffy's business. He's a good source for you?"

She grinned. "Hell, we use him as backup sometimes now that Johnny and Hap have retired."

Whitehall held up both hands as if surrendering. "I don't want to know about it." He stood. "Whatever's going on, you two need to watch your backs."

"We always do," Malone and I said in unison.

Mike was having a good chuckle as he left the office.

That was just about the last chuckle of the day.

CHAPTER THIRTY-SEVEN

After my partner and I mulled over the talk with Whitehall for a few minutes, I called Sonny Sampson. There was just too much mystery surrounding this latest attack and, with everything else going on....

"I want to hire you," were my first words after she said hello.

"What are you talking about? You think I'll take better care of your kid if you're paying me?"

"No, no, it's not that at all—but your extra twenty-four hours are just about up. You still haven't seen any sign of trouble, have you?"

"No, nothing. Certainly no hint of anything from Sabado. I'm thinking it's safe to head home."

"I'm thinking it's not. Two local guys tried to kill Malone and me earlier today. There's no indication they have anything to do with Sabado, but there's also no apparent connection to the other case we're working."

"My God, are you guys okay?"

"Malone got a minor flesh wound, but that's it."

"And the two shooters?"

"Both dead."

"Good job." She paused only a second. "So, not being a big fan of coincidence I would guess, you're still feeling uneasy about the kids' safety."

"You could say that—but I don't want to impose on you anymore. Thus the hiring."

"Well, I'm a thousand dollars a day, plus expenses."

"Ouch."

"Las Vegas. Gangsters and high rollers. They can afford it. Tell you what: I'll give you guys a family discount."

"I appreciate that. We'll take it a day at a time."

"And, whether they like it or not, I'm going to move in

closer to Colleen and Hoke again. I do believe in earning my money."

"Sounds good. I'll deal with my daughter if she's unhappy."

"Okay. I'm moving. Talk to you soon."

We hung up and only then I noticed that Malone was also on the phone. I presumed she was talking to Carl Gunther. There was no way to tell for sure from her end of the conversation which, at this point, consisted of "yeah?" and "really."

She hung up on a final "okay."

"Gunther?" I inquired.

"He would be very surprised if this Smithers character wanted us dead, but he says that Holt and Morgenthal have been known to moonlight—just as muscle, though, not hit men. There's no connection between Smithers and Sabado or anybody else out of town that he knows of, but he'll do some more checking."

"So...nothing that helps."

"Not a fucking thing."

I picked up the phone again, deciding to be proactive.

Colleen didn't even say hello. "I was about to call you."

I went on alert. "Is there a problem?"

"You bet there's a problem. I just looked out the front window and Sonny Sampson is parked out there again. I thought she was leaving town, leaving us alone. Is that Sabado guy back already or has she graduated to stalker status?"

"Neither one. Quite."

"Quite?"

"I asked Sonny to stay in town an extra day until we felt comfortable that the threat was over. She's been watching you from a distance. Then Devon and I had a problem earlier today that made me uncomfortable enough to formally hire her to watch over you more closely. Just for a while longer, until we figure out what's going on."

"That's just great. What kind of problem?"

"Some guys took a couple of shots at us."

"Like, with guns? Like, trying to kill you? Are you all right?"

"We're fine. You worry about you and Hoke. Don't—I repeat, do not—try to lose Sonny. We don't know what's going on or who is in danger."

My daughter heaved a big sigh. "Okay, okay. We were mostly going to stay home this evening anyway. We've been running around all day, enjoying our freedom." Another sigh. "So much for that. Maybe I'll invite her in to eat with us."

"That would be nice."

"You take care."

"You, too."

CHAPTER THIRTY-EIGHT

We were back in the office right at eight the next morning. It was a gray day, threatening rain, unusual for August in Portland but matching our moods perfectly.

I'd finished out the previous afternoon by calling Agatha Pepper, Veronica, and Big Avenue to make sure they were all watching their backs.

Agatha assured me she still had both Rodney and Walter close at hand, Veronica said she'd be careful, and Big Avenue averred that he was always watching his back. Given his line of work, that was probably true.

Then we went home to feed the cats and ourselves. Neither one of us had slept well.

After starting the coffee and checking phone messages (two potential clients) and email (one online payment notice and the rest junk), I headed down the hall to see if Eleanor Ivory was in her office yet. There was no response to my knock and I knew why as soon as I turned back toward my own office: Eleanor was just topping the stairs and heading my way, loaded down with two briefcases and another folder under one arm. She looked like she hadn't slept much better than we did. She was also a little damp.

"Can you believe it's raining on August 14?" she asked as I hurried forward to give her a hand.

"Well, it's not unheard of," I replied as I took the folder and one of the briefcases from her.

"I know, I know. Thanks. It would have to happen when I don't have a hand free for an umbrella."

"Do you even own an umbrella?"

She used her now-free hand to unlock her door. "That's beside the point."

I followed her into the office, put the folder on her desk

and the briefcase on the floor next to the one she'd been carrying. Meanwhile, she more or less collapsed into her chair.

"I gather things aren't going well with your client," I offered sympathetically.

She groaned. "We finally agreed on a proposal just before midnight. It might fly. Maybe. There's a chance. We'll know tomorrow."

I eased down into one of her visitor chairs. "So...is there anything else you have to do on that today?"

She gave me a look. "Translation: Can I get to those real estate records today?"

I shrugged. "That's what I meant."

She glanced at her phone. No blinking light. She looked at her monitor as the PC booted up. Apparently there were no blinking lights there, either. "Yes," she said. "I will get to your records. I will attempt to find something that might get a real estate agent killed, as per your request. Check back with me this afternoon. Late this afternoon."

It seemed to me that it would be unwise to push any further. "You got it," I said, and made an expeditious exit.

I'd just given my partner a heads up about Eleanor's plan for the day and settled on my side of the desk again when I heard a quick knock on the door, followed by the appearance of Martha Mondragon.

I stood and gestured at the visitor chairs. "Mrs. Mondragon. How are you doing? Have a seat. Do you want some coffee?"

She chose the seat next to Malone. "Coffee would be good." She sounded totally exhausted. I didn't blame her.

"I'll get it," I said to my partner and headed for our coffee maker where there was still more than half-a-pot of fresh. As I poured cups for our client and myself, I could hear Malone softly reassuring our visitor that it should be okay for her to go back home today.

I returned to the desk, setting Mrs. Mondragon's cup in front of her and taking my seat.

She was shaking her head. "I don't know if I can. I don't know if I ever can. Bernie is dead and now those two men...." Tears spilled down her cheeks. "That was our house! There's blood all over the floor! How can I live there now?"

Malone put a hand gently on her arm. "In the first place, you don't have to live there. You can decide that later. We can recommend someone who'll do a good job of cleaning up that room and make it look like nothing ever happened. Maybe you'll decide there are more good memories than bad in the house. Meanwhile, you have the hotel to stay in and you have us on your side."

Mrs. Mondragon looked up at my partner, her eyes wide. "Do you know who killed Bernie?"

"No, I'm sorry. We don't know yet."

The older woman sat back, pulling her arm from under Malone's hand. "Are you making any progress at all? What am I supposed to do? The police still suspect me and now strange, horrible men are tying me up in my own home.... There were bullets flying around.... I could have been killed!" She wiped away more tears. "What am I going to do?"

I grabbed some tissues out of a desk drawer and leaned forward to hand them to her. "You shouldn't be in any more danger, Mrs. Mondragon. Those men were after us, not you, and they're dead. We haven't identified Bernie's killer yet, but we're making progress. We have people to talk to. Meanwhile, if it will make you feel better, we'll arrange some extra security at the hotel."

She wiped her eyes. "I would like that," she sniffled.

It took another quarter-hour of tissues and reassurances, but Martha Mondragon finally left to return to her hotel.

Whereupon Malone gave me her classic gimlet eye. "How exactly do we arrange extra security at the Embassy Suites? We can't do it ourselves and the two old guys are retired. I don't think Reuben or Big Avenue would exactly fit in."

I grinned and picked up the phone. "No problem. I happen to know the head of security there. We worked together on a case four or five years ago. We've kept in touch and I'm sure a couple of his people wouldn't mind overtime—which we'll ultimately bill to Mrs. Mondragon, of course."

"Ah, sometimes I forget that you had a life before I came along."

"It was a mere shadow of my life now, but I did have one, yes. Hello, could I speak to Fred Findley, please? Thanks."

I waited while my partner smiled.

CHAPTER THIRTY-NINE

Fred did indeed have a man with a second kid on the way and a great need for overtime. He was sure he could come up with one more for a few days, considering that the hotel didn't have to pay for it. So that took care of Mrs. Mondragon's security.

Now, as for Mrs. Mondragon's case....

"You know it's probably not going to do any good to talk to their friends," Malone pointed out as she shut down her PC in preparation for us to go do exactly that. "I doubt Bernie was killed by a jealous husband."

"I know," I replied with a sigh, "but maybe one of them knows something that Martha doesn't, something that will point us in the right direction. Maybe even to a jealous husband."

Malone shrugged. "Maybe. On the other hand, we're just heading off to see if they're home? Not even renewing the two appointments we had to cancel yesterday? It could be a complete waste of the day."

I shoved back a small surge of irritation. I knew she had a point, but I needed to be doing something. "Or maybe," I snapped, "we get more if somebody's not expecting to talk to us today." I took a breath. "Look, Sabado's gone and even your buddy Carl has no clue why Holt and Morgenthal would ambush us. If you can think of something more productive we can do, please share and we'll get right on it."

She held up her hands in surrender. "Okay, okay. It's better than sitting here grumping at each other. Hell, maybe a couple more guys will try to kill us while we're out and that will give us the clue we need."

"That's the spirit."

We strapped on our guns and put on our jackets and headed out.

Rupert and Dorothy Barnes were the closest, on Ankeny about twelve blocks the other side of the Willamette River from downtown. They lived in a four-story apartment building on a tree-shaded block that probably appreciated the mid-morning drizzle more than I did.

I found a parking spot about half a block down and we just sat there for a minute, making sure that no one had followed us. Paranoia pays when people are trying to kill you.

"This time of day on a Tuesday," I began as I surveyed the street, "if there's anybody home it's probably the wife. So why don't you take the lead?"

A full ten seconds of silence drew my attention back into the car and onto my partner, who was glaring at me.

"Because I'm so good at connecting with housewives?" she finally asked.

I conceded defeat. "Forget I said anything. I don't know what came over me. Must be stress. We'll just play it by ear as usual."

"Yeah," Malone sneered as she opened her door, "we'll gang up on the poor little woman while she changes a diaper or whips her cream or whatever housewifely thing she's doing."

I got out and looked at her across the top of the Subaru. "You're not going to forget I said anything, are you?"

"Not a chance in hell."

The drizzle was tapering off, which was good since neither of us owned an umbrella. No upstanding Portland resident owned an umbrella.

"They're in apartment 101, which should be on this floor right in front," I said as we approached the entrance. There was an intercom box but the outside door was neither locked nor obviously monitored. We stepped directly into a nicely carpeted and fresh-smelling hallway and the first door on our right was 101. I knocked.

Just as I was going to knock a second time, an older man, mid-60s I'd guess, opened the door and looked at us inquiringly. He was heavyset, casually dressed in jeans, plain gray sweatshirt, and sandals. His face was florid and his hair more than a little thin. He carried what looked like a dishtowel in his left hand. I didn't need to look to know that my partner was smirking.

"Rupert Barnes?" I asked.

"Yes. And I see they haven't fixed the entrance door lock yet. I hope you two aren't here to rob me." He seemed remarkably sanguine about the possibility.

"No," I assured him. "We're private investigators." I pulled out my ID and flipped it open. "I'm Clint McCall and this is my partner Devon Malone. We have some questions about Bernie Mondragon."

The corners of his mouth turned down. "I heard about Bernie. Such a tragedy. I should call Martha." He stepped back. "But I'm forgetting my manners. I don't know how I can help you, but please come in." He hefted the dish towel. "I was just washing the breakfast dishes. I believe there's some coffee left in the pot."

I couldn't help seeing Malone's smirk as we seated ourselves in the tidy living room.

It turned out that Rupert was retired and a house husband (more smirking) while his much younger wife continued to work as an accountant. Bernie was one of her clients, which is how they all became friends—although it soon became clear that the primary friendship was between Mrs. Barnes and Bernie. She, of course, was at work on a Tuesday morning.

After one cup of tepid coffee and fifteen minutes of an unproductive interview, we made our excuses and left. Rupert seemed disappointed to lose the company.

"So," I said to Malone as we walked back to the car under cloudy skies but no more drizzle, "Rupert apparently believes Bernie to be a faithful husband and all-round decent guy. Whoopee."

"I wonder if his wife knows about Bernie's extracurricular activities," my partner replied as she opened the passenger side door. "In fact, I wonder if Rupert's much younger wife might *be* one of Bernie's extracurricular activities."

I mulled that over as I got myself settled in the car. "If we don't get any other leads, it would be worth following up. Rupert didn't seem like the jealous or violent type, but...." I turned the ignition and checked the side mirror before pulling out.

"But you never know," Malone finished for me.

Nobody pulled out behind us.

CHAPTER FORTY

Thomas and Evelyn Anders were next on our list. They turned out to live on another nicely shaded block, of N.E. Hancock, in a substantial house that looked newly painted blue with white trim.

I was able to park right in front and we headed up the brick walkway to the small porch and front door. The grass was well-trimmed and looked as new as the paint.

There was a somewhat ornate knocker on the door, rather than a doorbell, so I knocked. Once, twice, three times.

I was just turning away to announce that we couldn't win them all when the door was opened abruptly by a very tall woman, maybe mid-30s, dressed casually in shorts, sweatshirt, and flip-flops. She was breathing as if she'd run a hundred-yard dash.

She looked at the two of us. We looked at her.

"I really need to stop smoking," she said.

I had to tilt my head up a bit. She was at least six one. "Mrs. Anders?"

She caught her breath and smiled sheepishly. "Yes. Can I help you?"

We both pulled out our I.D. "I'm Clint McCall and this is my partner Devon Malone. We're private investigators looking into the death of Bernie Mondragon. We understand that you were friends."

Her expression shifted to sorrowful. "Yes, we loved Bernie and Martha. She wouldn't have hurt him, despite all his faults." She kind of squinted at me. "You aren't working for the police, are you? Trying to prove she did it?"

Malone leaned a little forward. "Working *with* the police, *for* Mrs. Mondragon, trying to prove she didn't."

That brought a smile back to the woman's face, along with

more normal breathing. "Oh, well. Good. Come in then." She stepped aside with a welcoming gesture.

"You're lucky you caught me at home," she said as she escorted us through the small entry alcove into a large living room that was predominantly tan and light green. It was a pleasant, lived-in space with overstuffed chairs and a big couch (on which resided a medium-size mutt who barely managed to cock one slightly open eye in our direction), and a flat screen TV on the far wall. There were several ashtrays in evidence and hints of smoke in the air.

"Normally I'd be in my office this time of day," she continued as she indicated we should sit on the couch, "but my daughter is home sick from school and I decided to keep her company for a while."

I hoped it wasn't asthma.

"I thought school was out for the summer," Malone noted as we seated ourselves.

"She's in summer school, special classes for college bound students. She's very bright." Mrs. Anders settled in the biggest recliner with appropriate parental pride.

"Mind if I ask what you do in your office?"

Anders smiled at my partner. "Not at all. I'm a psychologist with a private practice. My husband, who *is* in his office, is a real estate agent. A different agency than Bernie's, but that's how we got to know them. How is Martha doing? I want to call her with my condolences when she has a little space. I imagine she's somewhat preoccupied right now."

"She is that," I replied. "But doing pretty well, all things considered." The woman seemed open and cooperative, so I just went for it. "Can you think of any reason someone would want to kill Bernie? Or who that someone might be?"

She sat back as if I'd taken a swing at her. "Oh. Wow. Straight for the bottom line. Okay." She took a moment to think, which was in her favor. Then she shrugged. "It could have been one of his prostitutes or one of their pimps, of course. Bernie played in dangerous waters."

"So you knew about that."

She shrugged again. "He didn't go out of his way to hide it. Sometimes he and Martha would bicker about it right in front of us. They had an unusual relationship."

"But," Malone interjected, "you're certain she didn't kill him?"

"Oh, absolutely. Like I say, she'd known for quite some time that he had an obsession with ladies of the evening. She'd give him grief about it, but no more than that."

"Was it only prostitutes? Never anyone from his business life, no friends or acquaintances?"

A grin flitted across Mrs. Anders' face. "Like me? No, not that I ever heard of. I think his turn-on was that they were working girls."

"And his wife just put up with it?" I was thinking back to Martha and her gun in front of Bernie's motel room that had started all this.

"Oh, she had a problem with it. Thus the bickering. She was always looking for some way to get his head on straight, as she would put it. But she loved him. She really loved the guy, despite his disgusting little hobby. She wouldn't have hurt him." She grinned a little. "Not seriously, anyway."

Malone shifted on the couch next to me; I could feel her impatience with another dead end. "Any thoughts at all on who might have done it or why?" she asked.

Evelyn Anders shook her head. "Not specifically." And then raised one finger. "But there was something...."

"What?"

"The last six months or so, Bernie seemed uneasy, maybe guilty about something—not the women, something else. It was bothering him."

"His wife didn't say anything about that."

"I'm not sure Martha picked up on it. There were little signs, a shift of the eye, a twitch of the shoulder, the sorts of things I'm used to looking for when I'm in a session. Martha was really focused on the prostitute problem and none of the reactions I saw had to do with that."

"Any idea what they did have to do with?"

"Well, I only saw them when he was talking about the office, his work. It was something there. That's all I can tell you."

"There's no particular reference you remember, like a type of business or a client?"

"No. I'm sorry."

I took up the questioning again, just for another two or three minutes, but it was clear we were done. We thanked Mrs. Anders and took our leave.

"So," Malone said as we settled back in the Subaru, "something about his work. How many people work in his office, I wonder?"

"Something we need to find out, but...." I pulled away from the curb. "...what could be going on in a real estate office that might get you killed?"

"There are people there," observed my partner. "That's all it takes."

CHAPTER FORTY-ONE

The next couple on our list, Christopher and Camilla Bracken, lived in a somewhat dilapidated brown clapboard house on Yamhill, on the edge of our own Hawthorne District. This time three knocks didn't do the trick. There was nobody home.

We were making our way back down the walk when an elderly bald head appeared over the whitewashed plank fence to our left. "You lookin' for the Brackens?"

I stepped over to the fence and saw that it was a gnomish old gentleman in dirt-stained pants and long-sleeved shirt. He carried a hoe in his left hand.

"Yes," I told him, "we are looking for them. Do you know when they'll be home?"

He shook his head. "Nope. But not for a while, I 'spect. They're out of town. On vacation would be my guess, seeing as how they had a lot of stuff packed in that car. With the kids. And the dog."

"Oh, okay. Thank you."

"You want me to tell 'em you came by?"

"No, that's okay. Thanks for your help."

I rejoined Malone and we finished our hike to the car.

"Nothing like a nosy neighbor," she muttered as we walked.

I looked at my watch as we regained our seats in the car. "It's nearly lunchtime. The Pen and Pastry?"

"Why not?"

It was only about a six-block drive and, as usual, I parked in my own driveway. We stopped in to say hello to Stella and Maxine, then walked around the block to the coffee shop. We could have put together a meal at home, of course, but I was curious to chat with Veronica Fortune about her new love interest, the Las Vegas P.I. that we found ourselves relying on so much.

It's not that I didn't trust Sonny Sampson, but I figured that Veronica would have a very different, shall we say, non-professional, take on the woman. And the more you know, the better off you are.

I wasn't wrong.

"Sonny was a late bloomer," Veronica told us over our early lunches. Business was just slow enough that she had grabbed a curried chicken salad and sat down with us. I was having a chicken club sandwich and Malone a turkey BLT with chips that she had brought along from the house.

"She was married to a guy for a few years," Veronica continued, "before she got in touch with her inner woman and came over to our side."

"Ah," I said. "We didn't know that."

"Yeah, he was one of the casino owners, in fact."

"Really?" I could see that Malone was perking up, too.

"Not one of the huge casinos that you always hear about. At least I hadn't heard of it and I don't even remember the name offhand, but I gather it was on the strip and doing well. Probably still is, since she's only been divorced a few years."

"How long were they married?" Malone asked after swallowing her last chip.

Veronica shrugged, her attention pulling away toward the kitchen. "Three or four years, I think."

The place was beginning to get busy. It was only about three minutes later that Veronica made her apologies and dashed off to help her staff deal with the rush. She'd provided no further information in the meantime. But good enough.

"Huh," Malone said as we watched her go. "A casino owner married to a private investigator. That must have been complicated. Then you toss in that the PI was deciding she'd rather be with a woman...."

"I wouldn't have wanted to be a fly on that wall," I said, "but here's what interests me. Her ex-husband could be one of the people backing the legislation to legalize prostitution within city limits. Which would go a long way toward explaining why she's so eager to take Sabado down. Other than the fact that he's disgusting scum, anyway."

My partner mulled that over as she finished her BLT.

"You think she's doing all this for her ex-husband?"

I shrugged. "Maybe not literally, but once she learned what Sabado was really doing, she certainly would have known right away how that would impact the interests of the casino owners, assuming she paid any attention to her husband's business. And I bet she did."

"Okay."

"I'm not saying there's anything hinky going on with the woman. Quite the contrary. I'm glad to hear she might have even more reasons to be on our side."

"I thought we trusted her already."

"We do," I agreed as I tossed money on the table and we both stood, "but it's always good to verify."

We made our way out of the Pen and Pastry, hiked back around the corner to my driveway, and got into the Outback. Next on our list were Leo and Melissa Cavanaugh, who lived a couple of blocks off Sandy out beyond 82nd.

I had just turned onto Sandy when my cell phone signaled. I pulled it from my jacket pocket and glanced at the display. "Eleanor," I said to Malone as I handed her the phone.

Malone hit the speaker button. "Hey, Eleanor. It's Devon. Clint is driving. You're on speaker. You have something?"

"Hi, guys. Yes, I think I do. Are you going to be back in the office soon? I think we should go over this in person."

I immediately took a right at the next corner.

"We're on the way," I said.

CHAPTER FORTY-TWO

We hit the office right at one o'clock and Eleanor must have had her door open, listening for us, because she appeared in the hallway before I had our own door open.

A minute later we were all settled around the partners desk.

"Okay," I said, "what do you have for us?"

"Money laundering," Eleanor announced, looking very pleased with herself.

I think I might have frowned a bit in confusion. "So this is about Antonio Sabado and not Bernie Mondragon?"

"No, it's Bernie—or at least Bernie's real estate agency."

Needless to say, that riveted our attention.

Malone leaned forward. "You have evidence that the agency was laundering money? Who for?"

Eleanor's expression was rapidly going from pleased to pouting. "I wouldn't say that I have evidence. Not hard evidence that you could use in court. And I don't know who it was for."

I gave Malone a look and jumped in before she could jump all over our accountant. "Okay, so what do you have?"

"There are indications that Bernie Mondragon's real estate agency was serving as a conduit for a form of money laundering called under-valuation. Are you guys familiar with that?"

I looked at Malone and she shook her head.

"No clue," I said to Eleanor. "I have a general idea of what money laundering is, but we've never had a case that involved it."

She took a breath and seemed to settle herself for a lecture. "The agency records the property value on a contract of sale which is less than the actual purchase price. The difference between the contract price of the property and its true worth is paid secretly by the purchaser to the agency using illicit funds.

The purchaser is able to claim that the amount disclosed in the contract as having been paid is within their legitimate financial means. Then the property is sold at the market or higher value and the apparent profits serve to legitimize the illicit funds."

I gave all that a minute to sink in. It didn't. Again I looked at my partner. "Did you understand that?"

"I'd need pictures," she said, "but not right now." She focused on Eleanor. "I'll take your word that it works, but...you said 'indications.' I gather what you found falls short of evidence."

"It falls outside my area of expertise. What I see in the records looks like under-valuation and I may be looking at evidence, but you'd need a forensic accountant to verify that."

"Fine. Do you see anything there that indicates our client's husband was specifically involved in the money laundering?"

Eleanor shook her head. "No. The transactions I'm looking at are associated with names of agents who don't exist or at least don't work for that agency. Probably codes for whoever actually handled it. No telling if it was Bernie Mondragon or one of the other agents or all of the agents, for that matter."

"And there's no indication of whose money is being laundered?" I asked.

"None that I can discern. All shell companies and, again, I don't have the expertise or resources to track them down."

By this point my brain was buzzing. It was too much information and at the same time not enough. "Okay," I finally said, "I have to think about this. You've obviously hit on some important information, but I don't know if it helps us." I glanced over at Malone. "You?"

She shrugged. "Thinking is good."

Back to Eleanor. "Write up everything you've found, including what you suspect and what you think needs to yet be determined, attach the relevant files, and then sit on it for a day or two. It has to go to the feds for further investigation, but we need a little time first."

She nodded and stood up. "Good enough. I'm happy to have a day or two to get it together. I do have other work."

"Of course. And we appreciate your efforts."

She grinned as she turned toward the door. "Don't worry. The bill will be in the mail."

I think we sat there silently, both of us swiveling away, for at least a full minute after she closed the door behind her.

"So," my partner finally said. "Have we started believing in coincidences?"

I cocked an inquiring eyebrow at her.

"Antonio Sabado was in Portland supposedly to deal with his money laundering business and Bernie's real estate agency appears to be involved in...guess what."

"That's a stretch. The two cases are totally unrelated. Once in a great while, a coincidence is nothing more than a coincidence."

"Maybe. It's something to think about. It would certainly fit with what Evelyn Anders was just telling us, Bernie being involved in such a scheme or at least knowing about it."

"Oh, I'll certainly think about it."

And, in fact, I didn't have to think about it for long. We were tossing around the idea of checking out the rest of the couples on Martha Mondragon's list when Malone's line lit up.

She looked at the display. "Gunther," she muttered, and hit the speaker button. "Carl. You're on speaker. Clint is here. You have something?"

"I do. I did some more checking on your two amateur assassins and confirmed that they were not working on anything associated with Stuffy Smithers."

"Okay, and the punchline is?"

"They were hired by a company that is a subsidiary, about three times removed, of a corporation based in Las Vegas. Guess who controls the corporation in Las Vegas."

"Oh, shit!" I exploded. "Sabado did hire the hit?"

"That's what it looks like."

"Except, why would he hire two third-rate thugs like Holt and Morgenthal? He had a lot better firepower than that with him in the hotel lobby."

"Yeah, but he agreed that all of those men were going to

leave with him and he had to figure that I'd be watching to confirm their departure. Maybe he was desperate to see you two dead and did the best he could during his remaining hours in Portland." Pause. "Why would he be desperate to see you two dead? I ask because I'd like to keep one of you alive."

Malone snorted. "We don't know, Carl. We'll have to let you know about that. Thanks for the information, though, and keep an ear out for anyone else being hired by Sabado."

"Yeah," I said, "thanks, Carl." I'm sure I didn't sound nearly as sincere as my partner had.

He hung up laughing.

My brain had been churning away as we exchanged final pleasantries with the crime boss and it had produced a picture.

"What if," I said to my partner as she sat back from punching off the speaker, "you were a Las Vegas crime boss who came to Portland to deal with possible exposure of your sex trafficking operation and, while you were here, check up on the Portland branch of your money laundering operation. What if, in the course of looking into both those things, you came up with the names of the same two private investigators? What might you conclude?"

Malone's eyes went wide and her lips pursed as she took that in. "Huh. I might conclude that somebody was onto me really big time and that they needed to be eliminated along with the original leak."

"And maybe also the money launderer who seems to be a loose end."

Eyes even wider. "Sabado had Bernie killed?"

"It's a theory."

She sat back. "If you're right, we're looking at the coincidence to end all coincidences here." She scowled. "We hate coincidences."

"I know," I said with a sigh, "and I hope I'm wrong. I probably am." I met her scowl with one of my own. "I gotta say, if I'm not wrong, this is a hell of a good reason to hate coincidences."

I picked up the phone. "And just in case I'm right, we have

to make sure everybody's protected again. You call Agatha, I'll call Colleen."

"On it," she said and picked up her handset.

Nobody answered. Not Colleen. Not Hoke. Not Sonny Sampson. Not Agatha Pepper.

CHAPTER FORTY-THREE

I felt half-numb as I bullied my way through heavy Tuesday afternoon traffic on the way to Colleen and Hoke's house, hoping that we would find them with cell phones they'd forgotten to charge. Or at least some evidence of where they'd gone. Why they'd gone.

I'd already checked with Veronica as we rushed down the stairs and across the street to our parking lot. They weren't at the Pen and Pastry and she hadn't recently heard from them or Sonny.

We were about two-thirds of the way there when Malone finally spoke.

"I'm sorry for snorting."

I glanced over at her. "What? What are you talking about?"

"When you said Sabado might come back after everybody, I snorted. I'm sorry."

"I wasn't aware that you kept track of your snorts."

"The important ones."

"Ah. Well, you have nothing to apologize for. If you'll recall, it was my idea that Sabado would go away and stay away. Plus, we don't know yet that he's coming back or that he's behind any of this. Not for sure."

I moved into the slow lane to pass another car, hit the fast lane again, and pressed the accelerator down.

Eight minutes later I parked right in front of Colleen and Hoke's place. I got out of the Subaru and looked around. The air was hot and almost steamy after the recent rain. I didn't see their car or Sonny's car. The house was quiet.

"They aren't here," I said.

"Let's confirm," my partner responded as we headed for the front door. "If nobody's home, I'll pop the lock and we'll see if there's a clue inside."

Apparently, no one was home. Malone popped the lock.

There was no clue inside. No sign of struggle or disturbance, either, which made me feel a little better. But where the hell were they and why wasn't anybody answering their phone?

We were heading back to the car when Malone tapped my arm. She pointed off to the right. "Check it out."

Sonny Sampson's green Miata was turning the far corner and coming our way. It slowed as it approached us and pulled into a spot across the street. She was just opening her door as we got there.

I did not consider it a good sign that the woman looked absolutely miserable. She stared at Colleen's house rather than meeting our eyes, another bad sign.

"Sonny!" I called as soon as she started to step out of the vehicle. "Where are Colleen and Hoke?"

"They aren't here?" she asked in a discouraged voice. "I was hoping they would be. I was hoping I could find them before I called you back."

I grabbed her by the arm. "What do you mean, you were hoping? Where are they?"

She didn't even try to pull away. "I don't know. I lost them."

"You lost them? How did you lose them? Did someone take them?"

"No, no, they must have spotted me, which is very embarrassing. They went to a little restaurant in your area, a few blocks down from Veronica's café, and apparently ducked out the back as I was watching the front. Eventually I went in to see what they were doing and by the time I'd confirmed they weren't there, they'd retrieved their car and disappeared. I got stiffed by two amateurs and I feel like an idiot." She looked at me with glistening eyes. "I was going to call you next, but I wanted to do one more check back here first. I was hoping they'd come home."

I looked at my wife. "Oh great," she said.

I didn't know what to say, or do, but right then my phone rang. I put it to my ear. "Colleen?"

"It's Reuben."

"Reuben, this isn't a good time...."

His response was abrupt. "What did you have Big Avenue doing?"

"Bodyguard. For Colleen and Hoke. Why?"

"He just got fucking shot. That's why. Somebody tried to take him out right on the street. A drive-by."

"Shit. Is he all right?"

"No, he's not fucking all right. He was shot. He's in emergency at Providence downtown. Did he piss somebody off when he was doing for you?"

"Not that I know of. Is he going to make it? Are you there with him?"

"I'm here and I don't know yet if he's going to make it."

"Well, we'll get there as soon as we can—which might not be really soon. Colleen and Hoke are missing. Call me if you hear any news in the meantime."

By the time I hung up on Reuben's sputtering, Malone had her hand on my arm and Sonny was looking at me wide-eyed.

"Who's down?" my partner asked, almost in a whisper.

"Big Avenue. A drive-by. He's in emergency now and Reuben is there."

"Shit. That's one too many coincidences."

"No kidding," I said as I punched a button on my phone. "I'm calling Whitehall."

Not everything was running against us: Mike Whitehall was at his desk and picked up on the first ring.

"Hey, Clint, more trouble with Sabado?"

It always takes me a second before I realize it's Caller ID rather than precognition. "Uh, no. He left town. We think. But I need a favor."

"Okay, what?"

"I need to know where Colleen's cell phone is."

"You want me to have it pinged? Is she in trouble?"

"I don't know. That's the point. We were still worried about her and Hoke, so we had Sonny Sampson, that Vegas PI, keeping an eye on them, but she lost them. And now neither one is answering their phone or calling back. I'll give you both numbers, actually. We think Sabado is gone...but maybe some of his people are still here. I need to know where Colleen is, asap."

"All right. I'll call you back when I get the info. You want me to send officers if it's here in town, just in case?"

"Call me first. If I don't answer, send the cars if you can. Otherwise, let's decide once you get the location."

"Will do."

I gave him both Colleen's and Hoke's cell numbers and he hung up. I looked at Malone and Sonny Sampson. "I don't know how long that's going to take. I guess the three of us might as well head back downtown, unless somebody's got a better idea."

"No," my partner said. "I wish I did."

Sonny didn't look like she was having any revelations.

"Follow us," I instructed her. "We'll head for the hospital to check on Big Avenue, but we'll divert if we hear from my cop friend in the meantime."

She nodded. "Of course. Again, I'm sorry."

I did not tell her it was okay, since it wasn't. Malone and I crossed back to the Subaru and I handed her my cell phone as soon as we were both settled in. "Put it on speaker if Whitehall calls back," I told her. I got the car started and pulled out, checking the rearview mirror to see that Sonny was following.

"We don't know that they're in any trouble," Malone said as I got us back on Sandy headed downtown. "Maybe they just got tired of having a protective detail."

"And maybe whoever got Big Avenue got them first," I gritted back, trying to stay focused on my driving.

"Oh, man. Don't even think that. Mike will come through and we'll find them."

Neither of us said another word the rest of the way. The cell phone did not ring.

CHAPTER FORTY-FOUR

The Providence Hospital Emergency Room was just off NE 47th, north of Glisan. The waiting area was only about half-full—the half not occupied by a mean-looking black man with serious scars and a furious expression. He was clearly agitated, pacing back and forth in the substantial space that everyone else had left for him. Apparently his head-to-toe light blue outfit did not sufficiently soften his image.

He saw us a moment after we entered and met us halfway to the check-in counter.

"How's he doing?" were my first words.

"Still under the knife," was Reuben's response. "Not easy to dig a bullet out of that big fucker, I guess. But it looks like he'll make it."

"They told you all that?" asked Malone. "Did you say you were his brother or something?"

"I'm his emergency contact. He doesn't have any family here."

That surprised me. "I didn't know you and Big were that close. Mostly I hear about your rivalry."

"They must be frenemies," Malone interjected.

Reuben gave her a look. "I don't know what the fuck that is, but I'm his emergency contact. Plus I know the emergency doc who saw him first. She's keeping me posted."

I thought back to Agatha Pepper's experience here, the sharp and attractive black doctor who had treated her. "Let me guess: Latisha Morningside."

"How...?"

"We were in here recently working a case and talked to her. I just took a wild swing."

"Well, home run. Latisha's from my old neighborhood. Known each other a long time. Lemme see if I can get her out here. Maybe she knows more by now." He headed for the counter. Meanwhile I saw that Sonny Sampson had stopped just inside the entrance; apparently she was going to hang back, which was fine with me. It would take time to explain her and Reuben to one another.

Besides, I was reminded that we still had to track down Ms. Pepper and ensure her safety. If we weren't too late. I tried her cell again while Reuben managed to get his friend paged. Agatha didn't answer.

Dr. Morningside did, looking harried and mildly disheveled, about what you'd expect in the middle of an ER shift. She came around the corner and headed straight for Reuben.

"I told you I'd let you know...." Then she noticed us stepping up to join him.

"You two! Has something else happened to the old lady?"

"No, she's fine." I hoped. "We're here with Reuben to check on Big Avenue."

That gave her pause, clearly. She looked from Reuben to us and back. "You're all friends?"

"We work together sometimes," responded my partner.

"How badly was Big Avenue wounded?" I asked.

"A bullet grazed his head and there was another in his upper thigh. The head wound amounts to a concussion, probably not too serious since he was conscious when they brought him in. The bullet in his leg missed the femoral artery, thank goodness, but it's close so they're being extra careful removing it. Once he's out of surgery and awake, we'll know more, but he should fully recover. Do any of you know his legal given name? The driver's license that he has on him says Big Avenue and he claimed that that's his real name. I find that hard to believe."

"His name is Na'hahu Kemaoutu," I said. "He's from Samoa. I've no idea how he would have a license with his street name on it. Reuben?"

He shrugged. "Big knows the same people I do—and he doesn't want to use his real name 'cause nobody but him can pronounce it." A little grin. "You probably didn't get it right."

"Okay," Dr. Morningside sighed. "So fake ID. That's what I thought." She looked at me. "I don't suppose you know how to spell what you just said."

"No clue."

"Then I guess his chart will say Big Avenue for now. This is Portland. We've had weirder." She glanced over at the half of the area that was occupied by waiting patients. "I've got to get back to it. I'll tell the nurse to let you know when he's out of surgery."

She scurried off and I turned to Reuben. "Where did it happen?"

"He was talking to one of his girls on 82nd, near Sandy."

"Was she able to describe the shooter or at least the car?"

"Nah. Heard the first shot, saw Big start to go down, and dropped. By the time she looked up, the car was gone. She did call 9-1-1 and put pressure on the leg until they got there."

"Which is no small thing," said Malone. "She could have just run off."

"She's a good girl." He motioned to the nearby seats. The three of us were still alone in our half of the waiting area. "Now, tell me what the fuck's going on. Did you guys get Big shot up? Does this have somethin' to do with Tony Saturday?"

The three of us sat down, though I stayed on the edge of my chair. I was desperate for some reassurance that Colleen was okay, and Agatha Pepper as well, but I didn't know how to get any of it right this minute.

"Yeah," I said, "I'm pretty sure it does. Big was staying at a safe house with Colleen and her boyfriend," I began, "and some other people that we thought might be in danger from...Saturday."

Reuben's eyebrows went up. "Well, shit. Do I gotta worry??"

"There's no threat to you. But nobody who was in the safe house with Big Avenue is answering their cell right now and we need to find them. Have you heard anything else on the street about Saturday causing trouble? Putting a hit out on anybody? We know he's hired at least some local talent."

"I ain't heard shit. Nothin' since you called me the first time."

I could see over his shoulder that Sonny Sampson was getting pretty antsy over by the entrance and I didn't exactly feel calm myself. I stood up. "We need to get moving," I said to Reuben as my partner also stood. "Give me a call when Big is out of surgery."

"I will. Go find your daughter."

We headed for the entrance where Sonny joined us. "That was one scary-looking dude you were talking to," she said as we all headed back to our cars, "except for the sky blue outfit. That's Reuben?"

"That's him." We're heading for the office. Follow along." I glanced over at Malone. "It's time to do some cage rattling."

CHAPTER FORTY-FIVE

The three of us were back in the office twenty minutes later. As I had discussed with my partner on the way, I immediately left her and Sonny to settle around the desk while I hiked down the corridor to Eleanor's office.

I knocked and got an immediate "Come in!"

"I've changed my mind about you sitting on the info you gave us earlier," I said as I stepped inside and dropped into one of her visitor chairs. "Have you written it up yet?"

"Well, hello to you, too."

"Sorry. Hello. Have you written it up yet?"

She lifted off her chair far enough to reach the printer. "Jeez, yes. I just printed it out. You don't want me to hold it after all?"

I shook my head. "No. Things are moving too fast. Send it off to the local FBI office from our agency with an urgent request that they have a forensic accountant analyze it for possible money laundering. Maybe a little pressure from the feds will distract Sabado. Plus I need to know for sure that Bernie was part of the money laundering."

"Okay, but it's not like they're going to do it this afternoon, you know."

"Do the best you can. Sabado's already worried about what's going on here in Portland. Maybe he's monitoring it closely enough to pick up that the feds are involved, even if they aren't actually following up yet. There's no point in waiting, in any event."

She gave me a look. "What is going on with you? I don't know that I've ever seen you so jumpy and stressed. What's happened?"

"Yesterday Devon and I were ambushed and today Colleen has gone missing. It's possible Sabado is out to kill everyone involved with either of two investigations we've been doing."

"When...? What?" She focused past me at her door as though they might burst in any second.

I held up a hand. "Not you. They would have no reason to go after our accountant, nor would they have any way to know what else you do for us. But Big Avenue is in the hospital with gunshot wounds and it's probably because we had him bodyguarding Colleen and Hoke."

"Shit! You were ambushed? And Big Avenue was shot? I didn't see anything on the news about any of that. And you don't know where Colleen is? Do you think...?"

"All I know is that she's not answering her cell. Whitehall has put in a request to her provider to ping the phone. I should hear from him any minute now." I hoped. "The attack on Big Avenue just happened a few hours ago. As for the ambush, Mike kept our names out of it. You might have seen a story about two men shot to death inside a home on 28th."

"That was you guys? I assumed the homeowner did it. You shot them?"

"Yes. The homeowner was tied up at the time."

Eleanor shuddered. "Wow. Well, I hope Colleen's okay. And her boyfriend. I'll send these files off with a cover note from the agency right away."

I stood up. "Good enough. I've got to get back to the office."

"Stay safe!" Eleanor called as I closed her door behind me. I could not assure her that I would.

I hurried back down the corridor; the phone was ringing as I opened the door. Malone was looking at the display and she glanced up at me as she reached to push a button. "Mike," she said, both to me and to the caller, "you're on speaker. Clint and Sonny Sampson are both here."

"Colleen's phone is in Hood River," he said without preamble, "somewhere in the downtown area, which is only a few blocks in length anyway. I've asked the local cops to cruise through and see if there appears to be any young couple in trouble. That's about all I can do. The phone is still not being answered, but at least it's not turned off."

I sat down in my chair, trying to process the new information. "Hood River? What the hell are they doing in Hood River?" It was a small windsurfing community about an hour east of Portland up the Columbia Gorge.

"Beats me," Mike responded, "but I'd like to hear more about what's going on because I have another good reason to be calling you."

"What's that?" Malone asked.

"Your client. Agatha Pepper."

"Did something happen to her?" I asked with a feeling of dread as I locked eyes with my partner.

"You could say that. She and her nephew are here in the Justice Center again because she was involved in a gunfight downtown."

CHAPTER FORTY-SIX

I had a sudden image of Agatha Pepper in Stetson and fancy boots, blasting away with Walter at high noon. I wasn't far wrong, as it turned out.

I talked right over the gasps I heard from my partner and Sonny Sampson. "A gunfight? What happened? Is she all right?"

"She's not been wounded, if that's what you mean. Even better, no one else was hit—no thanks to Ms. Pepper. Apparently, she and her nephew were walking the dog near Nordstrom when a car pulled up and someone started shooting at them. Ms. Pepper, instead of taking cover like her nephew, pulled her gun and started firing back. I guess that wasn't what the shooter expected because the car took off in a hurry after being hit several times."

"Jesus Christ," I said. "This was right next to Pioneer Courthouse Square and nobody was hurt?"

"A couple of scrapes and bruises from people diving at the sidewalk, but otherwise not. Your client was very lucky, apart from all the charges that she now faces. And she's probably going to be famous, too. Everybody not in immediate danger went for their phones, of course. I'll bet there are already a bunch of hellacious viral videos out there."

"Great. Any ID on the shooter?"

"Nope. According to witnesses, the car was black, dark blue, or dark green, American or foreign, brand new or slightly used. They all agree it was a sedan, but nobody got the plate."

"Huh. So how much trouble is Ms. Pepper in?"

"A lot, starting with carrying concealed without a permit and reckless endangerment—with more to come, I'm sure. She used her one call to get a lawyer and asked me to call you, which I was going to do anyway because of Colleen. You guys going to come down here or head for Hood River?"

Remarkably, the news about Agatha Pepper doing a John Wayne had momentarily distracted me from the news about my daughter. That brought me back. "Probably Hood River, but I'll let you know." We hung up.

I looked at my partner and she looked at me. Sonny Sampson looked at both of us as if she were visiting an alternate universe.

"It's got to be Hood River," Malone finally said. "Big Avenue and Agatha both? Not even the slightest chance that's coincidence. We need to round up those kids."

"I agree," Sonny chimed in.

I held up a finger. "Let me try Colleen one more time. It would help to know exactly *where* they are in Hood River and why they're there, for that matter." I didn't think that Sabado would have kidnapped them and taken them to the purported Windsurfing Capital of America, but I really had no clue what else could be going on. I punched in my daughter's cell phone number.

And she answered on the first damned ring. "Hey, Pops."

"Colleen! What the fuck are you doing in Hood River? Are you okay?"

"Whoa! Calm down! We needed a break from your protection detail and figured the safest thing was to skip town. There are some Facebook friends here that we've been wanting to meet in real life, so we just drove on out."

"Without telling anybody or answering your phones? That isn't like you."

"We really needed a break. I'm sorry if you were worried, but...."

"Goddamn it, Colleen, we were a lot more than worried. Big Avenue's been shot and somebody tried to shoot Ms. Pepper. It looks like, rather than giving up, Sabado is escalating and intends to take everybody out who was in the safe house. Maybe more than that. Maybe everybody who's had any contact with Hoke. We don't know."

"Oh my god. Are Big and Agatha okay?"

"Agatha's fine. Big Avenue's in the hospital and was undergoing surgery last we heard."

"Oh my god. What should we do?"

"Get back here as quickly as you can so we can find you another safe place."

"Maybe we'd be safer staying here."

"You want to hang out in Hood River with no cover or protection, with me and Devon more than an hour away?"

"I guess not."

"You start back and we'll meet you halfway, at Multnomah Falls.... Hold on." Sonny Sampson was trying to get my attention. "What?"

"I'll meet them at the Falls. I lost them. I'll get them back. You guys need to see what you can do for Agatha."

"Colleen's my daughter."

"And she was my responsibility. Let me do this. You go do what you can for your client. It'll take at least a couple of hours to meet up with them and escort them back to town. The action and the answers are in Portland, not out in the Columbia Gorge."

I thought about it. "Okay. All of you meet us here, at the office, as soon as you can." Back to the phone. "Colleen? Did you hear that?"

"Yeah. Tell Sonny we're sorry. We shouldn't have ducked out on her. We'll head home now and meet her at the Falls." She hung up.

I nodded at Sonny, who was already up and ready to leave. "It's a go," I said. She went.

I took a deep breath as I looked at my partner. "We need to find another safe house for everybody. But first we've got time to see if we can keep Gunslinger Granny out of the pokey."

CHAPTER FORTY-SEVEN

"Of course I returned fire," Agatha Pepper said. "The man was shooting at us and I had to defend my loved ones!"

Ms. Pepper, Rodney, and Morty all sat in the conference room next to Mike Whitehall's office—Agatha defiant, Rodney subdued, and Morty asleep. Walter was no doubt confiscated.

In addition to Mike, Malone, and me, there was an elderly stranger present. Dour of mien and thin of hair, tall, wearing a plain brown suit that might have been as old as he was, he stood behind Ms. Pepper's chair. He was introduced as Horace O'Shea, her attorney.

Given the way he kept his hand on her shoulder while looking resigned to the fact that she was going to say what she wanted without regard to legal repercussions, I suspected he might be something more than her attorney.

"You could have hit an innocent bystander," Malone pointed out.

"But I didn't. I hit the car. Every shot. Probably got the shooter. There were two of them, you know. The passenger had the gun and I know I hit him. The way they tore out of there, they were probably heading for an emergency room!"

I looked over at Mike Whitehall. "We're checking," he said. "Nothing yet."

Lawyer O'Shea, meanwhile, was leaning over and whispering in Agatha's ear, probably trying once more to explain the concept of self-incrimination.

"Oh, Horace, I know I'm in trouble, but I didn't endanger anyone else. It's not like I couldn't hit a darned car!" She reached up and patted his hand that was still on her shoulder and gave us all a big grin. "Besides, it's so exciting, all these people trying to kill me."

He straightened up, squeezed her shoulder, and looked even more resigned. Rodney finally looked up from the tabletop he'd been staring at since we arrived and offered his aunt a guilty side-eye. Morty continued snoring.

Whitehall motioned Malone and me to step out of the room. The three of us trooped next door and settled around his desk.

"One of my detectives caught a drive-by on 82nd," he began. "Reuben's buddy, Big Avenue. Is that somehow related to this incident?"

"It's certainly possible," I responded. "We recruited him to help provide security at the safe house and Sabado may have found that out."

"You think Sabado is responsible for both shootings? He supposedly left town. You need to bring me up to speed, right now."

"We may have two related cases that created the perfect storm of gangster paranoia," I began. With Malone's help, I laid out what we'd recently learned about Bernie Mondragon's possible involvement in money laundering that could possibly be Sabado's operation.

"Wow," was Mike's initial response when we were done. "Do you think Sabado is back?"

"If he's not back, he could be hiring more local talent—assuming the two shooters at the Mondragon house were his."

"Or sending new people from Vegas," added Malone.

"Shit. I'm going to need a task force before this is done." He ran a hand over his head. "At least Ms. Pepper is out of it. I can hold her here on a variety of charges and her nephew along with her, at least for twenty-four hours. That will keep them safe. Colleen and Hoke are on their way back from Hood River?"

"Sonny Sampson is meeting up with them at Multnomah Falls," I said, "and escorting them the rest of the way back to our office. Then we have to find another safe house. A really secure location, this time. You got anything like that?"

"Maybe," Mike responded as he got up and stepped to his office door, "I'll have to check a couple of things. First, I need to get Ms. Pepper and her nephew secured. Any ideas what I can do with the damned dog?"

"Probably she can call her driver to pick him up and take care of him," my partner suggested. "That seems to be one of his jobs. Or maybe the lawyer can handle it."

"Good enough." He paused in the doorway. "Unless you have something else you want to say to your client, I guess we're done here for now."

Malone and I stood up as well. "Yeah, we'll head back to the office and wait for the kids."

"Good luck," Mike said and disappeared back into the conference room.

I checked my watch. Nearly five. Sonny should be meeting up with Colleen and Hoke within a half-hour or so. I still had no idea where we could keep them safe for sure. I hoped Mike would come up with something. If not, I was going to drive my daughter crazy by not letting her out of our sight. Collectively, we could make sure they were always covered, though it wouldn't make further investigating very easy. I had to find a really safe house.

But it wasn't going to happen right this moment.

"If nothing else is waiting for us back at the office," I said to my partner as the elevator descended, "we should give Mrs. Mondragon a call. She needs to know what we've found out about her husband's possible connection to Sabado's operation."

"At least she's safe with the extra security," my partner opined as the elevator doors opened onto the lobby.

"She's probably safe, anyway. Sabado's hired thugs could have killed her if he wanted her dead. She would have served as bait just as well."

"Right. If they were hired by Sabado."

"We have," I said as we stepped onto the sidewalk and did a quick survey for shooters or other threats, "too damned many ifs and probablys."

CHAPTER FORTY-EIGHT

The hotel desk put me through to Mrs. Mondragon's room and she answered on the first ring. I imagined her sitting there, afraid to go home, probably afraid to even go out, hoping that this call would somehow solve her problems. Instead, it was going to add to them.

"It's Clint McCall, Mrs. Mondragon."

"Do you have news? Do you know what's going on, who killed Bernie?"

"We've got some new information that may be relevant. And a theory."

"A theory?"

"Let me ask a question first. Did you get any hint that Bernie was uncomfortable or worried about what was going on at his agency? Any sense that he might be uneasy about something?"

She paused, apparently giving it some thought. "Maybe," she finally said. "I noticed that he stopped talking about work so much in the last six months or so. He always got a big kick out of describing his deals and that kind of stopped. Why? You don't think someone from the agency killed him, do you?"

"No, but we have learned that the agency was being used to launder money."

"What? Launder.... I've heard of that, but I don't really know what it means."

"Criminals were using the agency to turn money that looks suspicious into money that looks innocent."

"You think Bernie was helping criminals? That's your theory?"

"All we know is that one or more agents must have been involved. If your husband was one of them, that may have led to him being killed."

She didn't respond immediately, although I could hear her

taking deep breaths. "You're saying my Bernie was a crook and he was killed by other crooks?"

"We don't know for sure, Mrs. Mondragon. It's certainly a possibility. Even a likelihood."

"Do the police know about this theory?"

"Yes, and they're taking it seriously enough that I'd say you're no longer a suspect."

"I don't care about that! You can't go around telling the police that Bernie's a criminal!"

"Mrs. Mondragon, I...."

"You're fired! Don't call me again!" She hung up.

I slowly put the phone back down as my partner frowned. "Sounds like that went well," she said.

"We're fired."

"And you didn't even tell her that her husband was most likely killed because his money laundering accidentally connected up with something your daughter's boyfriend did in Las Vegas. She really would have loved that."

"If she even believed it. I'm still not sure I do. Anyway, fired or not, paid or not, I want to leave her security in place and make sure she has all the answers before we're done. We owe her that much."

"I agree. So. Now what?"

I looked at my watch. "It shouldn't be too long before Sonny and the kids get here."

"Depending on traffic. Maybe Mike has come up with a new and better safe house by now. You could check with him."

I slumped back in my chair and swiveled a bit side to side. "It's too soon. He won't have anything yet." I looked at my watch again. "I'm just anxious."

Malone got up, came around to my side, and stood behind me with her hands lightly massaging my shoulders. "I know. It will be good to have them in sight again."

Her line rang and she darted back around to her side, where she glanced at the Caller ID and punched the speakerphone on. "Hello, Carl. You're on speaker. Clint is here."

"Hello, Devon."

"What's up?"

"Anthony Sabado is back in town, with a dozen reinforcements."

"Shit. He called you?"

"No. He did not. But there's no place you can land a plane around here that I don't have eyes."

"Wait a minute," I interjected, my adrenaline heading off the charts already, "you're saying he came back and brought twelve men this time rather than four?"

"Give or take one or two, yeah. Certainly more than four. They landed in Hillsboro late yesterday, but I just got word a few minutes ago. I'm thinking that confrontation we had on Sunday didn't go as smoothly as it looked. Maybe the rumors were true."

Malone leaned in again as I picked up my cell phone and swiveled away from the desk. "Rumors?" she asked as I once again punched in Colleen's number.

"I've heard hints that he's paranoid and capable of, shall we say, extreme overreaction if he feels threatened," Gunther said as I listened to my daughter's cell phone going to voicemail.

"Like killing everybody associated with whoever has pissed him off," Malone continued.

"Yeah, like that."

Meanwhile, I was punching in Sonny Sampson's number.

"And you didn't think this was important for us to know before we confronted him in the first place?"

"It was just rumors."

"Until now."

"Maybe, yeah, until now."

My partner had been watching me as she spoke to Gunther and I shook my head at her, setting the phone back on the desk.

"Do you know where they are?" Malone asked Gunther. "Or anything about what they're planning?"

"No, I called you as soon as I heard they were here. You need to watch your back, Devon, but don't worry. I'm going to take care of it."

I was already on my feet, hooking my holster to my belt. Malone pulled her gun drawer open as she continued addressing the speakerphone. "What do you mean, you'll take care of it?"

"Sabado is disrespecting me and is a threat to my people. We'll find him and deal with him."

I exchanged a look with my partner as she holstered her gun and we both grabbed our jackets. She leaned down to the speakerphone. "Okay, Carl." She punched it off and looked up at me. "Multnomah Falls?"

"Multnomah Falls," I said.

Just in case, I scribbled a note telling Colleen to check in with Eleanor and call me. I taped it to the door on the way out.

I didn't expect her to be reading it.

CHAPTER FORTY-NINE

The drive from Portland up the Columbia Gorge to Multnomah Falls is a beautiful one, with forests and waterfalls and of course the river itself off to the left, all relatively unsullied by civilization because most of it is within the Columbia River Gorge National Scenic Area.

It's quite restful—if you aren't breaking every speed limit, hoping this is one of those days with no State Police coverage, and your partner isn't repeatedly calling your daughter, your daughter's boyfriend, and the woman who was supposed to meet them and bring them back home.

All with no answer. Time after time after time.

"I can't believe that Colleen blew off Sonny and left town without telling us," I finally said when we were nearly there. It was seriously bugging me. "She should know better than that with everything that's going on."

Malone put a calming hand on my arm. "She's not a kid anymore, Clint. She's a grown woman and if she wants to get away from all the stress, she has a right to do that."

"I'll bet it was Hoke's idea."

"Hah. You just don't like it that your little girl has a serious boyfriend. Don't you trust him by now?"

"Sometimes yes, sometimes no. It's hard to forget he was planning to kill me when we first met."

"Yeah, there is that." She took her hand away and focused on the upcoming exit to the Multnomah Falls parking lot. The State Police apparently being otherwise occupied, a drive that should have taken at least forty minutes took twenty-five.

"I'll tell you what I can't believe; I can't believe your theory about the incredible coincidence was actually right," she said as I took the exit.

"We don't know for sure," I replied.

"You got another possibility?"

"Not currently."

Multnomah Falls is by far the most "touristy" of spots between Portland and Hood River. There's a lodge, a nice restaurant, a big gift shop, a Forest Service information center, and of course the 600-foot falls themselves with a well-maintained trail leading up to a bridge that provides a magnificent view.

It was a little past seven as I cruised slowly through the huge parking lot located between the east- and westbound freeways. It was, as usual for a summer evening, nearly full and we soon spotted a familiar vehicle.

"There." Malone was pointing up ahead on her side. It was a bright green Miata and, a few cars further down in the next row over, Colleen and Hoke's old gray Corolla. Remarkably, I saw a car backing out of a space on my side. I sped up a little and nabbed the spot. My partner was bailing out even as the Subaru came to a stop and I followed as soon as I'd killed the engine.

"I couldn't see anyone in or around either car," she said as we trotted across the lot to the Corolla. It was indeed unoccupied. And unlocked, which was a little worrisome. Then I noticed a cell phone on the ground near the front left wheel well. When I reached down to pick it up, I saw it was smashed. I recognized it as Colleen's. Shit.

I held it up for Malone to see. "This is not good."

We stood surveying the lot for a moment. There were a great many people coming and going, but none of them familiar. "Let's check Sonny's car," I said with a sinking feeling. If they were on foot somewhere here in the facilities or on the trail, it could be extremely difficult to find them, especially if they'd been fleeing whoever smashed the phone.

As we approached the Miata, I saw something that took my breath away: Sonny Sampson slumped over in the front seat. I heard Malone gasp at the same time. We were on the passenger side and I jerked that door open, immediately reaching down to check Sonny's neck for a pulse.

"She's alive," I said.

"I see blood in her hair," my partner pointed. I hadn't even noticed. Too busy surveying the rest of the car interior as if I might find Colleen hiding somewhere in that very small space.

I gently parted the few strands of bloody hair and, to my relief, we saw a good-sized bump rather than a bullet hole.

Malone headed around to the driver's side, opened the door, and leaned in. "Let's get her upright," she said, "and see if we can bring her around. We need to find out what happened here."

I helped my partner reposition Sonny behind the steering wheel and that was all it took. Her eyelids fluttered and she groaned. "Shit," she said after a moment. "My head hurts."

I looked past her at Malone. "I should probably call for paramedics. She might have a concussion, or worse."

At that, Sampson's eyes came fully open. "I'm okay, I think. I just have a hell of a headache. Colleen...." She was looking around as if she expected to see my daughter standing with us.

Considering my urgent need for information, I was willing to wait on that 9-1-1 call. "What happened, Sonny? Where are Colleen and Hoke?"

"They're gone? Did they take off again?"

"Their car is still here."

She put her head back against the headrest and closed her eyes. For a moment, I thought she'd passed out again, but then she sighed and looked straight ahead out the windshield. "Shit. I fucked up. Again. I pulled in, saw them waiting in their car. I found this spot, then went over and told them to follow me back to your office. They said that was fine." She paused. "I came back over here." She closed her eyes again. "I started to get back in the car and that was it." She looked at Malone and then finally at me. "Someone must have followed me. I must have led them right to your daughter. I didn't have a fucking clue that they were behind me. I should turn in my fucking license."

I felt like I could barely breathe. "That's it? You saw the kids

211

sitting in their car, talked to them for a minute, and then everything went black? You didn't see anyone following you or hanging around their car here in the lot? Nothing?"

"Nothing. Not a fucking thing. I'm sorry."

I didn't know what to say, but I did notice that my partner had abandoned the driver's side opening and was examining the front left wheel well. I straightened up and looked over the hood of the car at where she was crouching. "What are you doing?"

"Looking for a tracker. Maybe she didn't see them behind her because they weren't right behind her. Or maybe they managed to put something on Colleen's car and they were already here. We'll have to check that if there's nothing on this vehicle."

"I'm more interested in where they've gone than how they got here."

By the time Malone had thoroughly checked the Miata and we were headed across the lot to Colleen's Corolla, Sonny was on her feet and accompanying us.

"You sure you don't want to get checked out?" I asked her as we practically trotted to keep up with my partner.

"I'm fine. No nausea, no blurred vision. Hell of a headache, but I can focus. If I get to feeling wobbly, I'll tell you. Meanwhile, I feel a powerful need to redeem myself." She glanced over at me. "Forget what I said about the action not being in the Columbia Gorge."

"It's forgotten." *As long as we get Colleen and Hoke back safely*, I didn't say. "And maybe you should stay out of parking lots from now on."

She huffed. "Yeah, they do seem to be a good spot for kidnapping people I'm supposed to be keeping an eye on."

Malone was just far enough ahead that she'd already checked the inside of the back bumper by the time we got to the car. She stood up holding a small, shiny object in her hand. "Bingo. It's a tracker, all right. They must have done it overnight and then waited for a likely spot to make their move." She looked at Sonny. "Your showing up could have provoked them to make their move here and now."

"Great. Another point for me."

My partner surveyed the lot. "It isn't a bad spot, actually. Lots of cars and most of the people over at the lodge or viewing the falls. A good chance no one would notice them slugging you or abducting the kids."

I also surveyed the lot, feeling as numb and helpless as I ever have in my life. "We don't have any idea which direction they went or what kind of car they're driving. Nothing." I locked eyes with my wife and partner and didn't have to ask out loud.

"So," she said, "there's no point in calling the sheriff or the state patrol. We can have Mike ping Hoke's phone again, but I don't hold out much hope for that. All we can do is go back to the office and start tracking these assholes down. If we can find any of Sabado's men or connections, we can find Colleen and Hoke."

"Without involving Gunther," I said.

She grimaced. "We have to do something with him. We have to somehow keep him from going after Sabado. His people start exchanging fire with Sabado's and the kids could be right in the middle of it."

"I'm so sorry," Sonny Sampson said softly, her words almost lost in the gathering dusk and the sound of waterfalls.

CHAPTER FIFTY

"We will find them," my wife and partner said yet again as the three of us gathered in the office. She'd said it several times as we were driving into town. In fact, that was about all that had been said on the trip after she called Mike and confirmed that Hoke's phone was not on. My brain was going in so many different directions, I could barely focus enough to keep the car on the road, much less carry on a coherent conversation.

It was nearly nine and, ridiculously, I found myself feeling guilty that the cats hadn't been fed—but I knew I wouldn't be able to go home until I got ahold of myself and we'd thrashed out at least the beginning of a plan. My daughter was out there somewhere, certainly frightened, maybe hurt, and my imagination desperately didn't want to go further than that.

"I'll get the coffee going," Sonny said as she headed for the little table that held the makings. We'd insisted that she ride back to town with us, even though she kept saying she was fine. Being wrong about a concussion is one thing when you're walking around a parking lot and quite another when you're driving down a freeway at seventy miles an hour.

Malone reached across the desk and I extended my hand to meet hers. "Breathe," she said. "We have things to do, and..." She glanced over at Sonny. "...you have to be present to keep me from slugging that woman if she says she's sorry again."

I took what must have been my two-hundredth deep breath since Multnomah Falls and began to focus. Being back in the office, holding Devon's hand, smelling coffee grounds was...grounding.

I looked at the glowing street out the window. "It's late. Mike will either be home or in the dojang. Probably Sabado's people brought them back here, to Portland."

She nodded as I heard the coffeemaker heating up. "Do you have his cell number?"

"No. We've been friends for a long time, but I always call him at the office or see him at the dojang. I don't even have his home phone—and a cop wouldn't be in the phone book, as you well know." I glanced around the office. "As if we have a phone book."

"Let me see if I can find the number." She had let go of my hand and booted up her computer as we were talking. She started tapping away on her keyboard. Sonny Sampson meanwhile brought over a cup of coffee and set it in front of me, then took one of the visitor chairs. I was beginning to feel a little more taken-care-of than I was comfortable with. I breathed in yet another of those deep breaths, very slowly, and let it out even more slowly.

"I know I told you to breathe, but are you doing some kind of Zen thing over there?" Malone muttered absently as she stared at the screen and kept tapping. "Ah," she went on before I could answer, "I've got it." She reached over, punched on the speakerphone, and then (presumably) Mike's home number.

"I thought the public couldn't access the private numbers of law enforcement," I said as the connection was made.

"True, though not much is private nowadays—and, anyway, cops know how to get a cop's number." My partner had been an officer with the Tualatin police and then a detective with the Portland Bureau before I got her tossed off the force. Or contributed to it, anyway. Long story.

"I could probably get you the home number of any Las Vegas cop," Sampson assured me as we listened to it ring. She was sounding a little more like herself, stronger, and that helped me focus. I had to be stronger as well. My daughter's life might depend on it.

"Hey, Clint...or Devon," came Mike's voice over the speaker. He obviously recognized the agency number on his display. I could hear a TV in the background.

"It's both," I responded, "and Sonny Sampson, the Las Vegas PI we told you about. We need you to put out a BOLO on my daughter and her boyfriend, just to report a sighting, not to approach. Antonio Sabado as well, while you're at it."

"I'm sending you photos of the kids from their social media now," Malone added. "I assume you can get Sabado's."

"We believe that Sabado has taken them," I said.

There was a long moment of silence on the line. "Whoa. Why are you calling me at home? Who did you talk to downtown? Just dispatch?"

"Nobody," I replied. "The abduction occurred in the Multnomah Falls parking lot earlier this evening and we've got nothing. No vehicle, no descriptions, no actual evidence that has anything to do with Antonio Sabado or that the kids were brought back here to Portland rather than taken somewhere else. Nothing. Sabado isn't even supposed to be in town, but is—according to Carl Gunther. The BOLOs would be a shot in the dark, but at least it would be some eyes on our side."

"Shit. Okay, I just got the pics. I have Sabado's already and can get them distributed to everybody who's on patrol with instructions to have dispatch notify me. Then what?"

"If it's the kids, depending on where they are and who they're with, then we maybe report a crime and definitely make a plan. If it's Sabado, have him followed."

"I don't like this."

"There's close to zero chance any of them are going to be out on the street, anyway, so you probably don't have to worry about it, but it's a base I'd like to see covered."

"Okay, you got it. And if you get onto them some other way, let me know. If it has to be outside the lines, I'd still have your back."

"I appreciate that, Mike. We all do."

"Take care, brother." He hung up.

We three sat there in silence for a few moments.

"What else can we do?" Sonny Sampson asked.

Before I was forced to admit that I didn't have any great ideas, my partner took a whole different tack. "So. You were married to a casino owner?"

Sonny looked surprised but not taken aback by the question. "Yes, I was. Where did you hear that?"

"Veronica."

"Ah. But...why did you bring it up now? You think I'm working with Sabado in all this?"

"You're in Portland in the first place because you were working *for* Sabado."

Sonny grinned, just slightly. "Fair point. But I quit. He knows that. He knew it before you met with him at the hotel and I assure you it's true. No question that I screwed up and lost the kids. Twice. But neither was at Antonio Sabado's behest. They were simply my own fuck-ups. I've already apologized, multiple times, and I can't do anything else but help you guys find them. If you'll let me."

Malone nodded. "Okay. A little more background might help." She looked at me. "You want to tell Sonny about Bernie Mondragon and your coincidence theory?"

CHAPTER FIFTY-ONE

Sonny Sampson was not a big fan of coincidence, either, but she did grant that it sounded like a plausible explanation in this case. Not least because, just like us, she couldn't imagine another one.

And, of course, there was the question of whether "plausible" could be applied to any of the crazy shit Sabado seemed to be doing.

One benefit of the back-and-forth was that I thought of something else I could do, even given the late hour. Ten o'clock in the evening was heading into prime time for Reuben Keys—and his ladies who operated in dark corners were more likely to see something than uniformed cops in patrol cars were.

I used my cell phone to call him and he answered immediately. "Yo."

"It's Clint."

"Yeah, I see that. I'm busy, man. I got my girls and Big's both for the next few nights. It's like herding fucking cats."

"Big Avenue's going to be okay?"

"That's what they tell me. He should be out of the hospital tomorrow. Maybe a day or so to recover at home. He's a tough motherfucker."

"I know that, but that isn't why I called. We think that Colleen and Hoke have been kidnapped by that Las Vegas gangster, Sabado."

"Shit. You think?"

"Somebody took them in the parking lot at Multnomah Falls. We believe it was Sabado and we hope he brought them back here to Portland. I'd like you to have all the ladies on the lookout for them. We can provide photos." I looked across the desk at Malone and she nodded.

"Multnomah fucking Falls? Why...? Never mind. All the girls have cell phones. I'll send the pics on when I get them."

I watched my partner tapping away as we spoke. "It should just be a minute," I told Reuben.

"What's going on, man? Why would that fucker take Colleen and Hoke? What's he want? Not money. You all don't have that kind of money."

"It's a long story, but I'm afraid he wants Hoke and a lot of other people dead, including Colleen, me, Devon, Big Avenue...."

"Shit. You saying he might have already killed them?"

"I hope not. I don't think so. I don't know what he has in mind, or even if it's him for sure, but the kids could have been killed on the spot if somebody wanted them dead right away. Get those photos to as many people as you can and call me if you hear anything."

"I'll do it—and you call me if you need backup. I like your kid and even that boyfriend of hers. These girls will just have to take care of themselves for a few hours if you need me."

"Thanks, Reuben. I'll do that."

We hung up and I looked at my two companions. "Well, we have both a homicide lieutenant and the scariest pimp in Portland as backup if we need it—but we won't need it unless we can figure out a move."

"I have an idea," Malone announced. It looked like she was scrolling on her cell phone.

"What?" I asked as she apparently found what she was looking for and pushed a button.

"Calling Gunther."

That brought me up short for a second, trying to process which reaction I needed to have first. "After ten o'clock at night? And you have his home number on speed dial?"

She squinted at me. "His office phone transfers to his cell after hours, or so he told me once. We'll see. Hush."

I squinted right back at her. *Hush?*

Either the phone transferred or he was still in his office. "Carl? Yes, it's Devon."

Normally, my squint would have become a glare at this

point, but we needed all the help we could get. However, I inferred from Malone's long silence and increasing color that help might not be in the cards.

"Yes, well, you too," she finally said and punched off the phone. Not gently.

"Considering that went from 'it's Devon' to 'yes, you too,' with nothing in between, I gather that Mr. Gunther was not inclined to chat right now."

"You could say that. Is the moon full or maybe there's some rare juxtaposition of planets? It sounds like Carl is going as crazy as Sabado. He basically repeated that he's not going to stand for being disrespected and that he didn't have any time for us until after he finds and deals with Sabado."

"Huh. That is definitely not good news. If Carl Gunther can't find Sabado, what chance do we have? His resources put both Portland police and prostitutes to shame."

Sonny Sampson, meanwhile, had collected our coffee cups, mostly untouched, and was taking them back to the counter. "You guys, it's getting very late and there's nothing more to do right now—except that I have to arrange to get my car back from the Multnomah Falls parking lot. Maybe we should all get some rest and meet up in the morning."

I looked at her and then I looked at my wife, as if through a faint fog. I really felt like I was in some kind of mental and emotional no-man's land, unable to find a way out. She was right. There was nothing more to do. We had not, in fact, done anything effective since Colleen and Hoke were taken. We didn't know for certain who had them, where, or even why.

Get some rest? Sleep? Sure. What the hell. We could go try that. Meanwhile, my daughter might be dead.

Devon and I made it home and fed ourselves and the cats, though I think the cats ate more than we did, and we finally fell into bed right around midnight.

"How the fuck am I supposed to sleep?" I know I must have sounded plaintive.

Devon turned off the lamp on her side and rested on one

elbow looking down at me. "How are you going to be any good tomorrow if you don't? We will find Colleen and Hoke and they will be okay."

I looked up at her face glowing in the light of my lamp. "I didn't think you were very big on faith."

The slightest shrug. "I'm even less big on despair. And so are you, usually. There's no point in worrying about the worst that could happen. We're going to need all the energy we can muster to make it the best."

I reached up and touched her cheek. *I almost wanted to say, You might feel differently if she were your daughter,* but that would be unfair. Now Colleen *was* her daughter—and she was right.

She eased down until her body was against the length of mine. "This has been one hell of a long day and you've got to try to relax," she whispered softly in my ear. "Maybe I can help."

She was right about that, too.

CHAPTER FIFTY-TWO

We were up at six the next morning. I could have used more than five hours of restless sleep, but it was better than nothing.

All four of us (cats and people) ate reasonably well this time, then Malone and I each took our own vehicle to the office as usual. I was desperately wishing as I drove downtown that I had a plan. So far there had been no sighting of Colleen or Hoke, no hint where they might be, or what was happening to them.

The downtown traffic was relatively light at a little after seven in the morning and we seemed to be the first arrivals at our building. The bookstore, of course, was closed and there was no sign of life on the second floor as we topped the stairs.

As I unlocked our door, I was really hoping to find some sort of message waiting for us. A sighting of the kids or Sabado, a ransom demand, a threat to back off, any kind of clue...something.

But there was nothing.

We hung up our jackets and Malone started the coffee as I settled at the desk and confirmed that no lights were blinking. I booted up the PC and started checking email—which looked at first glance to be mostly junk as usual. Nothing. A couple of potential clients, but they would have to wait or go elsewhere.

After a few minutes of staring out the window, Malone brought over two cups of coffee, sat down, and started checking her own email.

"Anything?" I asked after a couple of sips.

"Nothing."

"Shit."

"We will find them."

"So you keep saying. That will, however, require that we actually do something to find them. Any ideas?"

"One."

I was about to inquire what that one might be when there was a quick knock on the office door and it opened to reveal Sonny Sampson.

"Hey guys," she said as she headed straight for the coffee. She still looked a little subdued, which I thought was appropriate.

She sat in the visitor chair on Malone's side and took a sip, then set her cup on the desk, looking from one of us to the other. "Anything?"

"Nada," responded my partner. "You have your car back yet?"

She nodded. "I hired a service to retrieve it overnight."

"Anything on Sabado?"

"Nothing. It's not my town and my best source is in the hospital." She lifted the cup and took another sip. "I'm not going to apologize again, but I feel like shit that I didn't take better care of them."

"It is what it is," I said.

"What about your friend...?" She paused as we all heard an odd grunting sound coming down the hallway. "What the hell is that? Is that normal?"

The sound stopped outside our door. I grabbed my gun out of the desk drawer and crossed the room in a couple of strides, leveling it as I jerked the door open.

An extremely large black man with a heavily bandaged head and wide, bloodshot eyes stood there. He raised his hands. "Whoa, motherfucker, I already been shot once this week."

"Big Avenue? What the hell are you doing here?"

"I checked myself out. They let you do that, you know, even if you feel like shit. I want to help find Colleen and the boy."

"How did you even get here?"

"One of my ladies is driving me."

Malone's voice came from behind me. "Better duty than her usual."

That seemed to go right over all the bandages. Big Avenue just stood there looking at me, hands in the air. I realized that my gun was still pointed at him. I lowered it and stepped back. "Well, since you're here, come on in."

"And speak of the devil," Sonny Sampson said as he joined and eased down into the other visitor's chair which thankfully held up under his weight.

He squinted at her. "What?"

"Never mind," I said. "I'm not sure you're in any shape to help us, Big."

"I'm okay. I wanna help. I know people." He gestured at Sonny. "She can tell you."

Sonny nodded obediently. "He knows people."

"People that even Reuben don't know."

I held up my hands. "Okay, okay. If you're able to get around, check with your people."

"You all got anything?"

"Nothing," Malone responded. "We're pretty damned sure that Sabado has them but we have no idea where or what he plans to do with them."

That last part sent the cold down my spine again. "Just before Sonny showed up," I said to Malone, "you were going to tell me about an idea you had."

"Oh, yeah. It's not a wonderful idea. I could go talk to Carl Gunther again. We know he's looking for Sabado and he's got resources we don't have. Maybe he's learned something he'll share."

"He didn't sound in a sharing mood the last time you talked to him. He completely blew you off."

"I think it's worth a try. I have my ways."

"Whoa. You're not talking about seducing the son of a bitch, are you? I'm desperate to find Colleen, but I don't know if...."

She held up a hand to stop me. "Don't be an idiot. Of course I'm not going to literally seduce him, but he might be more receptive to my concerns in person than over the phone."

"And especially if I'm not with you." I took a deep breath.

CHAPTER FIFTY-THREE

Devon Malone was no fan of makeup. She'd not worn any as a police officer and not much since, but she was sporting lipstick and eyeliner as she entered Carl Gunther's building. Just a touch. Carl was a smart guy and would notice if she overdid it.

She hadn't changed her look otherwise. She figured her leather jacket and boots were part of what he found appealing. Just as Clint did. She smiled to herself as she crossed the lobby to the elevator, then sobered again as she pressed the button.

This was a Hail Mary, but she was going to do the best she could with it.

She took a deep breath as she stepped out of the elevator on the twenty-second floor and turned right. As usual, there had been no one in the lobby, no one else using the elevator, and there was no one in this carpeted hallway. It struck her that she had no idea who occupied the other floors of this downtown tower, but it was creepy that she'd never seen anyone coming or going.

Or maybe she was just feeling paranoid.

The smile that she got from the grandmotherly Mrs. Pinkerton when she opened the office door and stepped into Gunther Global Import/Export was somehow not reassuring. It was, in fact, somewhat tight-lipped. And she noticed that Mrs. Pinkerton's left hand was out of sight near the drawer where she kept her gun.

"Ms. Malone. What can we do for you today?"

"Is Carl in?"

"I believe Mr. Gunther is in his office, yes." No invitation to go right in this time.

"I need to speak to him."

Mrs. Pinkerton's visible hand tapped a few keys on her

keyboard as she peered over her glasses at the monitor. "He has an opening next Tuesday afternoon."

Malone snorted. "Oh, give me a break, Agnes. I'm not here to cause trouble. Carl and I need to have a conversation. There are lives at stake."

The no-longer-smiling lips firmed up even more. "I'm sorry. I have my...."

She was interrupted by a click from her intercom. "She can come in, Mrs. Pinkerton."

"Yes, sir." She gestured at Gunther's office door. "Go right in."

Carl Gunther, resplendent in his usual fine suit and expensive grooming, remained seated as Devon Malone entered his office and carefully positioned herself in one of his visitor chairs. She did notice a slight reaction when he first saw her in the doorway: a narrowing of the eyes and slightly elevated brows. Otherwise, he remained silent as she seated herself.

Malone folded her hands primly in her lap, looked Gunther in the eye, and sat equally silent.

It took almost a full minute, but he lost.

"Why are you here, Devon?"

"I believe Sabado has kidnapped my step-daughter and her boyfriend. I want you to back off until we've found them. I don't want them caught in a crossfire."

Again, the slightest reaction of surprise that immediately settled back into neutral. "There are always bumps when you acquire a new family."

"And I want you to tell me anything you know that might help us find them."

He sat back a little in the big, plush desk chair. "You have come with a lot of wants."

She nodded. "I have."

He broke eye contact and swiveled a few degrees to look out one of the office windows at the cityscape. "You know what it takes to be boss of a city like Portland?"

"Getting elected mayor?"

He glanced over at her and almost smiled. "That's one way, but I'm responsible for a lot more of the city than he is. He only deals with the visible."

Malone offered one of her snorts in response. "Enough with the metaphysics, Carl. I need you to back off until we have the kids. Do you have any leads on where he's holed up?"

He swung back to face her full on. "I do not have his location. If I did, he would already be dead. You have to understand, Devon: Antonio Sabado has come into my town, bringing a fucking fire team with him, without my permission or any notification. He's obviously here to cause serious trouble. I cannot let that stand. I let it stand and I fall. Simple as that."

"If we were to get to him first...."

"If you do, don't kill him. He's mine."

"I can't promise anything."

"Nor can I."

"Carl...."

He held up a hand, palm out, to stop her. "Devon, I'm sorry that your marriage has brought with it this grief. From choices come consequences. I will not back off. When I find Sabado and his men—and I will—I am going to take them out. None of them are going back to Las Vegas. If you want to get to them first, I suggest you get going."

She nodded slowly and stood. "Take care, Carl. You don't want me for an enemy."

At that, he did smile up at her. "No, I don't. Nor you me. I will tell my men that innocents may be present and it would be best if they were left alive, but...things happen. You know that."

She turned and left the office without another word. There was nothing more to say. She saw no one in the corridor, on the elevator, or in the lobby.

CHAPTER FIFTY-FOUR

I'd learned to recognize my partner's footsteps approaching the office door. I'd also learned that she tended to prance a little when she felt good and trudge when she felt bad.

What I heard now was a definite trudge.

"Hey," she said as she closed the door behind her and hung up her jacket.

Knowing that she wouldn't welcome my insights about her prancing versus trudging, I waited to get a good look at her face. "I gather it didn't go well."

She pulled out her chair and sat down. "You could say that."

"Any positives?"

She blew out a breath. "Gunther said he'd tell his men to try to avoid killing Colleen and Hoke. That was as good as it got."

"Shit. No hint where Sabado might be?"

"None. Gunther says he doesn't know and I believe him. So we still have a chance of finding Sabado first." She locked eyes with me. "I would strongly recommend that we do that."

"And all we have to do is figure out how."

Malone glanced around the office as she booted up her PC. "What are Sonny and Big Avenue doing?"

"Sonny is out rechecking the sources she got from Big Avenue and he's out looking for more."

"You know, I have to ask one more time: Do we trust Sonny?"

"I think I trust her intentions. I may have some doubts about her competence. She has lost Colleen and Hoke twice now."

"Outsmarted by the kids is one thing. Attacked by Sabado's goons is another."

"I know. I just...." I paused as I heard heavy footsteps approach our door. Big Avenue again?

I could see that Malone had also heard them and we sat quietly for a moment, waiting to see if they'd go on down the hall. They didn't. They stopped outside our door, but then started receding toward the stairs again. No knock. Nothing.

"What the hell?" I snatched my Smith and Wesson out of the drawer and stepped over to the door. It could have been a potential client who changed his mind or a person who realized he was in the wrong building...but maybe something else. I pulled the door open just enough to stick my head and gun out into the hallway.

The first thing I saw was the back of a large male disappearing down the stairs toward Stark Street. My foot nudged something and I glanced down to see that he'd apparently left an envelope on the floor.

"Guy dropped an envelope here," I said over my shoulder to Malone. I holstered the gun and took off for the stairwell. He was pushing the street door open as I reached the top of the stairs. "Sir? Hold on a second. I'd like...."

He glanced back up at me, revealing a pasty face with a prominent scar above one eye, then pushed out the doorway and took off to his right, toward Third. At least I could be pretty sure now that he wasn't a potential client.

I looked behind me to see Malone picking up the envelope and thought of all the recent news stories about letter bombs and deadly white powders. "Don't open it!" I yelled. "Wait for me!" Then I plunged down the stairs two or three steps at a time, hoping not to turn an ankle.

I hit the sidewalk and saw the guy had already crossed the street. He had stopped just beyond the intersection for some reason. I was about to take off running after him when a car pulled up beside him and he jumped in. It was a standard American late-model sedan, black or very dark blue, hard to tell in the bright sunlight, and too far away to read the plate. I watched it accelerate away and then headed back up the stairs.

What the hell was going on now?

I was still breathing heavily when I reentered the office to find my partner holding a sheet of paper and looking out the window, the open envelope on the desktop in front of her. So much for don't open it and wait for me.

I walked over and sat down. "Okay, so what is it?"

She handed it across the desk. "A love note from Sabado, on embossed letterhead no less."

And so it was: **Tony Saturday** emblazoned across the top in red, bold type. "*Dear Mr. McCall,*" it began.

> *I believe I have a couple of items that you value and I'm hoping we can come to an agreement about how you might get them back safely. There are several things that I will require from you to facilitate this.*
>
> *One is a list of everyone who knows about my heretofore secret operation in Las Vegas. I understand that you will be reluctant to do this because I may have given the impression that I intend to kill everyone who knows. And, frankly, I did intend that.*
>
> *But I have since gotten a better idea. Now the list would simply be for my information, a precaution if you will, and nothing more.*
>
> *So what is my better idea? To move the operation in question from Las Vegas to Portland. This strikes me as having a number of advantages that I won't go into here. I can tell you a few of them when we meet, if we meet, and if you're curious.*
>
> *So what else do I need from you? The cooperation of you and your wife in removing the primary obstacle to the transfer of my operation. I understand that you both, and particularly your wife, have a relationship with Carl Gunther that could aid in accomplishing my goals.*
>
> *There's no way I can go into detail about that until we've had a chance to meet and compare notes. I will be proposing a meeting, at which I will also provide proof of life for the two items I initially mentioned, but I want to first give you a day or two to think about all this.*

Think hard. It is not a decision to be taken lightly.
I'll be in touch.
Sincerely yours, Tony Saturday

I set the sheet of paper, high quality paper it was, carefully on the desk and looked over at Malone. "Well, this is bat-shit crazy."

"No kidding."

"I don't fucking believe it. He really expects us to give him a list of everyone who knows and then help him take out Carl Gunther?"

"I think door number two might be the more important one. The cat is way out of the bag on his Las Vegas operation. Which is probably why he's interested in turning it into a Portland operation." She shrugged. "I can think of several reasons without his help. Portland is less a center of attention, it's got waterways that offer more surreptitious transportation, and with Gunther out of the way there'd be no rivals to get pissed off about it."

"Surreptitious?"

"Hey, I know words."

I looked down at the sheet of paper again. "It's interesting that he goes back to the Tony Saturday persona for this letter. Maybe because he considers it official business." I tapped the sheet. "In fact, it's interesting how last century the whole thing is. An embossed letterhead in a plain envelope, hand-delivered? Very formal language. Why not send an email?"

"Says the guy who almost couldn't be persuaded to get a cell phone. There's always the danger somebody can trace an email, a call, anything electronic, if they have the expertise and the equipment. The only way to trace this would have been to catch the guy who delivered it."

I slumped a little. "Which I didn't do. I might be getting...."

"Don't even say it. You are not too old for this shit."

I took a deep breath and tried to get my thoughts in order. We couldn't just sit here while this son of a bitch held Colleen and Hoke captive. At least he claimed they were alive and, all things considered, they probably were.

"So Sabado has basically given us a day or two grace period while we supposedly consider his offer," Malone finally said. "One thing to consider: Do we tell Carl?"

"I would say no. If he knew Sabado was out to take Portland away from him, he'd be even more intent to stop him no matter who got caught in the crossfire."

"I agree. So. Grace period. We need to use the time. Any ideas?"

"Actually yes. There's one name that has come up in all this that we haven't checked out."

"Yeah?"

"Stuffy Smithers. He could be completely irrelevant but it was his men who tried to ambush us at Martha Mondragon's."

"You remember that Gunther said he checked them out and they weren't working for Stuffy at the time."

"And maybe that's true. But maybe Smithers knows more about what his men were doing than Gunther was told."

"Good point."

"It's a loose end." I stood up. "So let's go tie it off."

CHAPTER FIFTY-FIVE

"Yeah, whatcha want?" There were two boxes of tissues on his table and he spit out the question right before honking a major load of snot into an already dirty handkerchief. So much for the minor mystery of where Stuffy Smithers got his nickname.

The table was in a far and dark corner of The Venus Club, a hole-in-the-wall strip joint on Burnside, located between a non-franchise hamburger stand and a used clothing store. The man sitting at the table was probably in his forties or fifties, thin, totally bald, with pinched features and small, close-set eyes. Even sitting down, he was obviously very tall. If it weren't for the nose, his nickname would probably have been "Scarecrow."

He was wearing an oddly clean and apparently pressed white t-shirt under a well-worn and not-so-clean polyester suit coat that I'd be willing to bet didn't match the pants we couldn't see.

"You're Stuffy Smithers?" I inquired just to get it out of the way.

His beady gaze bounced from me to Malone and back. "Yeah, welcome to my office. Whatcha want?"

"I'm Clint McCall and this is Devon Malone. We're private investigators."

"Well, woo-fuckin'-hoo. Whatcha want?"

Without the invitation that was clearly not forthcoming, I pulled out a chair and sat down. Malone grabbed a chair from a nearby table and joined me. It was coming up on lunch time, but the dingy room was nearly empty. Not that anyone would want to eat here. There was a paunchy, middle-aged bartender and one old guy sitting near the stage (currently unoccupied) who looked like he was asleep. Or maybe dead.

"You had two guys named Holt and Morgenthal working for you," I said.

"Never heard of 'em." He blew his nose and pointed the handkerchief at Malone, who leaned away from it. "She talk?"

"When I have something to say. How about: we know you're lying."

"Sez you." This guy's repartee was a poor imitation of early '50s noir.

"And we're the ones who killed Holt and Morgenthal."

His eyes widened to almost normal size and he lowered the handkerchief to the table. Which was unfortunate, since his nose was still running.

Malone reached over, pulled a tissue from the box nearest to her, and offered it to him. "That's a bad cold you've got there."

He snorted, his version a good deal phlegmier than my partner's, but then refocused on what she'd said just before that. "I don't know nothin' about what they was doin' when they got killed...by you. You was there. I wasn't. They wasn't working for me at the time. Just now and then, but not then. They was, like, piece workers, you know?"

"Piece workers?"

"Well, yeah, when I had a little piece of work to do...sometimes they did it."

Picturing my daughter in hell somewhere, I decided it was time to take over the conversation. "You ever heard of Antonio Sabado?"

He gave me a blank look. "Nah."

"How about Tony Saturday?"

The blank look twitched. "Nah."

"You might want to rethink that. Tony Saturday has my daughter and her boyfriend and is threatening to kill them both. You do not have a poker face and you just gave away that you know something. If you want to keep your face, you're going to tell me what you know."

He looked around the nearly empty club as if hoping for backup. "You can't come into my office and...."

"Just did. Tony Saturday. Did he hire those guys through you? Did they tell you anything about the job? Do you know where he is now?"

Smithers had gone pale and looked even more like a cadaver than he had when we walked in. "I don't know him! I never met him! I sure as hell don't know where he is."

"But...?"

"But I did hear from a guy I know that Tony Saturday was looking for a couple of strong-arm guys for a serious job and I gave him—the guy—Holt and Morgenthal. I didn't know he was looking to hire a fucking hit. That's not what they do—did—for me. I don't even know anybody who does that."

"Okay," Malone stepped back in, "who was the guy that you know?"

He jerked several tissues out of one of the boxes, apparently having given up on the handkerchief, and blew his nose at some length. Finally he couldn't sustain it any longer and he tossed the soggy mass on the floor. "It was Slash, Slava Ragonovic."

"You're going to have to spell that."

"S-l-a-s-h."

"No, idiot, the guy's real name."

"Are you kidding? I don't know how to spell that foreign shit. Sound it out."

Now my wife was looking like she wanted to take his face off. "Where can we find the guy?" she asked through clenched teeth.

"There's a pawnshop over on Sandy, out near the airport. Slash works out of the back room."

"It's his pawnshop?"

A shrug. "I don't know. He's usually there. You want something, he can find it for you. Usually."

"Okay," I said as I stood up. "We're going to go talk to your buddy Slash. And you're not going to call him to tell him we're coming...are you?"

"Not a chance. I don't give a shit."

"Good man," Malone told him over her shoulder as she joined me on the way to the door.

CHAPTER FIFTY-SIX

"Now that is one ugly-ass pawnshop," Malone observed. We sat in the Subaru looking at the little building that could barely qualify as a shack. We couldn't see inside. The windows were too dirty.

There was, however, a PAWN sign above the door so we were probably in the right place.

"How in the world would a big-time gangster from Las Vegas know about a guy who works out of the back room of this shitpile?"

"Let's go ask," I replied as I opened my door.

There was no open or closed sign and even up close we couldn't see if there was anything displayed behind the window glass, but the door was unlocked.

Inside was a remarkably normal looking, though poorly lit, pawnshop. Everything was neatly displayed in locked glass cases and, even more surprising, the person behind the counter in back was a fresh-faced young woman with shoulder-length brunette hair, wearing a bright yellow sleeveless dress. She would have been just right for clerking in a high-end boutique. Not so much in a low-end pawnshop.

She offered us a big smile as we approached. "Hi, I'm Mara. Can I help you?"

Malone must have been thinking the same thing I was. "You work here?"

The young woman giggled. "Well, yeah. For the summer, anyway, while I'm home from college. It's a family business. Why?"

"Well, it's not the best neighborhood or probably the best clientele, either one. And you're here alone."

"Oh, I'm not alone. My uncle's in the back room. I've got a panic button under the counter here in case there's trouble.

He'd come running." Her smile was dimming. "What can I do for you guys? You buying or selling?"

"Neither," I said. "Actually, we're probably here to talk to your uncle."

"Probably?"

"Is his first name Slava?" I wasn't going to try the last name unless I had to.

Now she was looking downright uneasy. "Yeah, Slava Ragonovic. I'm Mara Ragonovic. What do you want with us? And who are you?"

We pulled out our ID and I gave her our names, noticing her left hand creeping under the countertop as I did so. My guess was that we would be meeting Slava Ragonovic at any moment.

I could see the family resemblance the second he burst out of the door behind Mara. The same nose, the same hair color, the same sharp features—only a couple of decades older, a foot taller, a hundred pounds heavier, and looking a lot tougher. He was dressed casually in jeans and muscle t-shirt.

"What's going on, Mara?" he asked as he stepped up beside her. He had the wary air of a man who had been prepared for a fight but didn't see one yet. Despite his name, he had no more accent than she did.

I held up my hands, one of them again displaying my ID. Out of the corner of my eye I could see Malone doing the same.

"We just want to talk," I said. "No trouble."

"Talk to who? About what?"

"Talk to you, about Tony Saturday."

That pushed his eyebrows up close to his hairline. He looked very hard at me, then at Malone. "Close up shop and go home, Mara. I'll deal with these two."

"But Uncle Slash...."

"It's been a slow day and there's nothing to worry about. Just watch your back until the bus comes, you know the routine. You got your pepper spray?"

"Yes, Uncle Slash."

"Okay. I'll see you at home. Nothing to worry about." He gave her a quick peck on the cheek and motioned for us to follow him back.

It was a medium-sized office with all the standard accoutrements: file cabinet, computer, phone. Plain and business-like. He settled in the swivel chair behind the desk as we took the two padded visitor chairs.

He looked from one of us to the other and Malone chose to speak first. "Uncle Slash?"

He sat back and almost smiled. Not quite. "Long story. You don't need to hear it."

"What we do need to hear," I said, "is what you can tell us about Tony Saturday."

"Why do you need to hear that?"

"We believe you put him onto two men who usually worked for Stuffy Smithers. He hired those men to ambush my partner and me. We killed them, in case you haven't heard."

The eyebrows went even higher than before and he visibly paled. "That was them? I didn't hear the names. That was you? Shit."

"So you admit it."

"Wait a minute. I didn't have anything to do with what happened. I just...."

"Just?"

"Ah shit. Did a favor for an old friend. Should have known better."

"How do you know Saturday," asked Malone, "and where can we find him?"

He gave my partner a long look and seemed to reach a decision.

"We grew up together in Newark, where he was Tony Sabado, and I don't know where he is. I suppose he's back in Las Vegas." He transferred his attention to me. "Look, I got a legitimate business here. Mostly legitimate. Maybe some items don't have the provenance they should, but no harm done. I had no idea what Tony was doing in town or why he needed two local guys."

"We need to find Sabado," I said.

"What's the big deal? Like I say, he's probably back in Vegas. Go ask somebody there."

"He's back in Portland. And the big deal is that he's abducted my daughter, who's only a little older than your niece, and is threatening to kill her. If you know him, you must have an idea what he's capable of. How would you feel if he had Mara?"

"Well, crap. I wouldn't like it. But I'll tell you again, I had no idea what he wanted those guys to do. I hadn't seen Tony for a long time and we weren't good friends growing up, but I guess he knew I was here just like I knew he was in Las Vegas. He showed up, looking all rich gangster, and said he needed a couple of guys who were reliable to do something here after he left town." He gave a little shrug at life's unexpected developments. "Tony's not the kind of guy you say no to; that was true even when we were kids. I didn't have anybody, but I knew Stuffy Smithers had some tough guys on his crew. Stuffy put me in touch with Holt and Morgenthal and I passed them along to Tony's people. The whole thing was weird."

"Why weird?" asked Malone.

"Well, when he showed up here Tony had *three* guys with him who looked a lot tougher than anybody Stuffy could come up with."

"He couldn't use them," I replied, "because he'd just promised Carl Gunther that he and all his crew were leaving town right away."

"Okay. That would explain it. But he's back? Does Gunther know that?"

"He does now. He's also looking for Sabado and we want to find him first so my daughter doesn't get caught in the crossfire."

"Shit."

"Yeah, so, is there *anything* you can tell us that might help with that?"

"I got nothin' about where he is or what he's doing now. I knew two of the guys he had with him because they're also from Newark. You might have a better shot at finding one of them if they came back with him."

"Why?" Malone asked.

Another little shrug. "They were loose cannons back in the day, really liked their booze and women. Maybe Tony has them under control now. People change. But that's all I got."

"What are their names and what do they look like?"

"Sander O'Connor and Mel Jackson. They look like big tough guys from Newark, like any other thugs; that's not going to help you much."

"We'll see what we can do with it," I said.

He held up a hand as I started to rise. "I really didn't have any idea Tony was looking to have somebody killed. He needed a couple of tough guys in a hurry and that's all I knew. If I'd known...."

"I believe you," I said. Malone and I were both on our feet by now. Ragonovic also stood and led us back through the now darkened and empty shop. He unlocked the front door and we stepped outside.

"Take care of your niece," my partner said to him, "and maybe don't do any more favors for out-of-town gangsters."

"She's a good kid," he said. "She wants to be a vet."

"We wish her well," I told him over my shoulder as we headed for the front door.

"We've got to get people looking for O'Connor and Jackson," I said to Malone as soon as we were back in the car. "They're more likely to be out on the street than Sabado is. Maybe we'll get lucky."

"We need all the luck we can get," she replied.

And my next thought was that Colleen and Hoke needed even more.

CHAPTER FIFTY-SEVEN

She was thirsty and hungry and hurting and needed to pee again.

She'd been blindfolded for what seemed like forever and she didn't know where she was. She could tell it was a large space, musty and dusty, mostly empty as far as she could tell, and a long drive from Multnomah Falls. The floors and walls were unfinished wood, at least where she had initially landed on her side in what seemed to be one corner. She could feel the occasional splinter as she squirmed to try to make herself more comfortable. Remotely comfortable.

She could sometimes hear someone breathing nearby. She hoped it was Hoke.

The men had come from nowhere. She and Hoke were sitting in the car at the Falls, getting ready to follow Sonny Sampson back to Portland. She turned to Hoke to say something, she didn't remember what, and saw that someone was just outside the car on his side. Then she realized that he, in turn, was looking wide-eyed past her and she glanced back to see that someone was on her side, too.

Both the someones turned out to be very large men with guns, who efficiently got them out of the car and very quietly across the parking lot to a nearby van where they were soon joined by a third man coming from another direction. The direction of Sonny Sampson's car.

In the van, they were gagged, blindfolded, and their hands bound. And then the long drive to here. Wherever here was. She'd heard a lot of freeway noise along the way. Probably Portland, but no way to know for sure.

How long had it been? At least a day, she was sure. What had happened to Sonny? Was it Hoke that she could hear breathing? What else were these men going to do to them?

They hadn't been rough getting them into the van in the

parking lot, probably because the men didn't want to attract attention, but upon arrival here she'd been dragged from the van some distance across the interior of what had to be a very large space and roughly thrown onto the floor.

She shifted again and found another splinter.

Heavy footsteps approached and she could sense someone leaning down close to her. She held her breath, not knowing what might be coming.

"Just like the other times, I'm gonna take the gag off and untie your hands," said a grating male voice near her ear. "You scream, you die. Understand?"

She nodded, at this point happy with anything short of death.

He didn't bother to untie the gag; he jerked it down over her chin and added another pain to her growing collection. Then he roughly unbound her wrists.

"Is my boyfriend here? Is he okay?" Her rasping voice didn't sound much better than the man apparently crouching next to her. She had asked every time he'd come to her, but he'd never answered before.

This time he did, to her enormous relief. "He's here. He's alive. He's getting bathroom breaks and food just like you."

"Can I see him? Talk to him?"

"No. I'm gonna give you a bathroom break and then I've got a smoothie here you can drink. Don't want you to piss yourself or starve. Somebody might want proof of life." He chuckled. "Or maybe not. I'm just doin' what I'm told."

"Who are you? Where are we? What do you guys want?" She'd also asked those questions before, but she couldn't help herself.

He gripped her arm hard and pulled her upright. "You aren't with the program, little girl. If we've got questions, you answer. You don't get questions."

She didn't point out that he'd finally answered one of her questions. She just let him half-carry her to what smelled like a very old and disused bathroom. Just as before, to her excruciating embarrassment, he stood right outside the open door as she did her business. She knew because she could hear him smacking his lips. When she was done he retied her hands and manhandled her back out of the bathroom—and, she assumed, to her previous spot on the floor.

After she was back among the splinters, she felt a straw against her lips. "Drink it," her captor said. "It's good for ya."

She sucked up what she was pretty sure was a kale smoothie; then he replaced the gag and she was left alone in silence.

She didn't even hear any breathing nearby.

CHAPTER FIFTY-EIGHT

"We found Sander O'Connor."

Our home phone had rung just as we were about to head to the office. It was Mike Whitehall. He'd put out a BOLO on both O'Connor and Jackson after I brought him up to speed yesterday.

"That was fast," I said. "So he's at the Justice Center?"

"Nope. The morgue."

I dropped the thumbs up that I'd been giving Malone. "Well, shit. I gather he resisted arrest?"

"Again no. Head shot, execution style, in a motel on Killingsworth. Found by a maid first thing this morning when she noticed the room door was ajar."

"Again shit. You think Sabado took out his own man for some reason?"

I could hear the shrug over the phone. "He's certainly capable of it, but there's no evidence of that at this time. No weapon. No witnesses. We've got people going over the room, but that probably won't give us anything, either. It was professional, Sabado or not."

"And no Sabado sightings." Whitehall already had a BOLO out on the Las Vegas gangster, but no one really expected Sabado to be walking the streets of Portland.

"I would have led with that, Clint."

"Of course. Thanks for the heads up. Let me know if they do come up with anything."

Mike assured me he would and I hung up.

"Who's dead?" Malone asked.

"Sander O'Connor. Execution style in a motel room. Sabado...."

"Gunther," she said simultaneously.

I mentally kicked myself that I hadn't gone there, yet. Not

enough sleep. "You could be right. Mike says it was definitely professional, so either one is a good bet."

We both just stood there a moment, Maxine and Stella staring at us from the couch and my wife looking not much better than I felt. Neither of us had gotten a lot of sleep the night before. "We can think more about it on the way to the office." Malone was heading for the front door.

"Righto." I followed her out to our vehicles after bidding the cats a good day.

It was a very bleary half-hour drive to the office. How the hell was I supposed to sleep when I didn't know where my daughter was or what might be happening to her? Then again, how was I supposed to help her when I could barely stay awake? I needed lots more coffee. And maybe Eleanor had some amphetamines.... No, I wasn't that sleepy. Lots of black coffee would have to do the trick.

Maybe we'd get some good news soon. That would wake me up. Slava Ragonovic was right about Sander O'Connor being out and about, easily found—even if dead. Maybe he'd be right about Mel Jackson as well. Besides Mike's BOLO, we had Reuben and Big Avenue (and their ladies) keeping an eye out. Maybe Jackson would turn up alive. That would be good. Maybe Sonny would come up with something....

I'm mentally blathering, I said to myself as I joined Malone crossing Third Avenue to the office.

"I'm going to talk to Gunther again," she said as we mounted the stairs. "We have to know if he's the one behind O'Connor's death and, if he is, we have to try again to get him to back off. He's going to get Colleen killed."

"You think he'll admit it?"

"If he did it, he'll be proud of it."

"Do you think he'll back off?" I unlocked the office door.

"Honestly? Not a fucking chance." My partner followed me inside.

"Then we should hope he didn't do it because that would mean he's close on Sabado's trail."

CHAPTER FIFTY-NINE

Devon Malone berated herself as she headed for Carl Gunther's office. This was pointless. She'd seen him just yesterday. He'd already said he was going after Sabado and he'd probably already had one of Sabado's men killed.

Still. Maybe she could use her feminine wiles.... Huh. She was much better with her Glock than with feminine wiles. Maybe.... Nah.

Nine-thirty in the morning in downtown Portland and again no one in the lobby, no one using the elevators, no one in the corridor on Gunther's floor. Did the man lease the entire damned building just for his office?

She turned the knob on the Gunther Global Import/ Export office door and was brought up short. Locked. Shit. Could it be there was no one in the building, not even Gunther?

She tried knocking and heard Mrs. Pinkerton's voice in response. "Yes? Who is it?"

"It's Devon Malone. I need to speak to Carl."

"Just a moment."

After maybe ten seconds, there was a buzz and then she was able to open the door. She was just thinking that an electronic lock on an interior office door was pretty heavy security when she saw that wasn't the half of it.

There was no welcoming smile from the grandmotherly Mrs. Pinkerton, not even the tight-lipped one that had been offered yesterday. She sat back slightly from her desk with one hand in the drawer where Devon knew she kept her weapon.

And that wasn't all. The receptionist wasn't alone in the room. There were two very large and mean-looking men, one on either side of the room, wearing equally grim expressions, with hands resting on their holstered weapons. So much for using the Glock.

Malone looked from one man to the other and then at the white-haired Mrs. Pinkerton. "Expecting trouble, are we?"

"Mr. Gunther said to go right in." Tight-lipped, nothing to add.

Devon took a deep breath. "Okay." She stepped carefully over to Gunther's door, both hands in plain sight, and opened it.

He was sitting behind his massive desk, looking exactly like a sleek gangster as always, a slight smile on his face. Perhaps a regretful smile, she thought.

"Come on in, Devon. Always good to see you, but nothing's changed."

"Something has changed for one of Sabado's men, a guy named Sander O'Connor."

"I told you what was going to happen."

She eased into one of the visitor chairs. "So you're officially at war. Are there other dead bodies around that haven't been found yet?"

"Not yet."

"So you still don't know where Sabado is."

"Not yet."

"Would you tell me if you did?"

That little smile again. "Not yet."

She leaned forward, putting all the intensity she had into it. "If you identify his location, let us go in first, get Colleen and her boyfriend out of there ahead of the firefight." She hated this. "Please."

The smile went away, replaced by an expression of sincere concern. She hated that even more.

"You know I value your friendship, Devon. I don't want you for an enemy. Far from it. If there is time and opportunity, I will let you know. Even so, that would probably just mean that you have the firefight instead of us. It might be better if we went in first. You want to be responsible for getting McCall's daughter killed?"

Malone shuddered, just inside herself, showing nothing to

Gunther. "I'm sure that Clint would want to take responsibility for his daughter rather than giving it to you."

Gunther nodded. "Very likely. All I can tell you is that when I find Sabado and the rest of his men, I will do my best to protect your step-daughter and her friend."

"Actually, you can tell me at least one other thing: How did you track down Sander O'Connor?"

"Ah, I have sources in Las Vegas, as I do in many places, and obtained a list of names, the men most likely to be with Sabado here in Portland. O'Connor was on the list—and used his own name to check in to that motel. Likely he was planning to meet a lady of the evening there."

"You get the names of everybody who checks into motels and hotels in Portland?"

"When I'm looking for people I do. My BOLOs are better than those of the police."

"I guess so. But none of the other names on that list have come up yet?"

"No." Again the slight smile. "Not yet."

Enough of this bullshit. Malone slapped her knees and stood up. "Okay, Carl. We appreciate all your help, really. Which won't keep us from coming after you if anything happens to anyone we care about."

He nodded and raised one hand as if in farewell. "Understood, Devon. Let's hope it doesn't come to that."

She left the office suite without even glancing at Mrs. Pinkerton or her two reinforcements.

CHAPTER SIXTY

Before the day was over, we were reduced to driving around downtown on the off chance we'd spot Sabado or Jackson. Malone had a mugshot of the latter on her phone that Mike had come up with, but so far we'd seen nothing of interest.

Mike couldn't find Sabado. Gunther couldn't find Sabado. Sonny had checked in to report she was fully recovered but had nothing new. She was going to keep looking. Nothing from Reuben or Big Avenue. So we drove.

And then my cell phone signaled an incoming call.

We were on a side street with available curb space, so I pulled over as I dug the phone out of my pocket.

"This is Clint."

"This is Reuben. Your guy is with one of my girls right now."

The electricity went straight up my spine. "Sabado or Jackson?"

"The Jackson guy."

"How do you know it's him?"

"Because he told her his damned name, she has that photo on her phone, and he bragged about being in town with a big-time Las Vegas gangster."

"Okay, that's pretty conclusive. How do you know all that?"

"She called me from the bathroom. They're in the house my girls use on northeast Stanton."

"I don't know where that is."

"I'm still downtown here. Are you in your office? I could lead you to it."

"No." I looked for the nearest street signs. "We're on 12th just south of Glisan."

"I can be there in five minutes and you can follow me to

the house. We can take the Steel Bridge. It's just north of Sandy near 57th."

"You sure your girl can keep him there?"

"She won't try to stop him if he wants to leave, but I wouldn't worry about it. She hadn't even started yet when she called me and I told her to give him everything she's got. He'll be there at least a half-hour, guaranteed."

"Let's hope so. Get here as quick as you can."

"On the way now."

He made it in four minutes. We followed him across the bridge and on to Sandy. He pulled over about ten minutes later and I pulled up behind him. Reuben sauntered back to our vehicle and leaned down to look in the passenger side window. It probably looked like we had a drug deal in progress, which fit right in with the neighborhood.

The house Reuben pointed out was a slightly rundown one-story peach-colored ranch in the middle of the block. There were no trees in the overgrown yard, so we had a clear view of the front door from across the street a few houses down. There was a rental car parked right in front that had to belong to Mel Jackson.

"How about we wait for him to come out?" Reuben said. "I don't want Rosalie to get hurt."

There was no part of me that wanted to wait even a second, but Malone and I had talked about it during the drive. "We're going to do better than that," I said to Reuben. "We're going to let him leave and then follow him. He has to rejoin his boss at some point and might even lead us straight to Colleen and Hoke." Before he could respond, I added, "You stay here and make sure Rosalie's okay. I don't want a caravan following Jackson."

He was a little grumpy about that, but finally nodded and trotted back to his car. Then we all waited.

Rosalie must have been very good indeed because it was almost an hour before a man matching Jackson's photo emerged from the house and got into the rental car. He pulled out and I followed when he was a block away.

Meanwhile, Malone was on her cell phone with Sonny Sampson. She'd contacted her while we were waiting and Sampson was currently parked two blocks behind us. No caravan, but Malone would give her a running description of our route so that she could follow but remain out of sight. We could have done that with Reuben, but I preferred another professional. Yes, she had been outsmarted by my daughter, but my daughter was very smart. And I did take my partner's point that there's no way Sampson could have anticipated being attacked in the middle of the Multnomah Falls parking lot.

Anyway, the decision was made. She was somewhere behind us as we kept Jackson's car in sight. He headed northeast, toward the airport. The traffic was typically heavy for mid-afternoon in Portland, so I wasn't very worried that he'd make us.

Apparently he did not, because after a short drive he pulled into the parking lot of the Airport Deluxe Motel, which—unlike the similarly named hotel downtown—was anything but deluxe. It was a standard old-fashioned row of motel rooms with parking spots in front of each and an office on the end.

"Crap," I muttered to my partner as I pulled into the lot right after him. "There's not much chance that they're keeping the kids here—or that Sabado is here, either."

"Maybe," she said as I slowed the car to a crawl, "but we have to decide right now if we're going to make a move or stake him out again."

I accelerated and pulled into the space next to Jackson. I noted that the curtains on the rooms in front of us and Jackson were fully closed. "Fuck it," I said. "Let's make a move."

So Mel Jackson got out of his car to be confronted by Devon Malone's Glock, held down by her side but in his clear view. I was coming around the front of the Subaru holding my Smith and Wesson so he could see it. At the same time, I saw Sonny Sampson's Miata pulling into the lot.

We were committed now. To what, we didn't know yet.

CHAPTER SIXTY-ONE

"Oh, shit," Jackson said as he raised his hands.

"Hands down," I told him as Sonny bailed out of her car and joined us with her gun drawn and down at her side. "Pull your gun, slowly, using just two fingers, and place it on the ground."

With three weapons that could be trained on him in a split second, he didn't have much choice. He reached inside his jacket as instructed, withdrew what looked like a .38 revolver, and crouched to put it down.

"Stand up slowly," I said. "Keep your hands down." Didn't want to attract undue attention. Just four friends gathering in front of a motel room. Nothing to see here.

"Who's in the room?"

His eyes darted to the door and back to me. "Nobody."

I stepped a little closer to him. "I don't care if someone hears the gunshot and calls the cops. Cops would be no problem. We're the good guys. So try again. Who's in the room?"

Tight-lipped. "Sabado."

That was a surprise, but I guess the point was that no one would expect him to stay in such a crummy place. And obviously it had worked since Gunther didn't know he was here. We'd have lots of company by now if he did. "How many with him?"

"Two."

So where were all the others? "Would you knock first?"

"Yes."

I looked over to check that the heavy curtains were still drawn. So far, so good. "Okay, here's what we're going to do. You're going to go knock on that door as you normally would. We'll be on either side of the door and, when it opens, you go on in and we'll be right behind you."

"Fuck. What if they start shooting?"

"You might try ducking."

"Fuck."

"If you don't make them suspicious, we'll be inside with the drop on them before they know it. You're sure there are only two guys with him?"

"I'm sure." He took a breath. "You gonna kill Tony?"

That brought me up short. "Not necessarily. Why?"

"I get you in there and he's alive when you leave, I'm dead. You gotta kill him."

"Your loyalty is touching, but the only thing I can promise is that I'll kill you if you don't get us in there."

"Let's move," Malone broke in. "We've been standing around out here too long already."

"I'll take the right side of the door," I said. "You and Sonny take the left. We go as soon as Mel here takes a step inside." I gestured him toward the door. "Like the lady says, let's move."

We all took our assigned positions. I nodded at Jackson and he knocked. "Yeah?" inquired a voice from within.

"It's Mel."

"Hang on."

I heard the chain dropping, the bolt turning, and then the door opened. Jackson took one step inside with Malone and me swinging around into view on his heels, Sonny right behind us.

The guy who'd opened the door had just time to exclaim, "What the...!" when I gave Jackson a good shove into him, knocking him back. He went down on his butt with Jackson landing on top of him as the three of us leveled guns at the other two people in the room.

One of whom was indeed Antonio Sabado.

Unlike his thug, he got to finish his exclamation: "What the fuck!"

"Don't do it!" shouted my partner at the man standing next to Sabado on the far side of the room, near the bathroom doorway. He froze with his hand halfway under his jacket. Sabado himself was looking only a little more casual than when we'd seen him last: dark suit pants, white shirt and plain gray tie. Same I'll-kill-your-ass frown. I kicked the door behind us shut and then we all held the tableau for a few seconds.

"Hey, Tony," said Sonny Sampson. "Long time no see."

It was a standard, dingy motel room smelling slightly of mold and something else, maybe pizza. All the table lamps were lit; with the heavy curtains closed, it might as well have been dark outside.

"Let's all just remain calm," I said as I surveyed the room. There was a little round table off to the side, conveniently provided with four straight-back chairs. "Sonny, check these guys for weapons, then grab those chairs and set them in a row in the middle of the floor. Jackson, you and your buddy get up and move over there with your boss. I wouldn't want Sonny to get caught in the crossfire if anybody decides to be stupid."

She disarmed the nameless thugs and patted down Sabado as he glowered at the rest of us. I noted that he didn't have a gun. Leaving the dirty work to others, I guess. That could make this a little easier.

As soon as the chairs were in place, I directed Sabado and minions to seat themselves, Tony and Jackson in the two middle chairs. I again looked around the room. "Let's see. Have we got something around here to tie these guys up with?"

"I have zip ties and rope in the car," Sonny announced.

Malone glanced over at her with eyebrows raised. "Your rental car comes with zip ties and rope?"

Sonny grinned back at her. "No, but we Las Vegas private eyes believe in being prepared. I'll be back in a minute."

"Retrieve Jackson's gun while you're out there," I said. "Somebody notices it lying on the ground and we could have company we don't want."

"Will do." Nobody said a word while she was gone.

Sonny was back within a minute or so and proceeded to

bind the wrists and ankles of the four men, gagging all of them except Sabado, while Malone and I kept them covered. She did Sabado last and, as she was finishing him, he said his first words since we'd arrived, to Mel Jackson on his left: "You are fucking dead."

Jackson glared at me as Sabado glared at him. I smiled.

"Okay," I said, "let's get this show on the road." I stepped in front of Sabado, leaned down, and carefully placed the barrel of my gun against his crotch. I was pleased to see that he flinched, just slightly.

"You have my daughter and her friend," I said, adopting a very business-like tone. "I want to know where they are and I want to know right now."

He was still trying to look defiant, but I was feeling more confident all the time. My assessment was that he didn't do violence himself, at least not anymore. He was used to relying on his men. My further guess was that he'd thought his crummy little motel room with only two armed guards was the perfect cover. He certainly didn't look like he was prepared to tough this out on his own. I smiled again. I'm sure it didn't reach my eyes.

"Don't worry. I'm not going to kill you, not directly, but if you don't tell me what I want to know, right now, I'm going to shoot your dick off. You might bleed to death. You might not. Either way, you're going to be dickless."

He opened his mouth and for a moment nothing came out. Then, "I don't...."

I shoved the gun down hard. "One lie and it's gone. I swear to god."

"All right! They're in a warehouse."

"Where is the warehouse?"

"Shit, I don't know. I don't know this town. I haven't even seen it yet. It's probably where they have warehouses. Shit!" He looked to his right. "Ask Hopper. He's been there."

I nodded to Sonny, who was still standing behind the men, and she loosened the gag of the guy named Hopper. He exchanged a look with his boss and apparently decided he was supposed to do his part in preserving Sabado's genitalia.

"It's on…York Street."

"Where on York? What's the cross street?"

"Fuck. I don't know. Somewhere in the 20s, I think."

I noticed Malone had holstered her gun and was looking at her phone. She glanced up and saw me looking. "I'm checking for warehouses on York in the 20s."

"How are you doing that?"

"Google street view."

"Okay." I had no clue what that was, so I kept my gun barrel snug in Sabado's crotch and waited.

She got something on her screen and held it up for Hopper to see. "Is that it?"

"Uh, no."

More tapping, swiping, clicking whatever the hell you do with whatever the hell she was looking at.

"How about this?"

"Uh…yeah, that's it."

She looked at me. "Corner of York and 21st." A few more taps. "Currently for lease, so probably unoccupied. At least legally."

Impressed with my wife's tech skills, I returned my attention to Sabado. He was developing a good flop sweat by now. "How many of your men are there?"

"Six."

"Where are the rest?"

"Motels all over town. I left it up to them, just so they do their shifts at the warehouse and here with me. Is that how you found me? Some dumbshit gave himself away and you followed him?"

"Two dumbshits. One of them's dead, the other one is sitting here beside you." Another glare from Jackson. "When was the last time you heard from the guys at the warehouse?" Nudge, nudge.

"Right before you showed up. They're supposed to check in every four hours."

"What happens if they can't get ahold of you?"

"I don't know. That's not supposed to happen. Kill the kids

and split, probably." He almost grinned for a second and I nudged a lot harder. He hissed at me.

That was everything I needed. I looked at Sonny again. "Gag these two and let's get out of here."

"You just going to leave us here?" That was Hopper.

"I'm sure as hell not taking you with me."

We were back in the parking lot and piling into our vehicles within two minutes. I looked at my watch. 4:05. So they'd probably try to check in with Sabado at eight. They might keep trying for a half-hour or even an hour before panicking, but we didn't have any later than nine this evening to do whatever we were going to do.

"Would you really have done it?" Malone asked as I backed out of the parking spot. She had her phone to her ear.

"He believed I would."

"Which doesn't answer the question."

"It's the only answer I've got. You calling Mike?"

"Gunther."

"Oh, that's nasty. But maybe you should wait. He's also going to want to know where the remaining men are."

"Once he has Sabado, he'll be happy to give us, say, a six-hour head start. And we'll be even."

"Okay. Nasty *and* smart. I love nasty and smart."

"I know you do. Oh, hey, Carl, it's Devon. I've got a present for you."

I pointed the Subaru toward the warehouse, counting down the minutes as I drove, Sonny Sampson following along behind.

CHAPTER SIXTY-TWO

It was a plain gray box taking up about half a square block, with two pull-down doors above a loading dock on 21st and what looked to be some kind of office with a big plate glass window on the corner with York. There was no signage. A broad, mostly undeveloped expanse began across the street and extended to the next street over.

I first drove by it at 4:25. There was no apparent activity, though a couple of cars were parked near the office entrance. There was no foot traffic and ours were the only moving vehicles.

About two minutes later, I pulled over on Wilson, which was the street on the other side of the open area. We had an unobstructed view of the warehouse almost two blocks in the distance. Sonny Sampson parked behind us. Malone dug a pair of binoculars out of the glove compartment and studied our target.

"Still no activity," she said as she lowered the binoculars and Sonny let herself into the back seat. "How do you want to do this? Just the three of us? If we call Mike, he'll probably want to mobilize SERT."

Which was the Special Emergency Response Team, the Portland PD equivalent of SWAT.

"Otherwise, what have we got," she went on, "the overworked Reuben and the walking wounded Big Avenue? We can't ask Hap and Johnny to come out of retirement again, not for this."

"Maybe we can," I said. "This is Colleen we're talking about. If they can still get around, they would want in."

"That's a big if, Clint."

"Let me think about it. Meanwhile, why don't you call Mike and have a cop-to-cop talk about him helping us off the books? You know SERT. They have to follow procedure, which means it would likely be either a hostage situation or a bloodbath. Maybe both. Try to get him here without them. I'll call Reuben; he probably knows how Big Avenue is doing."

"I'm afraid I don't have anybody to call," Sonny offered from the back seat, "but I'll be with you going in."

"Which is all we can ask," I said as my partner and I took up our phones.

Reuben answered his cell phone immediately. I could hear traffic sounds, so he was probably on the street with one of his girls. "Yo. You find 'em yet?"

"I'm looking at the warehouse where they're supposedly being kept. According to Sabado, there should be six well-armed guys with them and we have about three, maybe four hours to put the rescue together."

"Sabado told you all that. I thought he was a tough guy."

"I threatened to shoot off his dick. He decided to believe me."

"That would do it. Cops have him now?"

"Gunther."

"Fuckin' A. Anyway, where are you? You need backup?"

"The warehouse is on the edge of the Pearl District, corner of 21st and York. We're parked on Wilson, the other side of a big, undeveloped lot across York from the warehouse. And yes, I'm looking for backup. How about Big? What kind of shape is he in?"

"Good enough. He can move, pull a trigger."

"Okay. He still have that old Chevy?"

"That piece of shit? Yeah, don't ask me why."

"Use that. You park your pink pimpmobile here and it's going to attract attention even from two blocks away across an empty lot."

I ended the call and watched the warehouse through the binoculars until my partner ended hers, which didn't sound as if it were going well. Still nothing happening around our target, not even any other vehicles driving by. It was nearly five and there were no homes or open commercial operations in the immediate vicinity; it seemed entirely deserted.

"So?" I inquired when Malone lowered her phone from her ear.

"Lieutenant Whitehall is not a happy camper, but he will join us without reinforcements in tow. He'll have a few trusted guys ready to join us, though, because he thinks going in with just him and couple of pimps is a terrible fucking idea. His words."

"Good enough. I'm still thinking about Johnny and Hap."

She looked at her watch. "Think fast. We're down to three hours and counting." The corner of her mouth quirked up. "I imagine Gunther has collected his present by now."

"And good riddance." I thought for just another minute. My partner was right: the clock was ticking. "I'm going to call Johnny. Right now the odds are even, six to six. I don't like even odds."

She shrugged as I punched in Johnny Crew's number.

He and Hap Harbaugh were former Portland homicide detectives and retired private investigators with whom I had apprenticed for my own Oregon license. They were in their seventies now, but had been two of the toughest guys I ever knew and had long served as surrogate grandfathers to my daughter.

If they were around and ambulatory, they'd want to be in on this. Their wives would probably not be so enthusiastic about their participation.

"Johnny Crew," came his rumbly old voice over the phone.

"It's Clint."

"Hey, Clint, it's good to hear from you. What's going on?"

"Colleen's in trouble and I could use some backup."

"You're shitting me. Again? How bad is it?"

"Bad. We're parked on Wilson near 21st, across a big empty lot from a warehouse where she and Hoke are being held captive by six armed men."

"Fuck."

"Yeah. I already have Devon, Mike, Reuben, Big Avenue, and another PI from Las Vegas, but it would be good to have two more. How are you guys doing?"

"How are we doing? We're fucking old, is how we're doing. And you already know everything hurts on Hap's body. Always has. But we're both mobile, more or less, and we've still got our weapons stashed away."

"What about Geraldine?" I felt sure that Johnny's wife would not be on board with this. Nor would Hap's wife, for that matter.

"Ha. You're in luck. Gerry and Wilma are out doing some girl shit and I just talked to Hap a few minutes ago, so I know he's around and free."

I breathed a sigh of relief. That saved us at least an hour. And I had a thought. "Does Hap still have that big RV of his?"

"The monster? Yeah, he and Wilma go off to the hills every now and then in that thing."

"If it's gassed up and ready to go, drive it instead of your cars. It will accommodate everybody for planning the operation."

"Shit. Okay. He's usually got lots of snacks in there, too. And coffee."

"That's good. Call me back if it isn't available for some reason and we'll make another plan. Otherwise, when you come around the corner onto Wilson, you should see three or four cars parked together. Park on the other side of the street, not close but with a view across the open lot to the warehouse. Which is a plain gray box at the corner of 21st and York."

"Will do. I'll get on the horn and we'll be there as soon as we can. The clock is ticking?"

I glanced at my watch. 5:15. "Very loudly," I said and ended the call.

CHAPTER SIXTY-THREE

Reuben and Big Avenue were the first to arrive, in the beat-up old Chevy as requested. They pulled in behind Sonny Sampson's Miata and Reuben came up to my driver's side window while Big remained in the car. I was glad to see that he was wearing a somewhat subdued light blue outfit today.

"Hey," he said. I could see his attention was focused across the lot. "Is that it at the corner, the gray building? Anything happening?"

I glanced over at Malone, who again had the binoculars trained on the building. "Any sign of life?" I asked her.

"Nope," she muttered without even looking around.

"No," I said to Reuben. "We don't even know for sure they're in there. Sabado told us they were and the cars parked in front have rental stickers, so it's a good bet. But we don't know for sure."

Reuben contemplated the view another moment. "Tell you what. This neighborhood, this time of day, nobody's going to think twice about a black guy strolling past. I'll take me a walk around that block and see what I see."

"Good idea."

"If they ain't there, you gotta go back on Sabado, hard."

"Might be a little late for that," I said.

He leaned down to make solid eye contact. "Oh, right. Dead motherfucker." He slapped the top of the Subaru and walked off.

Reuben had barely rounded the corner behind us when I saw Mike Whitehall approaching, on foot, from the other direction. Then I saw that he had parked on 21st, just short of Wilson. Good thinking.

Which was the first thing I said to him after he reached our car and casually joined Sonny in the back seat.

He offered a little shrug. "Thanks. I figured four cars sitting here might begin to attract attention." After exchanging greetings with Devon and Sonny, he asked, "So, what's Reuben up to?"

"He's going to scout out the warehouse. Big Avenue is sitting in the Chevy back there. Johnny Crew and Hap Harbaugh are on their way."

He almost smiled. "Really? The old farts are out of retirement again?" The almost-smile disappeared. "How are we going to do this? We all gather around the car here and we'd better hope nobody in that building is looking in this direction."

"Hap has a big old RV. They're coming in that." I hadn't heard back, so I hoped it was true. "They'll park down the street, still with a view of the warehouse, and we'll use it as our operations center."

He looked across the lot. "Are you sure they're in there?"

I glanced over at Malone. "I wish we were. I hope Reuben sees something to confirm it." Anything. "We'll have to wait on that. You're here without backup, right?"

He grimaced. "As instructed by your partner...but I do have a few trusted officers on stand-by. They can be here in five minutes if needed." He gave Malone a look. "And I still think we should be five minutes behind SERT rather than doing it this way."

"Mike," she replied with a grimace, "we talked about this. They're good people but you know they can be cowboys sometimes. It's good that you've got some people close."

"Yes, it is," I announced, hoping to end the discussion. "Let's hope we don't need them." I glanced down at my watch. It was now 5:50.

At five after six, I saw Reuben returning and, almost simultaneously, an RV pulling to a stop about three-quarters of a block behind us on the other side of the street.

"Johnny and Hap are here," I said to my three companions. "Let's see what Reuben has before we make a move in that direction."

Malone lowered the binoculars and sat back. "I hope he's got something. I haven't seen a single sign of life."

I shuddered slightly at that turn of phrase and waited impatiently for Reuben to reach our car.

"Anything?" I asked him as he came even with the hood.

He stepped up to the window and leaned down, a big grin on his face—that faded slightly when he noticed Whitehall in the back seat. "There's a kind of alley on the other side, with an employee entrance, I guess. Three guys were just outside that door having a smoke, so somebody's there, all right, and I guess at least one of them don't like smoking indoors. Would be one hell of a coincidence if they aren't Sabado's men."

Oh wow, that was a relief. Not a guarantee. Not yet. But a big step in the right direction.

He pointed his chin at Mike. "We got cops in on this now?"

"Just the one," I answered.

He straightened up and I could see he was looking down the street. "What the fuck is that? Somebody fucking camping out here?"

"That's Hap Harbaugh's RV. He and Johnny brought it so we have a place to meet out of sight. Why don't you and Big wander in that direction and we'll follow along in a minute. Just keep it casual, nothing to attract a lot of attention."

"Okay, but I think we're good. I didn't see anybody behind that big window on this side and they're not seeing any of us from the other side." Still, he meandered away rather than walking fast.

CHAPTER SIXTY-FOUR

It was 6:20 by the time Big Avenue settled next to Reuben on one of the RV's side benches, the last to find a spot in the overcrowded interior of the RV. It wasn't as large as I had recalled, but it would have to do.

Malone, Mike, and I were on the opposite bench while Johnny and Hap Harbaugh occupied freestanding armchairs. Sonny Sampson was nearby in the passenger seat up front with binoculars trained on the warehouse.

No one spoke for a moment, everyone probably sizing up our resources and calculating our chances.

"Well," Johnny finally said, "ain't this a motley fuckin' group." He was a short and burly but well-groomed fellow with a full head of thick gray hair. At the Justice Center he had been known as "Dapper John." His long-time partner, Hap Harbaugh, had at least eighteen inches of height and a hundred pounds of weight on him. A completely bald mountain of a man, his nickname on the force had been "Hap the Hulk." They were both still reasonably fit even though Hap constantly complained about his back, bunions, knees, neck, and all the other parts of his body he could no longer reach.

"You better bring us up to speed, Clint," he rumbled.

Malone and I did so, as succinctly as we could. It was 6:40 by the time we finished.

"So," Johnny said, "we're all here ready to invade this warehouse and you're not even sure that Colleen and Hoke are inside?"

"I'm as certain as I can be. It's where Sabado said they were and those two cars parked in front are rentals, with at least the three guys that Reuben saw." I looked over at Reuben. "Did they look like they could be Sabado's men, Reuben?"

He shrugged. "I'm pretty sure they ain't tax accountants. They had the look, all right."

Back to Johnny. "If it's his men, the kids must be in there."

"Okay. So how do we do this?" Johnny asked.

"There's the office entrance that we can see from here," Malone responded, "and the entrance on the other side where Reuben saw the guys smoking. Did you see any other doors, Reuben, or windows that might provide access?"

"There's the roll-up doors on the loading dock and a few small windows but they're high up, near the roof."

"You're sure they're roll-up?" I asked.

"Yeah. I can tell the difference."

"What are you guys talking about?" Sonny Sampson asked.

"An overhead door raises up as a solid unit," I said. "A roll-up door is just what it sounds like. It rolls up into a coil overhead, meaning it has to be much lighter and more flexible than an overhead door."

"Ah. Easier to penetrate."

"If we have to, yeah. With any luck, at least some of these guys are heavy smokers and will be back outside soon."

"Set up and wait for somebody to come out for a smoke." That was Hap.

I looked yet again at my watch. Nearly 6:50. "Yes. If we can catch two or three of these guys outside in the next hour or so, that would improve the odds. Otherwise, we'll just have to enter the door on the other side and take our chances. The odds are good the door would be unlocked, anyway."

Johnny spoke up. "You said they'd bug out if they couldn't contact Sabado. Why don't we wait for that? Then they'd all be outside. We could even just let them leave and then...."

Mike beat me to the response. "We can't risk it. We don't know what they might do with Colleen and Hoke before they fled."

"Ah, you're right. I didn't think it through. We gotta go in."

I cocked an eye at Reuben again. "You think you can pop the lock on the office door in a hurry? It appears they're staying away from that area, so it would be another good entry point."

"I can do that."

"Plan on it whether we get ourselves a smoker or not. You

and Big Avenue and Hap park Big's car near the office door. Stay in the car for now. Apparently there's almost no traffic in this area this time of day. I haven't seen any cars, patrol or civilian, go by. A couple trucks. Anybody does drive by, they won't pay any attention to three guys just sitting there. You see anybody inside the office area, look drugged out until they go away again—and let me know if you've been seen. Otherwise, I'll call you when we're ready to go in."

I surveyed the group. "Everybody else good to go?" I got affirmatives all around.

"Good. Malone and I will set up around one of the back corners with Mike, Johnny, and Sonny at the other. You take your car, Mike, and we'll take ours. We each park a block over from the warehouse, us on 20th, you guys on 22nd, and we approach from the two sides to take our positions. Okay? On your toes, everybody. We've got a lot of moving parts here and one shot."

CHAPTER SIXTY-FIVE

It was 7:25 and my brain was screaming, *move! move! move!*

I peeked around our corner just far enough that I could see Mike peering out from the opposite corner. There had been no activity, no sound, no nothing near this entrance since we got set up. No call from Reuben, so nothing at that entrance either. And time was running out.

My daughter was in there somewhere, I was sure of it. Unharmed, I hoped, but surely frightened to death even if uninjured. What if we had to go in cold, eight of us against six of them? That would be a lot of bullets flying around...and Mike's backup was several minutes away. This could be bad. Very, very bad.

If only someone would come out for a nicotine hit! Come on! It's an addiction, for Christ's sake. Get out here!

The minute hand hit 7:30 and I was just about to call it when my wish came true. I heard the door open and a low-pitched voice as a man exited, a lighter already at the tip of his cigarette. There was another man on his heels. I reached back to tap Malone, signaling that we were about to move, and then held her back one more second as there was further movement in the doorway.

A third man closed the door behind him, joined the first two, and lit his own cigarette. Finally, some luck. If we could round up these three without alerting the ones inside, the odds would be pretty good.

Still more luck. The three men moved a little further out into the parking lot, chatting away and eliminating the possibility of crossfire if they decided not to make it easy. They looked quite relaxed. Apparently, nothing had worried them yet.

We were about to change that.

I edged around the corner with Malone at my shoulder and

saw Mike, Sonny, and Johnny following suit at their corner. The three men were puffing and chatting away, gazing off into the distance, still oblivious. They were at the apex of an equilateral triangle, both sides about fifteen feet. None of us could miss them at fifteen feet, so it was time.

"Just hold it right there, guys," I announced loudly.

They spun around to confront five people, all in shooter stance with weapons trained on them.

"What the fuck!" exclaimed the guy in the middle. He was the oldest of the three, clearly, and was apparently the spokesman; the other two just stood there, mouths agape. Nothing distinctive about any of them. Average height, build, even clothing—rumpled slacks and wrinkled dress shirts, one white, one blue, one...either gray or quite dirty.

I spoke again. "Very slowly, draw your guns—two fingers only—and lay them on the ground."

They didn't move right away but, after a few seconds that seemed like minutes, spokesguy very slowly reached around and brought a handgun out from behind his back, holding it with two fingers as instructed. He crouched and set the gun carefully on the ground. The other two followed suit as he straightened up. None of them looked happy about it.

"You don't know who you're messing with," the older man said. His close-cropped hair was graying compared to the blond and brown of the other two.

"Actually, we do," I responded. "What you don't know is that we already messed with him and he's dead." I didn't add that this was assuming Carl Gunther was predictable.

That shook the blond guy. "Tony's dead?"

"Very."

"Who are you people? Cops? Feds?" He was getting downright talkative all of a sudden. I guess finding out your crime boss is deceased can do that to you.

"Don't worry about who we are. Worry about staying alive. You can do that by answering a few questions. To start with, are you holding two young people, male and female, inside this warehouse?"

Blondie and still-silent guy looked at the older guy in the middle.

He scanned us for another moment and I guess still didn't see anything but five ways to die. "Yes," he said.

Quickly: "Are they hurt?"

"No."

I felt so relieved I almost lowered my gun. I had to stiffen my arms to keep it level. "And there are three more of your men still inside with them?"

The pause this time was probably him trying to figure out how I knew that. "Yes."

At this point, finally knowing for sure we were in the right place and I still had a daughter to rescue, my brain had begun to process other issues like, What do we do with these assholes now that we have them? It would take a lot of time and hassle to tie them up and lay them out in the parking lot—which might well attract unwanted attention even though the lot was off of what amounted to an alley rather than a street.

I quickly came to a conclusion. "Mike, how about you call in your officers to take these guys into custody and then the rest of us will go in after Colleen and Hoke."

"You don't want me to go in with you?"

"It will be seven to three without you and this way you're out here to be part of the rescue if we need it. At least a rescue would be entirely legal."

"Crap. Okay."

It took about two minutes for the patrol cars to show up; Mike's backup must have been even closer than he'd said. As soon as they pulled away again, bad guys and Mike within, I called Reuben's cell.

"We got three of the guys out back here," I said when he answered. "Mike took them away already, so there are four of us ready to go inside. Pop the lock."

"Already done," he rasped very softly back. "We're in the office and there's a little window that looks into the warehouse. I was waiting to hear from you before I take a peek to see if I can scope out where the motherfuckers are. That would be good to know before you hit your door, right?"

I took a deep breath. "Shit, Reuben. You could have blown this whole thing." Another breath. "But...you didn't and, yes, it would be good to know their positions—if you can take a look without them seeing you."

"I'll be quick. The odds are good."

I held my breath this time.

CHAPTER SIXTY-SIX

I timed it. Reuben was back in six seconds.

"I got a good look," he said, "and we got a lot of luck. The kids are tied up, gagged, and blindfolded in the far left corner from me, so they'll be on your right as you come in. The three assholes are clear on the other side of the big open space, sitting together. It looks like they might be playing cards."

"That sounds good," I responded.

"It ain't perfect. We need to take them down in a fucking big hurry because if they start shooting in your direction they don't have to miss by a whole lot to hit one of the kids. They're both flat on the floor, but you never know."

"We're ready to move back here. Can you safely check to make sure your interior door is unlocked? I'd like to be certain you're with us in there."

"No problem." His voice faded slightly as he turned from the phone. "Hey, Hap. Real careful, crack that door to make sure it isn't locked." Only about four seconds this time before his voice came back strong. "We're good."

"Okay. I'm going to count to three and wait one second. You go on three. I want them looking in your direction when we come through the door. Don't hesitate to shoot. And don't get dead."

"If anybody gonna die, it ain't gonna be us. Start your count."

I shoved the phone in my pocket, then counted with my left hand on the doorknob, Devon, Sonny, and Johnny crowded behind me. I hit three, took half-a-breath, and heard the first shot as I was pulling the door open.

You can take in a lot of information in a split second if you're totally focused and fueled by adrenaline. The warehouse was huge, dimly lit by windows high on the walls, and almost entirely empty. It smelled of dust and old chemicals. I didn't even glance to my right because I was already in the middle of a gunfight.

Our three targets, as I'd hoped, were all facing toward the invasion from the office. One of them was a few steps closer to us, probably wondering what happened to the smokers. The guy furthest from us was already staggering backward and going down. The other two were in shooting stance exchanging fire with Reuben, Big Avenue, and Hap.

So, by the time the guy closest to our entry began to react to us, we were already blasting away ourselves. It was a turkey shoot, seven prepared against three surprised, and it was over within ten seconds after we'd stormed through the entrance.

The noise had been horrendous and my ears were still ringing as I swung around to head for Colleen and Hoke. As Reuben had described, they were both bound hand and foot, gagged and blindfolded, laid out maybe four feet apart in the corner. Clearly they were both alive because they were flopping around like landed fish. They had to be scared shitless, with all the sudden gunfire and no way to know what was happening.

I called out to them as I ran, so they'd know rescue was at hand. I could feel Malone hard on my heels.

I dropped beside my daughter and first removed the blindfold so that she could begin to see she was safe. Her eyes were wild and red-rimmed, like I'd never seen them.

Next the gag. "Thank God you're here," she moaned. "Hoke. Is Hoke...?"

I looked over to where Malone was going through the same sequence on Hoke, just dropping his gag off to the side. His back was to us, but he appeared to be conscious and uninjured.

"He's okay," I said. I sat my daughter up and swung her around so she could see him as I was untying her hands.

"Hoke!" It was barely more than a rasp, but he must have heard her because he came back with an equally raspy "Colleen!" He squirmed to turn himself toward us while my partner tried to get his hands free at the same time. She paused that effort for a moment and helped him to sit up and turn, just as I had my daughter.

Once they could see each other, they gave up on trying to talk. I'd get them both some water as soon as possible. First, we needed to get their ankles untied and see if they could stand. We had to get out of here or we'd all be drinking from the Justice Center tap while trying to explain ourselves.

Which reminded me to pull out my phone and call Mike. I hit the speed dial, the speakerphone, and set it on the floor beside us as I continued to work on the last knot.

"We're right outside," were his first words.

"Do you trust the guys you're with?" were mine.

"Completely."

"Okay, stay outside then. Don't contaminate the scene with any evidence that you were here. The kids appear to be okay. Tired, scared, dehydrated, but okay." I glanced across the warehouse and saw that everybody was now headed our way, leaving the three bodies behind. "I'm pretty sure the bad guys are all dead."

After a short pause, "I expect to receive an anonymous tip the second everybody's clear—and make sure you don't leave any contamination of your own behind." Then a deep breath. "And, Clint?"

"Yes?"

"Let's not do this again."

"I promise. Thanks, Mike."

"See you on the other side."

By the time this exchange was finished, I had Colleen fully freed and on her feet. Wobbly, but upright. I stashed the phone in my pocket and hugged her.

"Oh, Daddy," she snuffled into my shoulder. My big, bad daughter hadn't called me that since she was seven. I wanted to go kill those three guys again.

Then Hoke was on his feet and staggering in our direction. Malone and I gave them a moment, then started herding everybody toward the back parking lot.

We needed just a bit more luck.

CHAPTER SIXTY-SEVEN

"Aack! Stella!"

My entire body convulsed for a second as a single claw carefully poked me right between the shoulder blades. I had been peacefully lying on my side, watching my wife sleep, both the peace and the sleep now disrupted by the claw.

She opened one eye and gave me a sour look. "The cats want breakfast," she said.

"At least Stella does." I knew it was her rather than her sister Maxine because cats are creatures of habit and the early morning claw in the back was one of hers.

"What time is it?"

I cocked an eye over at the clock. "Seven-thirty."

"So much for sleeping in on a Sunday." She tossed back the cover and got to her feet. She sleeps in the nude, so I enjoyed that even more than watching her sleep. "When are we meeting everybody?" she asked.

"At eight-thirty," I answered as I got myself up.

She stretched with a little groan. "Okay. I'm going to take a long shower."

"Yes," I agreed. "Let's."

Our luck had held Thursday night, Sabado having chosen his location well. There had been no one nearby to hear the gunfire and there was no one passing by as we spilled out of the warehouse and dispersed to our vehicles.

The headlines since had been about a gang war (true enough) rather than a vigilante operation by a motley crew of private investigators, pimps, and rogue cops.

Besides the people who had been in the warehouse, only five Portland police officers and one Portland crime boss knew what had really happened—and none of them were going to be talking about it. As for any of Sabado's men who'd been left standing around town, they had no doubt started running as soon as they heard their boss was dead.

We were, in every sense, clear.

So, following our very satisfying shower, Devon and I finally fed the cats and got ready to walk around the corner to the Pen and Pastry for breakfast with Colleen, Hoke, and some of the above-mentioned crew.

"What are we going to do if Martha Mondragon sends that check?" my partner asked as I locked the front door behind us.

We'd promised ourselves we'd provide the answers she needed and we'd done that with a phone call Friday. I don't think it helped her grief to know that the man who'd had her husband killed was now dead, but she thanked us and—over our protests—said she would send a final check for our time.

"I don't know," I said as we set out for our short but already sunny walk. "It would be an insult to send it back and it doesn't feel right to put it in the bank. How about we contribute it to Maxine and Stella's cat rescue group?"

"They have a cat rescue group?"

"They were rescued and fostered by the group, yes."

"Sounds fine to me."

The Pen and Pastry was already bustling with the Sunday morning crowd, mostly young men as usual, and the air was redolent with the scent of freshly baked delicacies. It was easy to spot my daughter and friends in the far corner; they were the only group large enough to require three tables shoved together. We headed in that direction.

I was pleased to see that Colleen was looking a good deal more healthy and happy than when last I'd seen her, settling in with Hoke at home after being checked out at the hospital. She and Hoke were at one end of the trio of tables with Sonny and Veronica sitting together in the middle and Johnny wedged next to the massive Hap on the other end.

I hadn't expected to see Reuben or Big Avenue. Their line of work required them to be up most of Saturday night and thus they were not much for Sunday morning breakfast meetings.

I was sorry to see that Mike wasn't in attendance, but he was still uncomfortable with his role in the rescue and our role in Sabado's death. He'd called to thank me for the anonymous tip he'd requested, duly recorded at the dispatch center, but I hadn't heard from him since and I knew that some friendship repair would be needed.

Everybody was smiling as we arrived at the table. "It's about damned time," Johnny said. "We're hungry!"

I glanced at my watch. "Weren't we supposed to meet at eight-thirty? We're right on time."

"I told everybody to be here a few minutes early," Colleen chimed in, "so we could"—she glanced around—"give you a proper welcome." At that, they all stood and started to applaud.

I felt my partner stiffen next to me. "Oh, for Christ's sake," she hissed. "This is embarrassing. Sit down. We're hungry, too." She pulled back one of the two empty chairs across from Veronica and Sonny and firmly plopped down.

I grinned as I joined her while the others also seated themselves. "Thank you all," I said, "but you should be applauding yourselves. You're all either survivors or rescuers. It took all of us."

Veronica frowned a little. "I wasn't there."

Sonny patted her hand. "You were my moral support—and you're sure as hell a survivor."

I cocked an eye over at my daughter and her boyfriend. "You and Hoke have your new phones all set up?"

"Right here." She held up hers and Hoke patted his on the table in front of him. I had bought them both new cell phones to celebrate their rescue. Hers had been smashed in the parking lot and Hoke's dumped somewhere we never found.

What they didn't know was that I'd had Eleanor Ivory install covert tracking apps on both phones. I wasn't going to tell the kids they were there, but neither was I going to misuse them. I didn't care where Colleen and Hoke went or what they did day to day, but I wanted a shot at finding them fast if they got in trouble again.

Malone meanwhile was looking over at Johnny and Hap. "How are you guys doing?"

Johnny shrugged. "Retired again."

"I busted a bunion charging into that warehouse," Hap announced.

Malone grinned at that. "I don't think you can actually bust a bunion."

"Felt like it." Hap tossed an entire donut into his mouth.

"You guys tell your wives what happened?" I asked as a waitress arrived at the table to refill coffee cups.

Johnny's eyebrows climbed up his forehead. "Are you kidding? They think we were out playing pool all evening. And they were still pissed."

"Well," I said, "thanks for your help."

"Anything for the kid," said Hap, to which Colleen responded with an "aww."

Sonny sipped from her newly-filled coffee cup and picked up a cruller. "Anything new with Agatha Pepper and her nephew? She shoot up anyplace else? She shoot him?"

I set my own coffee down and laughed. "You won't believe it," I told her. Everybody focused on me. Ms. Pepper was always good for a story and even more than usual now. "In the first place, Rodney, the nephew, is totally forgiven and is now an official part of the family. She's changing her will to give him half of everything."

"Half?"

"Friends of the Library gets the other half. But Rodney isn't the real news. Her downtown gunfight has gone viral and she's getting TV offers."

"Jeez," exclaimed Colleen, "they want her on TV?"

Malone took up the story while I took up a chocolate covered donut. "Not her, but they are talking a TV series about an old lady vigilante. Granny Gunsel."

That provoked a round of gasps and laughs, as it should.

"Granny Gunsel?" Veronica repeated. "I love it—but they might want to check the Urban Dictionary before they go with that. I don't think 'Gunsel' means what they think it means."

I saluted her with my coffee cup. "I'll take the author's word for that."

"So, Sonny," Malone began, "are you planning to stick around Portland now?"

Our visiting P.I. shook her head even as she took Veronica's hand. "Not yet. I'm heading back to help clean up Sabado's operation. Somebody will try to take it over and keep it going. I want to make sure that doesn't happen and that all the girls are rescued."

"Good for you," I said.

"Then," continued Sonny, looking fondly at Veronica, "I'll be back and we'll see what happens."

Malone chuckled. "Well, if you get married, try to have a better honeymoon than we've managed."

That brought big grins to the faces of both women. "We'll take that under advisement," Veronica said, "but we're not there yet."

After that, the conversation was mostly desultory, among other things bringing Johnny and Hap up to speed with the whole story. We munched pastries and drank coffee and enjoyed being in one another's company without any looming threats.

Finally Hoke stood up, his face reddening as we all looked at him curiously. He raised his coffee cup and cleared his throat as Colleen looked up at him fondly. I had a sudden, terrible fear that he was going to announce they were engaged.

But that wasn't it.

"Here's to Jacqueline Hudson, the girl in the Las Vegas lobby who wanted to tell me about Tony Sabado. You succeeded in the end, Jacqueline. You brought him down. Good job."

"Here's to Jacqueline," said we all.

We finished our coffee as I looked around at my friends, my daughter and the boyfriend I hoped would never become her husband, my new wife.... All safe and sound.

Back to the office tomorrow. Maybe we could specialize in finding lost pets for a while.

Watch for
A Killer of a Case
The ninth book in the McCall-Malone Mystery series
Coming in 2022

It isn't every day someone hires you to find out who they are. Is the client nuts or the victim of some event so traumatic that she really lost her memory? Are there powerful and dangerous people out there who want to make sure she doesn't remember? Clint McCall and Devon Malone find both themselves and their client in serious jeopardy as they try to sort it out. Oh, and they also have to find a kidnapped dog.

Visit glennharris.us
to be notified as soon as
A Killer of a Case
is available!

ABOUT THE AUTHOR

Glenn Harris lives and writes in the middle of the Columbia Gorge National Scenic Area (Hood River, Oregon). Besides creating detective novels and short stories, he serves as staff to the same two cats that live with Clint McCall and Devon Malone. His former lives include college English teacher, private K-12 school director, graphic design business owner, weekly newspaper managing editor, corporate manager, actor, and taekwondo instructor.

Keep reading the McCall and Malone mysteries! Stay tuned for A Killer of a Case and be sure to visit Glenn Harris' website www.glennharris.us where you can subscribe to his free e-mail newsletter to get updates and background of the series!

www.ingramcontent.com/pod-product-compliance
Lightning Source LLC
Chambersburg PA
CBHW060407260626
47160CB00006B/2461